PARADISE WILD

WILD AT HEART SERIES, BOOK TWO

BY CHRISTINE HARTMANN

PARADISE WILD

Limitless Publishing, LLC
Kailua, HI 96734
www.limitlesspublishing.com

Formatting: Limitless Publishing

ISBN-13: 978-1-68058-782-1
ISBN-10: 1-68058-782-X

DEDICATION

To Antje, my romance guru.

CHAPTER 1

"Taxidermy?"

The word conjured ratty, stuffed wildebeests in a natural history museum's savanna exhibit, with bald spots worn from countless curious children's fingers reaching past the sign reading *'Do Not Touch'*. Ellie retreated against the backrest of the basement restaurant's cushioned leather bench and camouflaged her dropping jaw with a sip of wine. The man in tweed with a two-day growth of thin facial hair leaned across the narrow table that separated them.

"You'd be surprised by the number of people who don't even know what taxidermy is." He glanced around the small, crowded, and dimly lit room. "Even here. Where we're all supposed to be..." He raised long, hooked fingers in the shape of bent quotation marks, exposing untidy nails, "*professionals* looking for dates." He lifted his bottle of IPA.

Ellie jumped gratefully into the ensuing pause. "Professions. That's a good speed dating subject. I cat sit." She laughed and pushed errant strands of hair from her face. "But it's not my life's goal. I'm in grad school. It pays the bills."

"I have a cat." Her companion groped through one jacket pocket and another, laying on the table an assortment of strangely shaped metal instruments Ellie didn't examine too closely. He finally stood and clutched intimately at his pants. "Ah." He extracted a gray flip phone from his front pocket, scrolled, and turned it toward her.

Ellie squinted at the tiny screen. "I can't really make out what your cat is doing."

"He's got a mouse in his mouth. Quite a trick. Getting the critter to fit in there." He flicked the phone shut with a click. "Small animals are hard to dissect."

The table between them felt suddenly disturbingly narrow. Ellie peeked at the smart phone in her lap. "Gee, time's almost up. And I've got one last burning question." She rubbed her nose to suppress a grin. "Do you generally have luck with speed dating?"

The shrill switch-partners tweet reverberating in the low ceilinged room obscured his response. His spindly hand hovered in the air like a bedraggled bird wing, waiting for Ellie to shake it. A sudden coughing fit seized her. She held her napkin to her mouth and shrugged. He sniffed, rubbed his nose on the sleeve of his herringbone jacket, and turned away.

Ellie circled "no" with thick black marks next to Mr. Taxidermy's number and looked to Celine, who was sitting a few tables down. Ellie mouthed,

"Watch out" and raised her eyebrows in the taxidermist's direction. Celine pointed a stealthy pinky at the retreating back of the man who'd just left her own table and rolled her eyes in crazy loops. Ellie smiled.

"Seems like you're having fun, number sixteen."

A tall, dark haired man of about thirty slid into the seat opposite Ellie.

She grinned and dropped the scorecard into her lap. "I'm learning that what they say is true."

"What's that?" He shifted his martini glass to the edge of the table and rested his hands where she could see them. Ellie examined the close-cut nails, the strong fingers, and the dark hair on the knuckles, neither sparse nor Neanderthal. She sensed rather than observed him scanning her and felt a soft blush warm her cheeks.

"That you learn more in five minutes face-to-face than you do in five hours of emails." She met his dark eyes, a grin still playing at the corner of her mouth.

He nodded, his expression open, welcoming. "I'm a believer. My company swears by performance-based interviewing."

Ellie cocked her head and gave him her best smile. "So tell me what you do."

The man opposite rattled off a distilled resume: CEO, mountaineer, and soup kitchen worker. His general demeanor matched his hands, manly yet approachable, tough yet seemingly warm. Ellie couldn't believe her luck. A gorgeous, approachable stranger, one fit for speed dating website advertisements.

Play this one right, Ellie, she thought.

She admired his career high points, skimmed over her own, and segued the conversation easily into hobbies and weekend activities. Her fingers played absently with her wine glass, watching his hands slowly fold and unfold, like wings on a giant butterfly.

The vibration of an incoming call in her lap made her jump. Her hands twitched and, before she could catch it, her glass toppled, spilling red wine across the table in a widening sea that threatened to engulf the CEO and his expensive-looking slacks.

Her date ricocheted out of his chair as though ejected. He stood far away, rubbing frantically with his fingers at a stain located embarrassingly near his zipper. Ellie leaned forward on her bench and shot him an apologetic look as she dabbed her cocktail napkin at the corners of the expansive puddle with one hand and waved frantically with the other for help.

"I'm sorry." She offered him a second tiny napkin, handed to her from the neighboring table. "I'm a klutz. Not a good thing for you to learn about in person."

She peeked at him to check for a smile. He took the proffered napkin without his eyes leaving the widening blotch. She sighed and concentrated on cleaning up the mess.

Minutes later, the time's up whistle echoed in her ears. She watched Mr. CEO draw large, repeated circles around the "no" next to her number before he moved with a grateful smile to his next table.

Celine winked at her. Ellie bit her lip and shrugged.

"Do I need a wet suit?"

Ellie looked up at an Asian man with inviting eyes.

"You're safe. I'm not drinking for the rest of the evening."

"Glad to hear it. I'm number fifty-two." He surveyed the room. "Although how I got that high a number, I'm not sure."

"Maybe a lot of registrants didn't show up."

"Glad you showed up." He crossed his arms and leaned back.

She stole a glance at the CEO, whose current date had sacrificed her sparkling water for the sake of a continued attack on the wine spot. "I don't think everyone shares your opinion."

"Don't worry about him. He's a frequent flyer."

She stared at her new date. "He comes often? But he must be flooded with matches after one of these things."

The man chuckled. "I don't know what he's doing wrong, but this is the third event I've seen him at."

Ellie peered at the person across from her, wondering why he'd admit to being here so often himself. "So you're a veteran?"

His head jerked up and spine straightened. "Navy. Five years. Surveillance. Still in that line of work."

Ellie blinked. "Surveillance?"

"Yes, ma'am. Work in a spy store. Do you know you can put a camera on someone that's so small, they won't even know it's there?" He pointed at the CEO. "I was thinking I could put one on him, to find out what he's doing wrong. Learn from his mistakes."

"Is that…legal?"

He smirked. "Depends on who's doing it."

Ellie pulled her hands slowly from the table, tucked her legs underneath the bench she was sitting on, and scrutinized his face. She wondered whether she'd mistaken the invitation in his eyes and decided she didn't want to find out. In her lap, she quietly removed the score card and pen from under her skirt and, as he prattled on about recorders, cameras, and under water listening devices, unobtrusively circled "no," making her number of rejections an even dozen.

***

The rooftop restaurant afforded intermittent views of glimmering boat lights in the dark San Francisco Bay. Ellie snuggled into her sweater, grateful for the large silver heat lamp towering over a cluster of tables.

"Girl, that was the most fun I've had in months." Celine's eyes sparkled with amusement. "A spy, a survivalist, and a wanna-be sommelier who gargled my wine and spit it back into my glass. Can you believe it? You can't make this stuff up."

Ellie laughed. "You forgot the taxidermist."

"I didn't forget him, honey." Celine shook her head. "I was saving the best for last." She stabbed her salad. "You've got to love someone who's so enamored with his hobby that he can't see he's freaking people out."

"How many yeses do you think he got?"

Celine squinted at miniature bulbs strung in sparkling rows across their table in the pattern of a grape arbor. "That girl with the pigtails. She was chatting him up afterward. So maybe one?"

Ellie chuckled. "That's probably one more than I got."

"Don't sell yourself short. Not too many of us twenty-somethings at these things. The spy shop guy was all about you."

"All over me, you mean." Ellie ran her fingers through her long hair and brushed down her sweater. "He probably planted cameras. Although I tried to stay out of arm's reach."

Celine chewed thoughtfully. "At least you got yourself out there."

A waitress stopped at their table and refilled their water glasses. Ellie studied the offices in nearby buildings, bright rectangles showcasing empty desks and the occasional hunched figure working late hours.

"I don't know if it counts if nobody picks me out of the crowd." Ellie twirled spaghetti around her fork.

"It counts. You're back in the running. Next time will be easier."

"Pretty much guaranteed to be less weird." She winked at Celine.

The waitress returned with two glasses on a tray. "Excuse me." She placed the goblets on the table. "These are from the gentlemen over there."

Ellie stared at the two businessmen looking in their direction while Celine raised her glass in a toast and flashed them a wide smile. Celine then turned to the waitress, her expression dropping immediately back to neutral. "Tell them we appreciate the thought. But we just finished a speed dating event. We're dated out for tonight."

The waitress nodded, turned to leave, and hesitated. "Did you really just speed date?"

Celine laughed. "Don't we look worn out?"

The waitress surveyed Celine's smooth, bright face, her short afro, her hot pink blouse. "I can't tell."

"We did. And we *are* worn out."

The young woman leaned over the table and lowered her voice. "I'm only asking because I've wanted to try it."

"Seriously?" Celine backed her chair from the table so she could look the waitress in the face. "Isn't that what you do for a living already? When I was a waitress, I thought the entire job *was* speed dating."

Ellie shook her head. "That's because you're confident and gorgeous, Celine. For us normal people..." She glanced at the waitress. The young woman smiled. "For us normal people, we need outside help."

The waitress straightened the tablecloth and wiped a few crumbs into her hand. She glanced in the direction of the bar and whispered. "Do you have any tips?"

Celine pointed at Ellie. "This woman can give you some."

Ellie thought. "Don't go with high expectations, keep your phone out of your lap, and don't let anyone touch you."

The waitress grinned. "I'll let those guys over there know they're barking up the wrong tree."

"You do that." After she moved away, Celine focused on Ellie. "Now. What's the next plan?"

"For what?"

"Dating."

Ellie concentrated on her food. "No plan."

"I thought you said you'd do this again?"

The cheese on Ellie's pasta broke into long strings as she pushed the noodles around her plate. "I just said it would be less weird the second time."

"You still thinking about Alberto? Really? You dumped him years ago."

The smile faded from Ellie's lips. "Eleven and a half months ago. But who's counting? And he's the one who broke up with me."

Celine dismissed the distinction with a wave of her hand. "Only because you didn't beat him to it."

"Still."

"Still nothing. A breakup doesn't mean you take yourself out of the running. Tonight ended your self-imposed monastic lifestyle." She lifted the complimentary glass of wine and clinked Ellie's glass. "Here's to new love."

Ellie left hers on the table without taking a sip. "I'll drink to friendship. Even lust. But not love."

"Oh, girl. Don't tell me you don't have serious FOMO."

"Nope." Ellie hoisted a forkful of pasta and stuffed it into her mouth. A loose noodle dangled and she shielded her face from Celine's eyes as she struggled with the vagrant strand. She laughed. "That's why you get the drinks, Celine. You aren't clumsy or messy like the rest of us."

"Don't try to change the subject." Celine's eyes reflected her serious tone. "I thought we had you back in the game tonight."

Ellie pushed the half-finished plate from her. "I'm in a new game. I'm done with serious dating."

"Because of Alberto? He's not worth it."

"Because of Alberto. And Elliot. It's too painful to break up with someone you love. I moved across the country for Elliot. I switched careers for Alberto. I'm done with all that."

Celine inclined her head and observed Ellie the way one studies an abstract painting in a museum. "This doesn't seem like the Ellie I know. The Ellie who believes in love at first sight. Who cries buckets at *Love Actually*. Who moved across the country and switched careers. All for love."

"That's right." Ellie raised her glass. "It's the new Ellie. The speed dating Ellie. Here's to her." She tapped Celine's glass and swallowed a large mouthful.

Celine didn't move, her face creased into unveiled skepticism.

"I want a fresh start."

In the chill night air, the chatter from other tables wafted across the ensuing silence. Ellie twisted her napkin, buttoned and unbuttoned her sweater, and shifted in her chair.

"You're making me nervous. Say something. It makes sense, doesn't it? Maybe I could get away

10

from San Francisco for a while. Away from the memories. I'm only twenty-four. I want to have some fun. Stop being so serious."

"Uh-huh." Celine drew the two syllables out to the length of an entire sentence.

"Come on, Celine. You know love's not all it's cracked up to be. Love sucks."

Behind them a tray clattered to the floor and conversations momentarily halted as patrons waited for the tinkle of cutlery, the splintering of glasses, the disintegration of flatware. Nothing more dramatic hit the floor. A man laughed. Conversations resumed.

"You've got that backwards." Celine raised her glass again and waited until Ellie lifted hers. "Losing love sucks. But finding love, girl, that's what makes it all worthwhile."

CHAPTER 2

Late August fog rolled across the small condominium balcony in waves. Inside, Celine and Ellie, bundled in sweaters around a tiny electric heater, sat on the sofa and watched their roommate's stunted avocado tree sway outside in the damp breeze.

"Nope. I'm too squeezed for funds right now. Speed dating's not cheap." Ellie leaned back against the overstuffed cushions.

"I know what your problem is." Celine sipped black coffee from a tall mug. "It's your 'I want to do good in the world' attitude. That's the same attitude that made you turn down the Twitter offer after your internship. If you were working for Twitter now, you wouldn't *have* money troubles."

"Maybe it was naïve." Ellie twisted her teabag around a spoon and dropped it in an empty cereal bowl where a few Grape Nuts kernels floated in a puddle of milk. "But I can't go back there begging them to let me in. They've hired tons of other people by now."

"So hang tight. In two quarters, you'll be waving a master's in computer science. Offers will flood your inbox." Celine zipped her fleece jacket to the top. "Why does it have to be so fricking cold? I wish I were back in sunny Berkeley."

Ellie grinned. "You're just saying that. You're a big city girl if I ever saw one."

"Only because you don't remember how close I came to becoming a nature girl." A momentary cloud passed over Celine's features, which she tried to disguise. She took a long sip from her cup.

Ellie screwed her eyes briefly shut and whacked her forehead, then peeped at Celine. "Sorry. I shouldn't have made you think of Kenji."

But Celine's smile returned as quickly as it had faded. "My advice is to take down your cat sitting website. Forget cats. Look what that fat one did to your shirt the other day. There are other part-time jobs."

Ellie laughed. "I was thinking about that. But this morning I got an email from another potential client. Someone who wants a full-time cat sitter."

"A cat that needs a full-time sitter? It's probably psychotic."

Ellie scrolled through email on her phone. "It's from the personal assistant to some woman named Vivyenne Lovejoy."

"Right. And Vivyenne has some money in Zambia she wants you to get for her."

Ellie grabbed a pair of socks from a laundry basket on the floor and tossed the pink ball at Celine, who backhanded it against the window, chuckling.

"Seriously. This sounds genuine."

"Because you're from Delaware, sister. Everything sounds genuine to you."

"So steer me straight. I'm tempted to call her."

Celine shot her an incredulous look and reached out her hand. Ellie passed the phone and watched Celine's dark eyes narrow, then widen as she read.

"So?"

"So maybe you should call."

"Right?"

Celine rose and stretched, her long arms almost touching the ceiling. "I'm getting more coffee. You get on that phone."

Ellie hit the call button.

"This is Devora."

"Hi. I'm Ellie Atherton. You sent me an email this morning about cat sitting."

"Cat sitting? Oh, right. For Viv."

"Yes. Vivyenne Lovejoy."

"Viv's the cat. Doctor Lovejoy is the owner."

"Sorry." Ellie made a face at herself in the window. "Cat sitting for Doctor Lovejoy. I mean, cat sitting for Viv."

"Right. So, I checked your references and social media. I couldn't find anything negative. I'll need a copy of your driver's license, your social security number, and proof you're really enrolled in graduate school. PDF scan is fine. Then I can set you up with a key. You can get it at the front desk of Doctor Lovejoy's condo."

"Hold on. I haven't said I'd take this job. I don't even know you."

"Right. Will you take the job? I think everything

14

you needed to know was in the email."

Ellie paced up and down the living room, as though trying to catch up with Devora and her rapid-fire proposals. "But I usually like to see the place. Get to meet the cat. You know, see if we like each other."

"Don't all cats like you? Isn't that why you're a cat sitter?"

Ellie halted. "Sure. Cats…they usually like me. But I really can't take the job without meeting you or Doctor Lovejoy first."

Celine returned with a second cup of coffee. She gave Ellie a thumbs up sign. Ellie shrugged.

"Right. We're in kind of a rush. You topped the list of candidates. But I just got a conference call cancellation, so I have a little time. Meet me at the Starbucks in Russian Hill on Polk and Vallejo this afternoon. Three-thirty."

"Okay. I can do that. But I need to tell you that I'm raising my rates."

Celine mouthed "yaassss" and raised her fist. Ellie bumped it with her free hand.

"Right."

"I haven't changed my website yet. But I'm charging ten dollars an hour more these days."

"Right. So I'll see you at three-thirty."

Ellie dropped onto the couch and looked at the phone. "She hung up."

"No way. Because you wanted more money?"

"No. I'm still meeting her. She's just seems super efficient. Doesn't like to waste time."

Celine plunked herself back on the sofa. "You don't have to take the job. Sitting on your butt for thirty-five dollars an hour in a three-million-dollar condo is tough." She ducked Ellie's imaginary throw.

"Did you see the pictures? It looks like the kind of place I want someday. And an Egyptian Mau."

Celine shuddered. "That cat looks like a miniature white leopard. Seriously. Be careful. All you have is an email. You still can't rule out human trafficking."

Ellie hopped off the couch, picked up her dishes, and headed to the kitchen. "Me, the naïve professors' daughter from the Diamond State. You, the cynical big city girl. How did we ever end up as roommates?"

Celine smiled. "I'm not cynical. Just West Side Chicago realistic."

Ellie turned and arched an eyebrow. "You grew up in Oak Park. That's not the West Side. Those are the posh suburbs."

Celine buried her head in her cup. "We had osmosis. The 'hood was right next door."

***

Slightly before three-thirty, four fashionably dressed women stood outside the Vallejo Starbucks entrance. They were all texting. Across the street, Ellie used her reflection in the window of a personal training gym to tidy her blowing hair. She pulled the bottom of her faux leather bomber jacket to straighten the wrinkles, took a deep breath, and crossed at the corner. Even from afar, she had no doubt as to which woman was Devora.

The petite blonde dressed in all black, carrying a slim Burberry bag at her side, looked up from her gold iPhone when Ellie stopped in front of her. Her face registered no surprise, as though she were used to being recognized for who she was.

"Ellie."

"Devora?"

Devora pointed to the outdoor table next to her on which stood two Grande cups. "I got us lattes. Thought it would save time. One's milk, one's soy. You can get sugar inside if you want." She pointed to the chairs near the street. "I cleaned them off already."

Ellie took the cup closest to her and sat. Devora's minimally made-up face radiated confidence, competence, and honesty, and Ellie regretted the increasingly ludicrous scenarios she and Celine had cooked up earlier in the day. The chances of Devora or her employer kidnapping Ellie seemed about the same as her being killed by a pedicure-acquired toenail infection.

Actually, probably less.

Devora removed an iPad from her bag and poised her fingers over the screen, regarding Ellie with a neutral stare. Ellie hesitated, a small, unexpected fist tightening around her stomach.

"Um."

Devora sipped her drink. "I thought you wanted to ask me some questions. I've got…" She tapped her phone. "Fifteen minutes."

Ellie held onto her cup with both hands.

Don't spill anything. Her iPad probably costs more than I make in a month.

17

"Your email said Doctor Lovejoy's looking for a full-time cat sitter. Can you tell me about the hours?"

"Right. I'm sorry I wasn't clear. Full-time means all the time. Someone to live with the cat."

"Like a cat nanny?" Ellie gestured. Her cup teetered and she clamped back on it in a flash.

Devora's head cocked to one side. "I can give you some background. The cat's not originally Doctor Lovejoy's. He belonged…"

"He? I thought its name was Viv."

"It is. And he's male. Doctor Lovejoy inherited Viv in a break-up." Devora inspected Ellie for a moment. She thought she perceived a tiny smile play briefly at the corners of Devora's lips. "Let me be candid. Doctor Lovejoy kept Viv when she and her boyfriend split up. Now she doesn't know what to do with him. The cat. The boyfriend's gone."

"She doesn't live in the condo?"

"Not most of the time. But the cat does. And he's going a little crazy." Devora lowered her voice. "Doctor Lovejoy can't stand him, although she would never admit it. Hence the need for a cat sitter. Until she figures out what she wants to do with him."

Ellie carefully released her cup and unzipped her jacket. She felt suddenly hot. She looked around for the sun, but it wasn't hitting their side of the street.

"I'm in graduate school. Classes start in a few weeks. So I couldn't be there all the time. I usually just look in on the cats I take care of."

"Right. Well, we thought you could take some time off." When Ellie regarded her quizzically, she

18

added, "From school."

"For a cat?" Ellie's mouth fell open. She brought the cup to her lips to cover her surprise.

"For a cat. And for twenty-five thousand dollars for the semester."

Ellie choked, splattering the table with drops. Devora shielded her iPad with her arms but Ellie watched in dismay as brown dots covered Devora's sweater.

When Ellie's coughing subsided, Devora raised her hand. "I'll be right back."

Ellie whipped out her cell phone. Her fingers flew over the screen.

Ellie: Offered me 25k to take semester off.

Celine: Wtf?

Ellie: Do it?

Devora returned. Ellie dropped the phone in her lap, where she felt it vibrate moments later with Celine's response.

"I'm sorry about your sweater."

"Right." Devora rubbed her hands on a napkin. "I cleaned it off."

"Look." Ellie shrugged out of her jacket and put it on her lap over the giggling phone. "The semester starts next week. I can't stop classes, no matter how much money you offer."

This time Ellie was certain she saw a smile flash across Devora's lips. "Right. Doctor Lovejoy authorized me to propose a second option."

Ellie dropped all pretense and rested her chin in her hands as she listened to Devora outline a scenario as ludicrous as the ones Celine had invented. When Devora finished, Ellie looked around them, scrutinizing the other customers and passersby.

Devora looked around too. "What are you doing?"

"There's a camera somewhere, right? One of my friends put you up to this? Celine?"

"It's not a joke. It's a regular job. Until December, with an option to renew if things go well. You'd get benefits. Doctor Lovejoy would pay for health insurance, since you'd lose what you're getting as a student, I assume."

Ellie lifted her jacket and held the phone toward Devora. She tapped the record button. "Tell me again. Nobody's going to believe this."

Devora leaned toward the orange case. "Fifty thousand dollars to take Viv to Hawaii and supervise the renovation of Doctor Lovejoy's recently purchased house."

***

The next day, Ellie stood in front of the glowing doorbell by the white door of Dr. Lovejoy's thirtieth floor Russian Hill condominium. She wore a flounced skirt with thick horizontal black and white stripes and a black boat neck top. A utilitarian gray messenger bag hung at her side. The bomber jacket lay over one arm.

Her hand hovered over the bell. She hesitated.

What's all this going to mean?

She closed her eyes, momentarily transported back to another door, one from her high school days. It was solid wood, with three diagonal rectangular windowpanes. It belonged to a house on the more glamorous side of the university professors' ghetto, the section where science and engineering faculty with lucrative industry side jobs lived. She'd shuffled the ten blocks from her parents' liberal arts professor section in twice as many minutes, her backpack clutched to her chest, feeling exposed and embarrassed to be carrying school books on a Sunday, even though a trip to the university library had been her excuse for leaving the house so early. As she stood at the door, hesitating, she found it difficult to believe that Elliot even remembered he'd asked her to come over.

She scuffed her Ugg boots on the tile porch, glancing up and down the wide, tree-lined street where nobody moved early on a Sunday morning. In the far distance a lawnmower revved. But the nearby inhabitants kept easier hours.

Deciding to act as if nothing had happened the previous night, Ellie poised a shaking finger over the bell and then dropped her hand to her side. She paced in the narrow space between the door and the large living room windows, head hanging low.

Her mind went back to the prior night's drive home. She thought of her friend Elliot, his hand on the gearshift lever as he pushed the car into first and pulled the parking break, nestling the Miata deftly into the dark shadows between streetlights near her house. She remembered how he'd slid his hand to her knee. His gaze hadn't left hers as he leaned across the levers, pulling her uncomfortably toward him. He'd explored her mouth, his tongue sticky and tasting of beer. His braces had pinched her lips while his fingers yanked at her top.

At that moment, all Ellie had been able to think was, *I'm not the kind of girl guys make out with.*

That thought had kept her from enjoying the long, fumbling, increasingly warm minutes in the car.

I'm his friend. Not someone he takes to parties. Not someone any *guy takes to parties.*

Although Elliot had taken her to a party that evening.

I'm his study buddy.

Even though Elliot had stopped studying with her months ago.

Guys don't hook up with me.

Despite Elliot's efforts to do exactly that.

What's going on?

The last time Ellie had kissed a boy had been at summer camp the previous August. He had chosen the last dance on the last night to walk her into the woods for a hurried embrace against a tree. Mosquitos had swarmed around them in increasing numbers until Ellie's partner, waving, scratching, and swatting, fled for the cafeteria. The next morning, he'd avoided her at breakfast and disappeared into the back of his parents' SUV before she'd had the chance to say goodbye.

That had seemed to her like a fitting precursor to another romantically arid year of high school. But parked by her home, with Elliot's increasingly heavy breathing, inept fumbling with her blouse, and hands sliding hesitatingly across her breasts, she'd reconsidered and wondered if he wanted to date her.

Standing in front of Elliot's door the next morning, she asked herself for the hundredth time what he had meant and how he felt. Did he like her that way?

A more intriguing and somewhat disturbing thought always followed. Did she like *him*?

In the cloudy light of a damp Newark, Delaware October morning, with orange fall leaves still sticking to her fuzzy boots, teenage Ellie closed her eyes and tugged a strand of long hair across her chin. The scent of her shampoo mingled with the faint aroma of her parents' morning coffee. It smelled comforting.

I got this.

She pumped her fist like her high school team did before its volleyball games.

Screw it. Whatever happens, happens.

She pushed the buzzer.

Years later, on the thirtieth floor of the Russian Hill condominium, Ellie opened her eyes and refocused on the reality in front of her. This wasn't Elliot's door. It was Dr. Lovejoy's. The plush maroon carpeting and muted light of elegant wall sconces pulled her back to the present. She trailed a strand of hair absently over her chin.

Still smells like shampoo and coffee.

In the quiet corridor she pumped her fist inconspicuously and depressed the bell.

After only a moment, Devora answered dressed

in what, on first glance, seemed like the same outfit as yesterday. A second glance told Ellie this one was even more expensive. She took a brief sniff as she passed. Devora's scent was subtle and reeked of money.

Inside the white interior, Devora stood out like a lone pine tree on a snow-covered mountaintop. The whiteness was so glaring that Ellie wished she hadn't removed her sunglasses.

She shielded her eyes. "It's intense in here."

Devora nodded. "Right. It's worse at certain times of day."

Their high heels clicked on the travertine flooring as they traversed a hallway as long as Ellie and Celine's apartment. Ellie took in the gleaming stainless steel kitchen to her right and the closed white doors to her left—doors that blended almost perfectly into the wall and were indicated only by silver handles.

The hallway ended at an enormous living-dining room. The view of Fisherman's Warf and Alcatraz Island framed in the row of floor to ceiling windows brought Ellie to a sharp stop.

A soft "wow" escaped her.

Devora continued without pause, crossing the line where the stone flooring yielded to nubby white carpeting flecked with specks of gray. "Doctor Lovejoy, Ellie Atherton is here."

Ellie hadn't noticed a woman sitting with her back to the view, her feet in a ceramic footbath, her hands on a small table, the entire scene dwarfed by the immense expanse of glass. An Asian woman in a white coat busied herself with polishing Dr.

Lovejoy's nails and ignoring the other guests.

Ellie teetered across the bumpy carpet, wishing the she could see her new employer better against the bright light. Ellie held out her hand. It hung in the air for a few seconds before anyone spoke.

"I can't shake your hand, as you can surely see, Ms. Atherton." Dr. Lovejoy nodded, indicating the woman at work. "But thank you for coming."

Ellie's arms retreated behind her back. "Ellie. Call me Ellie."

"Ellie then. Call me Vivyenne." She turned to Devora and asked her to bring Ellie a refreshment, showing her as she did so a square, chiseled chin in profile. As Ellie's eyes adjusted, she surveyed the rest of Vivyenne, unable to find a wrinkle of fat or hair out of place.

*Upkeep, refurbishing, and additions for a body like that must cost...*She paused to calculate. *Over thirty thousand dollars a year.*

Devora handed Ellie a scalding china cup of black coffee.

Oh, great. Ellie searched for a place to deposit the already shaking vessel. *This doesn't look like a Stainmaster carpet.*

Vivyenne glanced at a computer screen propped on a table at her side. "I don't have much time, Ellie. I know you want to meet Viv. And I believe Devora has told you my circumstances. I adore the cat."

Ellie stole a quick glance at Devora, whose face remained neutral.

"But I recently purchased a house on Maui and am thinking of moving there. So I would like Viv to get used to it. How better to adjust him than to have him go with you, while you supervise the work that must take place before I can take up residence?"

Ellie nodded absentmindedly, thinking only of the small, brown tidal wave gradually building in her quaking hand. The more she concentrated on trying to hold still, the more her hand wobbled.

If I don't find a place to put this quick, Vivyenne's going to kill me before I get to Hawaii.

Devora appeared at her elbow. "Let's go find Viv. And I'll brief you on the current situation." She steered Ellie by the elbow and, as soon as their backs were to Vivyenne, relieved Ellie of the coffee.

Ellie lowered her voice. "Hashtag grateful."

"I saw yesterday how you are around hot liquids. I would have brought you water, but she didn't have any. She would have flipped if I'd poured you some out of the tap."

Ellie grinned at Devora. "How do you stand working here?"

"Why are you taking a semester off to look after a house?"

"Money."

Devora raised an eyebrow in response.

Ellie nodded. "Oh, right."

A few minutes later, Ellie sat on a white bedroom carpet with her back against a white wall, a sleek, white and gray spotted cat curled up on her lap. She traced the two stripes on its cheek and a contented hum issued from the lithe form.

Devora stood erect, a few foot from the wall. "So you understand, right? I'll be your main contact. I'll do research on the contractors. You just have to make sure they do what they're supposed to do. I hear Hawaii's not the easiest place to get things done quickly."

"I got it. And you'll take care of the whole pet immigration thing?"

A characteristically rapid smile scooted across Devora's face. "It's not immigration. Hawaii and California are the same country. It's a rabies quarantine. And I'm passing that over to you. It's mostly done. You just have to get him through at the airport when you arrive."

"I think we can handle that, right, Viv?" Ellie pulled gently at the striped tail, which twitched out of her grasp.

Devora's phone pinged. "That's Vivyenne. I've got to get back in there. You can find your way out, right? I'll have the iPad and the credit card sent to your address. You buy your tickets and let me know the dates."

Ellie stood and cradled the limp cat in her arms. Devora paused at the door. "There's no way you can take Viv now, is there?" She glanced toward the living room. "She really hates the poor thing."

Ellie frowned. "I can't. Our place doesn't allow pets. That's how I ended up cat sitting in the first place."

"Right. Was just a thought." Devora reached out and tickled Viv briefly behind the ear. Then she was gone.

As Ellie waited for the elevator, she texted Celine.

Ellie: *All set. Cat's adorable. Boss is an ice queen. Assistant's better than I thought.*

Celine: *Good. But who cares. You're going to MAUI.*

Ellie: *Can I get an amen?*

The elevator that whisked Ellie to the ground floor dropped as smoothly as a Rolls Royce gliding over a red carpet. Ellie stepped into the glittering two-story lobby and sighed.

If this is her San Francisco place, I can't wait to see what she bought in paradise.

CHAPTER 3

Celine steered the tiny silver Zipcar along the freeway, maneuvering through thick traffic toward the airport exit lanes. "I still can't believe it. Three weeks ago you were lonely and broke."

Ellie grinned. "I could still be lonely."

"You'll be in a mansion walking around in a bikini surrounded by buff contractors. Explain to me how you're going to be lonely."

Ellie looked out the window at the Bay. "Seriously. I've never done most of this stuff before. Supervise electricians and gardeners and whatnot?"

"When it gets too much, drag yourself down to your private Maui beach and call me. I'll be feeling your pain."

The car sped by large corrugated iron warehouses over which a billboard proclaimed, *'The best days are play days'*.

Ellie laughed. "I feel like I might be veering off the highway I thought my life would be taking. Should be taking."

29

Celine glanced at her. "Didn't you want to get away from here?"

"Sure. But I also wanted to be a lawyer once. And for a while I thought I wanted that high-powered job at Twitter. But I'm glad now I didn't do those things. They didn't fit. They weren't me."

"Nerves. It's like you're walking down the aisle. You aren't quite sure you're doing the right thing." Celine patted Ellie's knee. "Well, I'm here to tell you, get a grip. You're moving to paradise. If you hate it, come back, and I'll take your place."

At the Alaska Airlines curb, Celine hopped out and opened the hatch. She hefted two enormous suitcases onto the sidewalk as Ellie slung her messenger bag around her shoulders and removed Viv's cat carrier from the foot well. She raised the black and yellow nylon bag to eye height.

"What's good, Viv?"

A pitiful meow issued from the interior. Celine joined them and scratched at the mesh.

"Don't complain too much, dude. There's still time for me to crawl in there and replace you."

Ellie put the carrier down and looked at her suitcases.

"What was I thinking when I packed these?"

Celine tilted her head to one side. "You can't blame me. I was the person who said all you need is a swimsuit."

"I wanted to be on the safe side." Ellie lifted the cat carrier and balanced it precariously atop of the smaller case.

A police officer pointed at the car and motioned. Celine and Ellie wrapped their arms around each other.

Celine pecked Ellie's cheek. "Don't forget your fam will be freezing in the fog."

Ellie slung the carrier over her shoulder. "Wish me luck."

Celine waved at the approaching officer and strode toward the driver's side. "Aloha, sister. Expect me at fall break."

Viv's carrier swayed from Ellie's shoulder as she struggled to pull the two suitcases behind her. Inside the terminal, a long line snaked to the edge of metal post boundaries. Ellie closed her eyes.

"Awesome. It'll take hours to get through that."

She panted, sweat dripping down from her temples despite the air conditioning, and joined the line behind a harried couple with three young boys attempting simultaneous escape in different directions. When the group moved forward, she nudged her suitcases with her feet and concentrated on keeping Viv level. She couldn't see well through the mesh and wondered what the feline was thinking.

She lowered her face to the bag. "With any luck, this will be your first and last plane ride, cutie. You'll spend the rest of your life sniffing plumeria flowers and eating pineapple."

Fifteen minutes later, the line had moved only half a revolution.

Ellie turned to the older woman behind her. "Wish we were over there." She pointed to where two relaxed-looking couples stood waiting.

The woman winked. "That's first class, honey. We're in steerage."

"First class?" Ellie blinked. "I've got a first class ticket."

The woman winked. "Then what are you doing over here with the peasants?"

As Ellie searched for a way out, other passengers stared with open resentment. Ellie felt her face redden.

The older woman tapped Ellie on the shoulder and pointed at her husband. "Ronald, be a gentleman and lift up that tape. This young lady's in the wrong line."

Ellie kicked her suitcases under the black nylon barrier.

"Sorry. I obviously don't fly first class often."

"Don't apologize." He lifted the tape higher. "We can't all be in that line, or it would be as long as this one."

Ellie ducked under the nylon and tried to stand on the other side. But something tugged her backward, threatening to dislodge Viv's carrier from her shoulder.

"Hold on there, missy…"

Ellie yanked the bag and her legs kicked out from under her. Then, as in slow motion, metal clanked. The crowd sucked in a collective breath. TSA officials stepped forward. And Ellie rolled to the hard gray floor with only one thought in her mind: *Don't crush the cat.*

The clatter of two heavy metal posts hitting the shiny floor reverberated throughout the large lobby. A stunned silence followed as people tried to classify the sound. Terrorist? Accident?

The kindly older woman bent down. "Are you

okay?"

Ellie sat up. "I'm fine. This stuff happens to me all the time." She spun toward the carrier, fiddled with the zipper, and lifted Viv out. He arched against her cheek. His silky warm fur felt comforting in the cold lobby. She plopped him in her lap as TSA officials righted the security posts and reassured passersby.

"Poor Viv." Ellie petted him. "Welcome to air travel."

***

Just inside the plane, a male flight attendant in a blue aloha shirt pointed Ellie to the second row. Ellie double-checked her ticket. The young man in the aisle seat raised his eyebrows.

"Are you the window?"

"Yes." Ellie stood up straighter. *Oh my God. I'm sitting next to a surfer god.*

"My pleasure." The tall blond in light blue O'Neill board shorts eased his bare legs and flip-flop clad feet into the corridor and stood. Ellie suppressed a grin as she slid past.

"Dog?" He nodded at the carrier on her lap. Ellie bit her lip as his loose curls bobbed.

"Cat. Egyptian Mau. Super cute and a little drugged up right now. He should be really quiet."

The man shrugged. "So much better than a baby."

Yikes. A baby hater. You'd better not start anything, Viv.

Ellie slid the cat container carefully under the

seat in front of her. The more she tried to think of something other than the gorgeous man next to her, the more she wanted to peek at him out of the corner of her eye.

What does a surfer who admits to a woman that he hates babies look like up close? Heck, what does a surfer look like up close?

Her inner battle raged when a flight attendant leaned over and interrupted.

"Champagne? Hawaiian mimosa?"

Ellie jumped, nearly knocking the tray from the woman's grasp. The attendant pulled back, the smile fixed on her lips, her eyes cautious.

Baby Hater took a mimosa.

"Champagne, please." Ellie took a quick sip to lower the level of liquid, and put the flute in the cup holder between the seats. A second glass after takeoff emboldened her to glance at her companion.

He lay reclined. A large leopard print eyeshade covered the upper half of his face. His ripped chest rose and fell gently with his breath. Long hands rested on his thighs. Ellie inspected the left one.

No wedding ring.

She dragged Viv's bag from under the seat and hoisted it onto her lap. The small flap retracted enough for her to reach inside and fondle the cat's soft ears.

Ellie turned her head to the window and whispered into the carrier. "Hey, Viv. I'm sitting next to Mr. Maui, 2016."

Viv purred against her hand. The champagne bubbled pleasantly in her stomach. And the effect of the two-thirty alarm that morning caught up with her. She drifted to sleep with her hand still in the carrier.

An urgent summons from her bladder woke her. She regarded with dismay the empty dishes littering Baby Hater's tray, blocking her exit to the aisle. Her stomach grumbled.

She leaned toward him. "Excuse me."

He didn't stir.

She tapped him gently on the arm, feeling a tingle as her fingers touched the unyielding muscle. There was no response. She shook it, patted his hand, and was considering climbing over him when the male flight attendant noticed her distress.

"Give me a second." He cleared the dishes and returned the tray to its rest. Then he clamped a hand on the man's shoulder and shook vigorously. "Sir. The lovely lady next to you would like to use the facilities."

Ellie caught no trace of irony in his use of "lovely."

Baby Hater grunted and swung his legs to the side.

"I think that's the best we're going to get."

Ellie leaned on the flight attendant's arm and crawled out of her seat, hanging onto the overhead luggage rack with her other hand, secretly wishing she might trip and land in the surfer's lap.

"Be glad you're not in coach." The attendant smiled at her. "I'll get you a meal when you're back. Chicken okay? That's all we've got left."

In the bathroom, Ellie wished she'd paid more attention to her hair that morning. It cascaded in crumpled tangles over her shoulders. She ran her fingers through it until it lay reasonably flat and dabbed her eyes with a wet paper towel.

Back in her seat, the attendant flicked a linen napkin expertly across to her. "I'm afraid you're going to have to eat quickly. We're only fifty minutes out."

Ellie found California wine helped the macadamia nut stuffed chicken breast go down rather well. She was working her way through the bananas Foster dessert when she remembered Viv. She shoveled the remainder of the ice cream into her mouth and retrieved Devora's air-dried New Zealand cat treats.

"He loves this stuff." Devora had passed Ellie the small bag on Viv's last day in Dr. Lovejoy's condo. "Give him some on the plane when you tell him hi from me."

Ellie had examined Devora's face for signs of sentimentality but saw only the usual neutral expression. "I'll text you a picture of him on the beach."

"Right. I know he's in good hands."

In the airplane, Ellie pulled at the rubber band around the package when…*snap*. With no warning, it broke. The projectile torpedoed across her seat, ricocheted off the tray table, and hurtled straight into Baby Hater's cheek.

He slapped his face, flung off the eye mask, and inspected his hand.

Ellie looked at him in dismay. "That wasn't a bug."

His bright blue eyes opened wide. He glanced from his hand to her and back again.

"Really. That was my fault." She felt color flood her face as she held up the treats. "My rubber band broke and hit you. I'm so sorry." A laugh that welled up from her stomach threatened to break free. She clenched her lips and gripped the bag, hoping his angry explosion would frighten her into silence. Anything would be better than giggling at this Adonis.

His face creased into a grin that left little space at the sides of his face.

"Was having a freakin' nightmare. Stoked you woke me up."

Ellie's chuckle grew into laughter that burst from her in hiccups. "I'm so. Relieved. I felt. So bad."

The man handed her a paper napkin. "I must have looked funny. No worries. My wife will be sorry she missed it." He reached out a firm hand. "Mike."

Ellie shook it, suddenly serious as her stomach sank. *Your wife? Knew it was too good to be true.*

"I'm Ellie."

"You and your cat live in Maui?"

"No." Ellie had to fight against sounding depressed. "We're just visiting. I've got a temporary job there."

"Where?"

"Wai...? I can't remember. I have it in my phone." She began to dig in her bag, relieved to have something to do other than to meet eyes with the *married* man she had been lusting after.

"Wailuku?"

"No."

"Wailea?"

37

"That's it."

"Nice area. You'll like it. My friend has a sick art gallery down there." He ran his hand through his curls. Ellie suppressed a sigh. "There's a gallery opening later this week. You should go." He lifted his bottom from the seat to retrieve a bulging wallet. Ellie turned away, embarrassed to look. After sifting through a large assortment of paper, he handed her a warm business card.

"Valley Isle Gallery." Ellie hesitated. "I'm not really an artist. And I couldn't afford to buy anything."

"Turn up. It's in a hotel. Validated parking." He unbuckled his seatbelt and stood over her, a picture of everything she had fantasized a man in Hawaii would be. "People on Maui are friendly. You'll make friends in no time."

***

The veterinarian met Ellie and Viv at the gate. After an uneventful inspection, she received a signed entry permit for Viv and dragged her suitcases from the open-air baggage claim into the bright Maui sun. She fished in her bag for sunglasses and stared at the Bali Hai-style mountains in the distance. Undulating green peaks folded into soft curves, creating a deep, majestic tapestry. Ethereal clouds cast dark patches into shadow and obscured the heights, leaving what lay above to Ellie's imagination.

She squatted and lifted Viv by the scruff of his neck. She clipped a cat harness around his chest and legs and put him on the ground. He looked around, blinking. She poured the remainder of her water bottle into her cupped hand. He licked it eagerly.

Almost an hour later, a cheery young Hawaiian woman slung Ellie's suitcases into the back of a passenger van. "I'm sorry about the mix-up, yeah? They should have told you to come to the bus area, not rental car. Local agencies are different."

"That's okay. It gave Viv here a chance to chase some chickens." Ellie fanned herself with the rental car company brochure. "Are they wild?"

The driver hoisted herself into the seat and turned up the air conditioning. "Feral chickens. Got loose in the nineties, they say. Your cat likes chickens?"

"I don't think he'd ever seen one before. But what he saw, he liked." Ellie tugged on Viv's leash and pulled him back from his inspection of the driver's lunch cooler.

"How long are you on the island?"

"December. Maybe longer."

"It's quiet season now, yeah? More winter visitors come after Thanksgiving and Christmas."

"Are you from here?"

"Upcountry."

"Where's Upcountry?"

The driver pointed left, toward the enormous, distant volcano. "Up there. Up Haleakala."

"That's Haleakala? I thought it would be higher."

"Ten thousand feet. Just looks short from far away."

"Does it get snow?"

"Sometimes. They close the roads if there's ice." The driver was silent for a while. "You heard about the changes on Maui? We have Target and T.J. Maxx now."

Ellie stared at her. "You didn't have them before?"

"They're new. Big grand opening last year. Traffic was crazy."

Ellie thought about Bay Area traffic jams and took in the intermittent cars passing them in the opposite direction. *Maui must have a different definition of congestion.*

The driver pointed at the wide, red-dirt fields on either side of the highway. "No more sugar cane. This year's the last harvest. The company's closing down. No more sugar from Hawaii."

Ellie stared at the vast openness, empty except for weeds. "What are they going to use the land for?"

"Don't know. It's, like, thirty-six thousand acres. They say maybe agriculture. Lots of people lost their jobs." The driver shrugged. "Could be dust storms later. Or maybe they'll build houses."

At the agency's main office, Ellie gripped Viv's leash tightly as a different attendant than her driver disappeared to get her car. Viv stalked back and forth along the pavement, antsy since his glimpse of the office fish tank. He stopped and cocked his head at a high-pitched engine squeak from around the corner. Salt-glazed headlights preceded a cracked hood, mottled roof, and dingy tires. Ellie's eyebrows fell.

"*This* is my car?"

"Two-thousand ten Nissan Sentra. Yeah." The attendant gazed at Ellie placidly, seemingly used to a less than ebullient initial reaction.

Maui sun beat down on white paint that had never seen the gloss of a wax job. She opened the door. The interior looked okay. The dashboard had been recently polished. Viv pushed past her, leapt on the seat, stretched toward the headrest, and began sharpening his claws on the upholstery.

"No. Bad cat." Ellie scooped him into her arms.

"You want an upgrade?" The attendant held up his clipboard.

Devora's admonition not to go crazy with the business credit card rang in Ellie's mind.

"No. I'm sure it runs fine." Her eyes shifted from the paint to the wheels. "Right?"

"Yeah. And if it breaks down, you call us 24/7. We come anywhere on island. Give you a new one."

Ellie pulled slowly out of the lot. "Somehow, Viv, his words weren't exactly reassuring."

Viv meowed.

"Got it. First things first. Food."

After a detour to a grocery store that could have come straight out of the Midwest, Ellie set her phone's GPS for Dr. Lovejoy's house. Her mood brightened as she cruised at twenty miles an hour past palm trees, open air restaurants, beach parks, barefooted men carrying surfboards across crosswalks, and a sapphire ocean that stretched to the horizon.

"Welcome to paradise, Viv."

She watched the laid-back beach town

41

atmosphere of South Kihei gradually transform into the manicured, high-end hotel atmosphere of Wailea. The road widened. Instead of a straight shot past restaurants, public parks, and condominiums, it wound languidly between golf courses and tall hedges above which peeped grand roofs. The ocean views disappeared behind gated, beachfront properties. Cars were larger and drove faster.

As their destination grew closer, her heart raced. She pointed at the enormous monkey-pod trees shading the road. "This, Viv, is what money looks like. Tough, I know. But we've got to get used to it."

The directions pointed her to a narrow road heading toward the beach. Ellie slowed to ten miles an hour, reminding herself that there would never be another first time to drive up to this house. She turned off the air conditioning and opened the windows. The sweet scent of mock orange blossoms drifted into the car. She willed herself to breathe more slowly.

"Your destination is on your right." The voice from the GPS sounded inappropriately neutral.

Ellie turned on her blinker and slowed to a crawl. *That's it.*

She braked and backed up a few yards to where a short driveway led to a large metal gate with embossed bamboo shoots. She pulled the car in front of it, got out, and inserted the key Devora had given her into the grimy lock. The gate creaked loudly as it swung open into the property.

Ellie wiped her hands and jogged back to the car. *I'm here. This is so awesome.*

Her grip on the steering wheel tightened as she eased the car forward. The house came into view on the right.

"Oh my God." Ellie jerked the car to a stop and laid her hand across her mouth. She closed her eyes and then opened them again. The house was still there. "Viv, that mother of yours is a piece of work."

Her gaze ranged rapidly over the large, overgrown structure that would be their home.

"She sent us to live in a dump."

CHAPTER 4

Ellie parked the car in the middle of the overgrown drive. Tropical vines encroached on all sides, covering much of the asphalt. She removed Viv from his carrier and let him wander, leashed, at her feet while she absorbed the dilapidated property.

"I bet the last time anybody called this home, people still went to Blockbuster."

The garden that lay between Ellie and the ocean evidenced former organization, even beauty. Overgrown floral bushes flowed along the edges in a pattern reminiscent of waves. A dry fountain lined with lava stones supported a life-size Hawaiian woman gracefully captured in mid-dance, her hula skirt billowing around her tapping feet, her arms raised to the sky. A small cream-colored guesthouse stood to the left of the fountain against the border of hedges. Beyond that, the ocean sparkled blue and clear, with two islands, one small, and one large, visible in the distance.

The main house stood back from the drive with a view of the garden and water. It was an expansive one-story structure with a red tiled roof that arched into Asian-looking peaks. Vines squeezed the massive square pillars of the wide wooden porch and clambered across the floor, where a lone deck chair lay on its side, sprawled like a parched traveler left to desiccate.

Ellie pulled a reluctant Viv up the steps.

"Welcome to the Maui Bates Motel."

Floor to ceiling windows shone with reflective one-way glass. Ellie stuck her tongue out as she passed. Devora's second key fit the tiny lock of the massive carved door that swung open noiselessly to Ellie's push. She inhaled the musty air.

Viv yanked free. She watched him chase something scuttling along the wide hallway.

"Don't even think about bringing that back to show me."

Ellie walked into the corner living room to her left and flipped each of the many switches by the door. Recessed lights illuminated the large, empty room. Overhead ceiling fans turned noiselessly. Blinds retracted.

At least Devora came through. The electricity is on.

Ellie turned the latches on the windows closest to her and slid them along their runners until they clicked into place. A fragrant breeze wafted through the screens and stirred her blouse. She sighed.

"Viv? Where are you?"

Muffled meows led her to the kitchen at the back of the house where the cat sat on the counter, the corners of his mouth curved around a struggling gecko. When he spied her, he jerked his head

45

toward the ceiling and gave her a leer that said, *See what I've got?*

Ellie lunged for his leash, but he dashed away before she could catch him.

She leaned on the dark granite counter.

"You little monster. Don't let that thing go."

She felt something crawling up her arm.

"Eek. Ants." She swiped at them viciously, turned on the lights, and surveyed the room. The floor and counters were littered with tiny black dropping the size of small rice kernels. Ant highways trailed along baseboards, up walls, and across the ceiling. The refrigerator was warm inside and she couldn't find a microwave, but the sink produced both hot and cold water and the gas stove worked.

In the master bedroom, she sat on the bare mattress and texted Devora.

Ellie: Arrived. House is a dump.

Devora: Keys work?

Ellie: Yes but house is filthy.

Devora: Electricity on?

Ellie: Yes but bugs in kitchen and massive cockroaches in bathroom.

Devora: Live ones?

Ellie: Not anymore.

Devora: Mattress there?

Ellie: Yes but nothing else.

Devora: Lost ur credit card?

Ellie: No.

Devora: So get to work.

Ellie sent an emoji with its tongue sticking out.

Devora: Viv pass inspection?

Ellie: Yes. He's lovin' the bugs.

Devora: Right. Stand ur shoes up at night. Helps keep out poisonous centipedes.

Ellie: WTF. How much she pay for this place?

Devora: Over 4M.

Ellie: She got shafted.

Devora: Location. Remember, ur in paradise.

Ellie wandered toward the front of the house, opening every screened window along the way. When she reached the porch, she righted the deck chair and called Celine.

"Thought I might hear from you about now. Been to the beach yet? Show me some video."

I should show you a video of the kitchen. I know how much you love the six-legged set. Instead, Ellie switched to a video call and panned across the long garden.

"Awesome." Celine's face registered genuine astonishment.

"See all the vines? The place needs serious work. And not only outside. The inside's a disaster area."

Celine brushed her hand across the screen as though chasing away an annoying fly. "Did you see those flowers? And the ocean? Walk me over there."

Ellie traipsed across the lawn. Celine informed her along the way about the plants they passed— sago palm, plumeria, pendent heliconia, ornamental bananas, blue ginger, longhorn.

"When'd you get your botany degree?"

"My mom loves gardening."

"My mom loves ancient Greek."

"Less practical. Now walk into the water and tell how warm it is."

Ellie kicked off her sandals and pointed the phone at her toes. She clambered over the black lava rocks that littered the shore's edge.

"Ouch."

"Be careful. Don't drop me."

Ellie laughed. "I appreciate the concern. You should have come inside when you dropped me off at the airport. I knocked over a whole row of those metal posts they have to mark the lines."

"Sorry I missed it."

Ellie reached a sandy section and stepped into the smooth, clear water. "Wow. It's warm."

"How warm?"

"Not quite like a bathtub. But comfortable."

"It's so clear."

"The sand is soft." She wiggled her toes to bury them.

"How soft?"

"Well, not like a rabbit. Kind of like…cream of wheat?"

"Thanks for the image of your feet in my breakfast bowl."

"How about a plush towel?"

"Better."

Ellie watched her own legs on the screen, her navy linen capri pants legs ballooning in the gently flowing ripples, her deep red toenails shimmering in the afternoon sun. She sighed.

"I heard that. Sounded like the sigh of someone in paradise."

Later, back on the porch, Celine suggested Ellie make a Target run.

"Your immediate problems are nothing a little elbow grease and Clorox can't fix."

Ellie nodded slowly. "And ant traps. Do you think they make gecko traps?"

"Probably."

"Should I leave Viv here by himself?" She turned the phone to show Celine the image of Viv throwing himself high against the living room wall to catch a gecko.

"He knows where his litter box is?"

"I showed it to him."

"Then leave him. That cat thinks he's died and gone to heaven. And if they don't sell gecko traps, you're going to be glad he got a head start on his new job."

***

Ellie pulled into an empty section of the Target parking lot so she could sit and admire the West Maui mountains glowing in the late afternoon light. Her hair blew in all directions when she exited the car, obscuring her vision. She held it back with one hand and typed into her long shopping list, "Hair elastics."

Inside the store, beyond an initial section of Hawaii-themed goods, she felt as though she'd never left San Francisco. The clothing and jewelry departments mirrored what she'd last seen at the Target on Geary Boulevard. She pushed a shopping cart along the aisles, throwing additions on the bulging tower of items. Mattress cover, sheets, towels, cleaning supplies, mousetraps, and soap jostled with a coffee maker, a blender, toys for Viv, and groceries.

She examined the prices of refrigerators and weighed the relative merits of buying one she could lift by herself with buying one that would hit Vivyenne's pocketbook with a kick she might register as payback for sending Ellie unprepared to a dump. A man's voice broke in.

"They might be cheaper at Costco."

Ellie looked up to see a heavy-set man with an astounding tan set off by startlingly white hair.

"Don't mean to give advice, eh? But Costco's sometimes cheaper for big items."

"They have Costco here?"

"Since 1995. Upgraded in 2012. Got gas now too."

"Gosh. Thanks."

The man nodded and pushed his cart away.

People are *friendly in Hawaii.*

At the checkout, Ellie, distracted by the candy shelves, said "yes" to the cashier's question about needing bags.

Why wouldn't I need bags?

She added gum and chocolate bars to the pile, paid, and only then noticed the heap of red dotted recyclable bags mounded in her cart.

She stared at the cashier. "Don't you have plastic bags?"

"No plastic bags in Hawaii. Only paper or recyclable."

"And you don't have paper?"

The cashier smiled sheepishly. "Sorry."

Ellie laughed. "No worries." She fingered a mass of handles. "I always wondered what I was going to leave my grandkids. Now I know."

Dusk settled across the island as Ellie drove home, the passenger seat next to her occupied by a belted-in mini-fridge. Pineapples, bananas, and a king-size bottle of rum peeked out of a cardboard box alongside a large bag of ice. In the bright kitchen at the back of the house, she unpacked paper towels to the music of IZ Kamakawiwo'ole's ukulele on her phone. After scraping from the counter what a solicitous Costco employee suggested was probably "only" gecko poop, she scrubbed the surface with bleach and deposited the blender. Next she chopped a pineapple, its scent evocative of her first summer in California.

For an instant, an image of a blanket spread near a rose garden in Golden Gate Park filled her mind. She saw Elliot stretched across it, gazing at the cloudy sky. She remembered the taste of the sweet fruit mingling with the bitterness that welled in her mouth in response to his words.

"Just because we've been together since high school, Ellie, doesn't mean we have to be together forever."

In the Wailea kitchen, Ellie shook her head and turned up the music.

I came here to get away from all that.

Viv lay stretched in the corner, sated from dinner and exhausted by more exercise than he'd had in the past months put together. He regarded her through half-closed eyes. Ellie sloshed coconut cream, rum, ice, and pineapple chunks indiscriminately into the blender. Her fingers hovered over its plastic levers.

"Plug your ears, baby. This cleaning crew needs an incentive."

The cat yawned, laid its head on its paws, and turned its ears flat when the screeching began.

After three hours of cleaning, close to midnight, Ellie regarded the voluminous kitchen trashcan, filled to the brim with sodden paper towels. She pushed strands of sweaty hair from her forehead with a yellow-gloved hand.

"I quit."

She traipsed to the porch and leaned against the vines snaking up a supporting pillar. The crash of ocean waves on the beach echoed louder in the dark, as though the sea had crept up the lawn in the night, like a living creature eager to explore. The air was still warm, a soft breeze bending the tops of the palm trees near the house, their silhouettes barely visible in the light of a crescent moon.

Using the flashlight on her phone, Ellie carefully picked a path across the middle of the yard. She steered clear of the eerie shrubbery. The forgotten Hawaiian dancer, appearing suddenly on the fountain in the semi-darkness, made her jump. She rolled her eyes at herself.

Nobody out here but you, Ellie. That's what Vivyenne paid the big bucks for. Privacy.

From the sound of the ocean, Ellie imagined large breakers smashing against the shore. But at the water's edge the surf appeared the same size as during the day, with only the stillness magnifying each reverberation. Too used to the city, Ellie couldn't help but turn toward the house, scanning the darkness for the sign of another person, straining her ears above the waves to check for footsteps, unable to quell completely the sense that she wasn't alone.

Give it a rest. It's just like that night with Alberto. Nobody was out there then, either.

She thought back to that night only a few years ago when she had wanted nothing more than to drive straight to their cramped studio apartment after closing the microbrewery for the night. But Alberto had steered the car to a neighborhood near Ocean Beach, parked in a friend's driveway, and walked with her to the shore. Ellie's exhaustion masked her nervousness until they stood alone on the vast, dark expanse of sand, the San Francisco night enveloping them like a thick, damp, uncomfortable sheet. She struggled to make out sounds above the consistent crash of the waves.

"Can't we come back in the morning?" She tugged at Alberto's sleeve. "People get murdered out here."

Alberto, silent, had pulled her farther onto the beach. Ellie bit back her resentment, feeling as though she'd been doing a lot of that lately. She distracted herself, organizing the following day's activities, prioritizing those she could squeeze into the few hours between the morning alarm and the eleven a.m. opening of the restaurant attached to the brewery.

When am I ever going to get enough sleep again? Maybe if somebody stabs us out here, I'll end up in the hospital and can get some rest.

She smiled at the thought.

I could sleep in and get meals brought to me for a change.

She swung Alberto's hand. This kind of crazy detour from life's normal course was one of the things that had attracted her to him. His sense of adventure. His willingness to take risks. His boldly stepping forward without regard to the consequences. She decided to make the best of it.

He stopped by the water's edge and launched into a speech about the vastness of the ocean. It blended in Ellie's weary mind with the rush of the water. The words entered her mind as blurry, indistinct sounds, their meaning irrelevant, only

Alberto's physical presence a comfort in the semi-darkness with the city's glow at their backs.

"...break up."

The short phrase registered in Ellie's thoughts seconds, perhaps minutes, after it had been uttered.

"What?" Ellie's head snapped to look at her companion. "Did you just say 'break up'?" She struggled to make out the details of his face in the gloom.

"I said, I don't really see you fitting into my future. Our dreams don't align."

Ellie jerked her hand from his. "You walked me out here in the middle of the night to break up with me?"

"I thought doing it here would make it something you'd remember."

She shuddered, suddenly afraid of much more than the myriad possible strangers roaming Ocean Beach at one in the morning.

"I turned my life upside down for you. And now you want to break up?" Ellie put her hand on her hips, anger flashing from her eyes in the darkness. "How the hell did you think I'd forget this moment?"

Back on the beach in Maui, Ellie sighed.

Alberto was a shit. Celine was right. I would have broken up with him eventually. He just beat me to it.

She kicked at the shallow water dancing in the light of her phone, realizing for the first time that Alberto had been right too.

We didn't align. Maybe if we'd been more honest

with each other from the beginning, instead of always doing what we thought the other person wanted, something could have worked itself out. But the way it was, it had to end.

It felt like a revelation, and with it, the Maui darkness seemed to lift slightly. The constant washing of the sand sounded less grating, more soothing. The deep stillness behind her felt less creepy, more inviting. The stars above floated less distant, more glorious.

Ellie strolled back to the house and crawled, unwashed, onto the bed next to the already dreaming Viv, whose nose twitched eagerly on the pillow.

"First day in paradise." She rolled on her side and gazed out the window at the flickering stars. "Wonder what tomorrow will bring."

CHAPTER 5

Ellie awoke with a start, disoriented and sore. A rhythmical thumping issued from the corner of the room. She shielded her eyes against the strong sunlight that streamed in through the window above her bed. The rays illuminated Viv pouncing periodically against the wall.

"I spent thirty bucks on toys for you yesterday, buster." She glanced at the undisturbed pile of pink and purple furry animals in the corner. "Should have known better. There's no gecko like a real gecko."

For breakfast, Ellie, clad in shorts, a t-shirt, and flip-flops carried a cup of coffee and a small banana across the scraggly lawn to the shore. The powerful morning sun warmed her back. The blue ocean shimmered. The two distant islands, one nestled in the embrace of its much larger cousin, glowed a deep pink. Birds chirped, cawed, and cooed all around her in the fragrant trees and bushes. Palm fronds rustled, bending slightly in the northern breeze.

She waded into the water above her knees, still surprised by its warmth, and turned back to look at the house.

From this distance, it looks like a fixed up rich person's house. Kind of.

She relaxed. Warm, velvety air caressed her. The tide lapped at her legs.

Then a large wave broke half way up her back. She stumbled forward, coffee sloshing. She barely regained her footing.

And that, folks, ends any idea I had about swimming here. She scanned up and down the shoreline. The only figures were two stand up paddle boarders in the distance, smaller than grains of rice on the horizon. *I want me a beach with a lifeguard.*

An hour later, Ellie drove slowly along South Kihei Road in search of lifeguard stands. When she had passed a few, she pulled into a small strip mall to turn around. While she waited for a Mustang convertible to back out of a spot, the banner in front of a snorkeling shop caught her eye: **'*Free mask and fin rental with lessons*'**.

Ellie pulled into the convertible's slot.

In the store, photos of sea turtles and brightly colored tropical fish covered the walls alongside snorkels and masks that dangled from the ceiling.

"Aloha." The teenager behind the counter stepped out to greet her.

Ellie pulled her long ponytail over her shoulder. "Hi."

"Can I help you?"

"I saw your sign outside. About free lessons."

"Snorkeling lessons, yeah? They're forty dollars. But you get a free rental set when you sign up."

Ellie looked at the boxes of fins on the floor. "How long is a rental?"

"Twenty-four hours."

Ellie's eyes glittered impishly. "Twenty-four makes it sound like a long time."

The youth looked at the floor. "Well, it's one day."

Ellie tapped his arm playfully. "I'm teasing. Look, I'd like to sign up for a snorkeling lesson if you have something this morning. I'll buy the gear. I'm going to be here for a few months."

"Do you live here? I can give you the kama'aina rate."

"The what?"

"The rate for locals."

"Thanks. But I'm not local. The only ocean swimming I've done was at Rehoboth Beach. In Delaware."

"Delaware? What state's that in?"

Ellie laughed. "That's a trick question. Do you have lessons this morning?"

The boy returned to the counter. "Yeah. Noa's teaching a class in an hour." He nodded to the back of a darkly tanned man patiently helping a gray-haired woman with fins.

"Okay. Sign me up." She handed him the business credit card with only a twinge of unease.

Learning to snorkel must fit in my job description somehow.

The class met at the north end of the first of three beaches all called Kamaole. Ellie deposited her tunic, towel, and flip flops above the high tide line and joined the small group standing near the water. They were easy to identify, with identical orange snorkels and masks hanging from their hands. A man approached them from a stairway tucked between the palm trees and rocks, yelled something, and waved. He limped slightly and Ellie's fantasies of meeting another Baby Hater fell away as she took in the instructor's brown hair that had been cut so long ago all style had faded to fringe, his wiry, almost emaciated body, and the baggy board shorts held up precariously on jutting hips.

The other students were two Vancouver families with three children each and an older couple from Dallas. Ellie recognized the older woman as the one from the store. The instructor, Noa, made them laugh with his short bio of how he moved from the Bronx to Maui. Then Ellie made them laugh when she blew into the bottom of the snorkel instead of the mouthpiece.

Noa brushed her arm and whispered as he passed her. "Wish you were holding something else in your mouth."

Ellie narrowed her eyes and shot him a look, but he was helping adjust a young girl's mash. She shrugged.

In the water, Noa took a hands-on approach to instruction. He held the children up under their stomachs, one floating on each side of him. He carefully eased the older couple into their fins, submerging to made adjustments while the woman giggled.

"Ooh. I'm ticklish. Oh, my."

"Don't let him do anything I wouldn't, eh?" Her husband peeped anxiously beneath the surface with his mask.

The woman splashed water at him. "Honey, the last time you removed my shoes was on our wedding night."

During Ellie's turn, she wondered about Noa's needing to support her flat stomach while she practiced kicking. When he moved his hands to her thighs to adjust her style, she pulled slowly away. He gave her the thumbs up sign and motioned for the group to follow him.

The shimmering blue world beneath the waves amazed her. Ridges in the sand far beneath reminded her of Italian marbled paper. Cream-colored fish with whiskers sifted for food. Black lava rocks loomed in the distance. Ellie pushed to one side the "Jaws" theme that had been playing softly ever since she entered the water.

The older man pointed to long, skinny fishes that looked to Ellie like silver sticks. A small maroon box dotted with white spots darted beneath her. Schools of glittering flat yellow and white gems inspected the expanse of coral ahead. Sea urchins shone in hues of black, gray, white, and red.

Suddenly, something brushed her chest. The snorkel muffled her scream. She whipped around to see Noa at her side and shook her head at him. Her bikini, her hands pantomimed, was off-limits. He shrugged, gave her another thumbs up sign, and paddled toward the two families.

Ellie kept the others in sight but steered clear of Noa. As the coral grew thicker, fish swam in greater profusion around her, their color and variety beguiling. She followed a lustrous blue and green shape with a funny bump like a BMW antenna between its eyes. Out of nowhere, a large bulk caught the corner of her eye. She screamed down her tube again and turned toward it.

The enormous sea turtle swam unconcernedly past, its shell longer than her torso, its yellow and brown flippers blending in with the mottled light. Ellie followed it at a respectful distance, transfixed. After surfacing for air, it floated gracefully downward, limbs outstretched like a Star Trek Klingon Bird-of-Prey, to a resting place under a rock.

Ellie surfaced, awestruck. She struggled in the strangely heavy waves to look around for her companions.

I have to show you this.

But she didn't see anything. Except the moored sailboat she had noticed from the beach. It had been small and enticing then. Now it loomed large and parallel to where she swam. The umbrellas on the beach, in contrast, seemed miles away. She looked down.

Oh, no.

The ocean floor was distressingly distant. Music reverberated in her head, this time at much higher volume.

Dah-dum. Dah-dum.

Ellie spotted orange dots close to shore.

Snorkels.

A high wave swamped her. Water filled her snorkel. The gurgling noise of her own breathing

62

terrified her. It sounded like she was drowning. She sucked in salt water with her next gulp of air and spat the snorkeling tube out. She gasped.

Dah-dum.

All her limbs tingled.

What was that?

She stuck her head in the water and spun around like a top, checking the deep for an approaching shark. Her head emerged, sputtering. Another wave splashed against her face and she took in more water.

Dah-dum.

She felt the jaws clamp her arm. She yanked it free, screaming and kicking.

"Hey, don't panic."

The words took a few moments to register. Ellie swiveled toward the speaker. She saw a black-masked man with a snorkel dangling from the side of his face. The eyes visible through his mask registered concern. He held his hands above the surface.

"You looked like you were in trouble."

Ellie coughed as another wave sloshed against her.

"Put your snorkel back in."

She shook her head, hacking.

"The waves will keep coming. Put it back in and let me get you back to shore, okay?"

Ellie nodded and replaced her snorkel.

"That's it. Now give me your hand."

The man held his hand out to her. She clenched it with a strength borne of terror.

The man chuckled. "What a grip." He smiled and

Ellie exhaled. She nodded and gave him a thumbs up.

"Okay. Here we go. Kick along with me and we'll get there faster." He replaced his snorkel and put his head in the water. Ellie followed suit.

As they traveled slowly toward shore, she periodically glanced at her companion. He met her looks and nodded. She felt her heartbeat gradually slow. As the ocean floor ascended to meet them, her breathing grew steadily calmer. Finally, he motioned for her to stand.

Ellie ripped off her mask.

"Tera firma. Thank goodness."

The man looked pleased. "Welcome back." He pulled off his own gear. His wavy, dark brown hair glistened. Ellie noticed for the first time his thick, smooth chest and bulging biceps.

She rubbed the tension out of one shoulder at a time. "I don't know what would have happened if you hadn't been there. I totally panicked."

"Was this your first time out?" He bent to remove his fins.

"I was in a class."

"An invisible class?" He squinted at the ocean. "I didn't see anyone out there with you."

Ellie had trouble removing her eyes from her intriguing savior. But she finally shaded them and scanned the horizon. "Over there. By the rocks. I think that's them." She smoothed her hair, preparing to put her mask back on.

The man shook his head derisively. "You've got a lousy instructor if he hasn't noticed you're gone. You should get out and rest. You had quite a scare."

Ellie tugged with elaborate nonchalance at a string of seaweed tangled in some strands of hair. Her face reddened. She held her hair back with one hand and turned the seaweed side away from her companion. "I should get back out there."

He put his fins back on his feet and pulled on his mask. "Then I'll go with you."

Ellie blushed. "You don't have to."

"I was a life guard in high school. Humor me."

Ellie laughed, took another ineffective yank at the seaweed, and donned her outfit. The man held out his hand. Ellie looked at it, reddening further. But she acquiesced when he didn't let it drop. His grip felt warm and comforting. It banished the horrible theme music from her mind. They strode together into the shallows.

Under pretext of watching fish, she stole glances at her swimming mate as they headed out to the group. His muscles rippled as he glided by her side. She tried to relax her hand in his, but something in her didn't want to let go.

She kicked more slowly as they approached the class. Noa swam toward her.

"Hey." Noa scrutinized her rescuer, who still held her tightly. "You didn't pay. This class is for participants only."

Ellie felt her companion's arm stiffen. "Some class," he said. "You didn't even notice she was in trouble out there."

"Try doing my job, dude. They give me more people than one person can handle. Besides, I've got my eye on her, don't worry."

Ellie turned away from Noa, lifted her mask, and

rolled her eyes at her new friend. "Thanks."

He grinned. "You be careful."

"I will."

Ellie watched him swim away, wishing she had the guts to race after him.

But he's bound to be like Baby Hater, she told herself. *Wife. Kids. Pet hamsters.*

She jumped at a voice in her ear. "Stick close to me." Noa smirked behind his mask. "I can show you plenty."

***

Later on the beach, the children from the class carted wet sand from the ocean in conveyer belt fashion to craft their growing sea turtle sculpture. Ellie, wrapping her hair, seaweed and all, in a towel, watched them.

"Hi."

The familiar voice made her heart quicken. She turned and blurted out the question that had been consuming her since she'd left him in the water.

"What's your name?"

One corner of the man's mouth rose. "Denver." The slight movement transformed slowly into a broad smile. "How about you?"

"I'm Ellie. And I'm so glad to see you." *Way to go. Just let it all hang out.*

"I'll take that as a compliment."

"I mean, I didn't really get to thank you out there." *Easy. Remember his wife.*

She glanced quickly at his left hand, but it was holding a duffle.

He shrugged. "I'm glad I found you." He removed a GoPro from the bag. "Got some good shots. Have some of you too."

"They can't be very flattering."

"I think they're pretty decent."

Ellie grinned. "You must not take many pictures."

"I know what's good when I see it."

Her eyes held his gaze. She tried to ignore the thumping in her chest.

Remember. Wife. Kids. Hamsters.

He searched again in the bag. "Send me an email if you want the pictures."

He held out a card with his left fingers clearly visible.

No ring.

She took it and read. "Denver Edgerly. So you…and your family…are from Seattle?"

His eyebrow shot up and then settled just as quickly. "My parents are there." He bounced the camera lightly in his hand. "But otherwise I'm a family of one."

Ellie's toes drew a heart shape in the sand before she realized what they were doing. She hastily stepped on the outline.

"I'll send you an email, Denver."

"I'll look forward to it, Ellie."

The rhythmic pounding of the waves on the shore echoed in her head as she watched Denver's retreating back.

He beats Baby Hater. By a mile.

CHAPTER 6

Noa flashed a shaka gesture to the teen managing the snorkeling shop counter and headed to a jacked-up pickup in the parking lot. The rusty door hinges squeaked as he entered and threw his empty lunch bag on the ripped upholstery of the passenger seat.

On Mokulele Highway, he rolled down the windows and gunned past two Mustang convertibles. The asphalt road stretched straight between the detritus of the former sugar cane fields that cast long shadows in the afternoon light. His mind wandered to the highlight of the morning's snorkeling lesson, the long-haired brunette in the bikini.

She let me touch her body. Came back to me after that dude 'rescued' her. That was sick.

He patted his pants pocket, feeling for the registration information he'd swiped from the store's folder.

She's my girl.

The truck whined reluctantly uphill into Macawao. Noa pulled a torn sweatshirt from the backseat and tugged it over his head, one hand on the wheel. He slowed and eased into an empty spot in front of the Pukalani Superette, a phone with a cracked screen held to his ear.

"Just pulling into Puk Sup. Need anything? …Got it."

He shuffled through the aisles, his flip-flops slapping the shiny linoleum as he picked items from the displays. Plastic tubs of Chef Boyardee beef ravioli, a six-pack of Budweiser, a bag of rice, some carrots, a daikon, a container of eggs, and a few cans of Spam filled the basket he brought to the checkout.

"Hey, Lisa. Howz it?"

"Howz it, Noa. You shopping for auntie again, yeah? How she doing?"

He shrugged. "She's okay. Up and down. You know."

"Yeah. Say hi for me."

The clerk bagged the ravioli and beer separately from the remaining items and waved to Noa as he walked out. A few minutes later, he pulled up in front of a gray, one-story house with corrugated metal roof and faded green shutters. A scraggly overgrown plant evoking only the faintest memory of tending and watering battled for life in a blue stoneware pot on the entrance steps. A sloping-roof concrete structure with a separate entrance and two small, shutter-less windows leaned against the side of the house like a black-sheep relative.

Noa parked on the grass by the side of a chain link fence. An elderly, stooped Asian woman in gym shorts and a tank top leaned against the doorframe of the main house, waiting. Noa raised the bag of groceries. The woman smiled, showing a large gap in her lower front teeth.

"Mahalo." She swayed sideways with the weight of the bag.

"No problem. You need some help?"

"You come for dinner tomorrow?"

"Sure."

The woman nodded, pushed herself from the door, and disappeared into the dark interior. Noa watched until she vanished into an adjoining room.

He kicked an outdoor washing machine hose from the path and pushed open the adjacent building's unlocked door. An uncovered rack of fluorescent lights on the ceiling illuminated a bare concrete floor and sparse furnishings. A TV and mattress rested on the ground opposite a sink, refrigerator, cabinets, and a two-ring burner on a short counter. A white plastic table with a matching chair occupied the center of the space. A surfboard leaned against the one empty wall.

Noa flicked a remote and opened a tub of ravioli. He flopped onto the mattress and ate, staring blankly at the football game on the screen. When he finished, he pulled the fuzzy bolster pillow against his chest and dozed.

A nearby revving engine roused him. He looked at his phone.

"Almost eleven."

Back in the truck, the cans of Bud rattled next to him and his hair whipped in the cool night air as he drove the nearly empty roads down to Kahului and then up to Wailuku. On a back street east of town he shut off his lights, cut his engine, and coasted in neutral until the truck reached a series of small but well-maintained stucco houses. He braked by one with flat metal sculptures of the Hawaiian island chain drilled to its outside wall.

Shadows behind a curtained window outlined two figures inside. Noa broke off a beer and swallowed the contents in a continuous gulp. One of the figures passed to the curtain-less window nearest the street, where an overhead light illuminated the blonde head of a woman walking and then bending over a sink. Noa crushed the empty can and threw it across the street. It bounced on the lawn beyond the light cast by the window.

"Two-timing bitch."

Noa sat in the dark, scrutinizing his ex-girlfriend.

"Putting that fuckin' restraining order on me."

Another can quickly followed the first.

"Whining about a few bruises."

And another.

"Better life my ass."

One more.

"My father beat me worse than I hit you. And he did it every fuckin' day."

He eased open the driver's seat door, wincing at the noise it made. The woman in the kitchen continued washing.

"Then my stupid-ass mother. Moved us out. Gets laid all she wants. With whoever she wants. And twelve-year-old me gets what? A fuckin' better life?"

A shaven-headed man appeared behind the woman. Even at a distance Noa could make out the muscular tattooed arms that wrapped around the woman, who leaned into him as he nuzzled her neck. Noa took a step forward. The man looked up. Noa quickly retreated behind the truck, his neck craned from behind the cab as he peered at the entwined couple.

"Who needs you. I got someone better."

Noa felt in his pocket for the registration, took it out, and lodged it against the window where he could see it. He unzipped his pants, felt the stiff warmth in his hand, and jerked. He closed his eyes and thought of Ellie.

***

That afternoon, Ellie used both hands to steer the car home from the beach so she wouldn't be tempted to email and drive.

"Viv." She scooped up the cat waiting at the front door and swung him to and fro by his armpits. "Guess who I met at the beach today? Give up? A totally awesome Hawaiian surfer dude."

Viv patted mildly at her face with soft paws. She cradled him in her arms and tickled his stomach. He squirmed and writhed his way back to the floor, where he stalked off toward the kitchen. Ellie followed.

"Okay. Maybe not a surfer. But a lifeguard. Used to be. And drop dead gorgeous."

Viv emerged from behind the counter with a desiccated gecko in his mouth.

"Ha. Good try. Even that can't spoil my mood. Now drop it."

Viv slinked off toward the bedroom. Ellie raced after him, laughing.

On the lanai, leftover slushy piña colada in hand, she crafted an email to Denver. She read it aloud to Celine.

"Good." Celine's image on the iPad nodded. "You don't sound desperate."

"I'm not desperate."

"Just frisky."

Ellie's gaze drifted to the ocean. "What I really am is flattered."

"Don't start the 'who's gonna be attracted to little ol' me' routine again. Thought I talked you out of that."

"You should have seen him."

"Don't need to. He saw you. And what he saw, he liked. That's all you need to think about. Give him your phone number and push send."

"Sent."

"You go, girl. Now take me out to that beach again."

Ellie worked on calling contractors for the two remaining hours before her self-imposed Hawaiian quitting time. She called companies from the long list Devora had emailed first thing in the morning, starting with the cleaning service Devora said she hoped would be up Ellie's standards.

That's Devora's version of a joke, right? My standard right now is no dead animals in the kitchen sink.

She coordinated logistics, checked references, and set up appointments, all the while willing herself not to look at her email unless work demanded it, which, somehow, it did, frequently.

But Denver didn't reply. And the next morning Ellie didn't even think about email until after coffee, when his name stood out like a beacon in her inbox.

Ellie read,

Here's a link to the uploaded pictures.

Her eyes shone as she sat on the lone deck chair, shielding the phone from the morning sun's glare.

Sorry it took me a while. Work was a bear yesterday. Business calls and emails. Didn't even have dinner. Fell asleep with the phone on my chest.

A vision of Denver's broad chest glistening with seawater spun through Ellie's mind like a slow motion throwback to a *Baywatch* commercial. She shook her head to dispel the image and read on.

Hope the rest of your 'lesson' went okay. Instructor looked like a scumbag to me. But I'm glad you got your feet wet. Snorkeling's one of the best ways I know to spend a Hawaii morning.

Ellie's fingers could hardly type fast enough. But progress on the actual content of her reply was slow.

I'm so glad I met you yesterday.

Delete.

`Thanks for the pictures. Love the ones of the turtles. Might want to Photoshop the ones of me.`

Delete.

`My parents in Delaware will love the ones of me.`

Delete.

`My friends in California will love the ones of me.`

Constructing the final sentence took more time than the rest of the email put together. She settled on,

`Maybe I'll see you on the beach again sometime.`

She closed her eyes and hit *send*.

In the kitchen, she hid the phone in a cabinet and turned her back on it. Then she stuck a sticky note on the door to make sure she remembered where she'd hidden it. Viv regarded her quizzically from the tile floor.

"I've got to get some work done. I won't check until lunch."

When she opened the cupboard at eleven-thirty, eight missed work calls stared up at her from the screen. She didn't finish replying to all of them until after two. The reward email from Denver made her sit down.

"Ugh, Viv." She stroked the cat who was stretched his full length in the sun on a kitchen windowsill. "He's on a flight back to the mainland. Says he'll text me a picture of Seattle when he gets there."

She wrote back, *Safe travels,* and attached a selfie of her and the cat before she thought better of it.

"He's got enough bad photos of me."

***

A few evenings later, Baby Hater's gallery opening beckoned from Ellie's calendar, a lone evening entry in a sea of white space.

"Should I go?" She stood in front of the full-length bedroom mirror in a sleeveless dress of red hibiscus prints on a white background.

"You asking me or yourself?" Celine's image gave her a questioning glance.

"You."

"Hell, yeah. Mr. Gorgeous Lifeguard isn't the only fish in the tank. Go see what else you can catch."

"That's easy for you to say." Ellie played with clipping her hair back in a bun. "Men fall all over you."

"If things get tough, pretend you're drowning. Worked last time."

Ellie made a face into the phone and laughed.

An hour later, a white-clad attendant whisked to

her car door under the softly glowing lights of the hotel's massive, pillared entrance.

Ellie blushed. "Sorry about the rent-a-wreck."

The young man smiled as though she had just handed him the keys to a Rolls Royce.

Ellie's heels clicked on the polished marble floor as she strolled past exotic flower arrangements taller than a child. They traced the air with the faint breath of tropical perfume. The open lobby encircled an enormous water feature, beyond which stretched more marble, glittering chandeliers, and enough flowers to fill a botanical garden. Ellie sunk into a chair at the edge and watched guests pass in quiet groups. The only sounds were the splashing of the fountains and the hushed hum of conversation in Russian and French from the concierge desk.

Ellie sighed. *This is my kind of paradise.* Her dress fluttered around her knees as she rose to ask her way to the opening.

On one of the hotel's lower levels, Valley Isle Gallery occupied a corner location in an alley of high-end real estate. Soft Hawaiian music drifted from the white-carpeted interior. Ellie stood in front of a large picture window framing a purple glass octopus. She gazed past it, trying to get a lay of the land.

People have drinks. And they're eating. I probably want to avoid both unless I'm looking to get kicked out for spilling something on a fancy painting.

"Ellie."

She turned to see Baby Hater with a buff, beautiful blonde on his arm, his female twin in all things perfectly surfer.

"Epic. Here's the person next to me on the plane. Brigie, meet Ellie. I'm getting you two drinks."

Ellie waved to deter him but his back was turned. She faced the stunning Brigie.

Oh, great. What's Baby Hater's real name again?

Ellie fumbled. "It was awesome of…your husband to invite me here. I don't know anybody on Maui yet except…your husband."

"He's always stoked to make people feel at home."

"He's a great introduction to Maui. Perfect for the plane. Gave me a really awesome picture."

Brigie smiled as though she understood exactly what Ellie was talking about.

Which is good, because I have no idea what I'm talking about.

Baby Hater appeared fortuitously with champagne. Ellie buried her face in the glass. She grinned at his explanation of the octopus in the window and then dove, drink in hand, into the heart of the gallery.

A marine theme dominated the displayed art. Ellie marveled at the mediums used to depict creatures of the deep and at the imagination that morphed a turtle into a coat rack and a humpback whale into a miniature piano.

"Do you like cephalopods?" An eerily tan man of about fifty materialized at her elbow.

"Cephalopods?" Ellie blinked and tried not to scratch her head. "Sure."

"Which do you prefer?" The man leaned toward

her.

Her eyes flicked from his to the glass in her hand. "Uh, they're all kind of nice?"

"I agree. Everyone likes Nautilus. But I prefer octopuses." He took a step forward, nearly rubbing arms with her.

"Oh."

He inclined his head conspiratorially and whispered in her ear. "Did you know they're a kind of mollusk?"

"Gosh, no." Ellie looked around for Brigie.

"Most people don't know they're related to clams and oysters. But if you visualize their construction…"

Ellie suddenly jumped. Champagne splashed on her dress.

Did he just pinch my butt?

Mr. Octopus stared blankly. He solicitously proffered his napkin and reached forward as though to help wipe the front of her dress. Ellie pulled back. As she did, her bottom collided with a zebra-painted sculpture of two dolphins cavorting with a ukulele.

"Whoops-a-daisy. Don't want to break this one." A smiling woman in flower-print leggings and a cropped dark top steadied the black and white creation. "It's worth more than you think."

Ellie shot her a grateful glance. When she pivoted to glare at Mr. Octopus, he had disappeared into the crowd. She swiveled back to the woman.

"Thanks for the save. I have a history of being clumsy."

The woman took a sip from a Perrier bottle.

"You should try yoga."

Ellie searched for a tray on which to deposit her glass. "For my history?"

"For moving effortlessly through space."

"That's a nice way of putting it."

The lithe woman stretched out her hand. "I'm Jacqui Novotny. I teach yoga here at the hotel."

"I'm Ellie Atherton." Ellie shook the proffered hand and bent to examine the price tag of the piece she almost knocked to the floor. She stood quickly, her face drained of color. "I've got to go. I have no business being in a room where I could break things worth that kind of money."

Jacqui grinned. "I'll walk you out. I've done about all the schmoozing I can stand for one evening."

Near the exit, Jacqui grabbed two fresh Perrier bottles from the buffet and handed one to Ellie.

Ellie unscrewed the top and took a long gulp. "You don't drink?"

Jacqui raised an eyebrow. "Oh, I drink. But not on the job."

Ellie stood at the wide stone railing opposite the gallery and looked out over the manicured garden with palm trees surrounding a Maui-shaped swimming pool. "You work at the gallery?"

"At the hotel. Tonight's not part of the formal job description. But if they think there might not be enough guests at something like this, the word's passed around." She rubbed her hands through her short, bleached hair, making it stand in all directions. "Like stuffing the bottom of the tip jar before you put it out." She regarded Ellie. "Why are you here? You don't look like a hotel guest."

"What gives that away?"

"You're unattached, for one. Not many single women come to Maui without girlfriends in tow."

Ellie explained her circumstances, giving Jacqui a brief history of Vivyenne and Viv. Jacqui leaned against a carved pillar, listening and nodding.

"Sounds crazy, right?" Ellie laid her purse on the broad railing and put her hands on her hips.

"I'd have made the same choice."

"I got totally suckered by the money." Ellie flung her hands wide. Both women both watched Ellie's purse sail a graceful arc into the garden below.

"It's Maui, honey. We're all suckered by something." Jacqui took Ellie by the arm. "Let's go find your purse. And then I'm giving you a free yoga lesson."

CHAPTER 7

Later that evening, Ellie's white Sentra pulled over crushed vines into her uninviting driveway. She parked the car and locked the gate. The house looked dark and uninviting after the lights and excitement of the hotel.

When she pushed open the heavy door, Viv sat statuesque in the wooden foyer. She slung him over her shoulder.

"I sometimes wish you were a big, scary German shepherd."

Viv rubbed his face against her cheek and purred.

"I know." She stroked against the grain of his fur. "Nobody protects me from creepy crawlies better than you."

She laid her phone on the kitchen counter. The screen indicated two text messages from an 808 number.

Great. More creepy crawlies to worry about.

Viv hopped from her arm and batted the phone across the granite surface. Ellie rapped his paw.

"Bad cat. This is *not* an eight-hundred-dollar cat toy."

She spun the phone around and read the first message:

Hey it's Noa. Hope 2CU soon.

And the second:

JTOU.

Well, I wasn't *thinking of you, Noa. What I* was *thinking about was how you got my number.*

She swiped delete and jumped as the device jiggled with a new text from another number she didn't recognize:

It's Denver. JTOU.

Sounds much better coming from you. She added him to her contact list.

Ellie: Thx. U busy?

Denver: At work. As usual.

Ellie: Not me. Gallery opening tonite.

She poured cat kibble into Viv's bowl and got herself a bottle of beer from the refrigerator.

Denver: Jealous.

She used one finger to punch her response as she fished in a drawer for an opener.

Ellie: Would have been more fun if u'd...

Don't go there. Keep it light.
Delete.

Ellie: Was fun. Did yoga.

Denver: At gallery?

Ellie: Private lesson in ritzy spa.

Ellie gave up the search for the opener and put the beer back in the refrigerator, bumping the door shut with her hip.

Denver: Now really jealous.

Ellie: Might go back. Liked the instructor.

Ellie sucked on her little finger.

Denver: Was it a man?

She grinned.
Gotcha.

Ellie: Woman. Jacqui.

Denver: Glad u made a friend.

Ellie followed Viv to the master bedroom and flopped on the comforter next to him.

Ellie: Me 2.

Denver: What u doing now?

Ellie rolled to her side and fondled the cat. She slowly typed a response, closing one eye as she pushed *send*.

Ellie: In bed.

She flipped quickly onto her back and nervously tapped her feet on the mattress. Viv glared at her and hopped from the wiggling surface.

Denver: Sweet dreams.

Ellie's feet stopped their thumping.
That's all you have to say?

Ellie: U2.

She boosted herself off the bed and headed back to the kitchen.
Where's that damn bottle opener?

*** *** ***

Chimes woke her the following morning. Her hand fumbled across the nightstand until she found the phone. She held it to her ear with her eyes still closed.

"Hello?"

"Hey. It's Noa."

"Noa?" She sat up and quickly tugged her nightshirt up under her chin, hiding her cleavage, feeling as if he'd invaded her personal space.

"You get my texts? Just calling to say hi."

Ellie felt exposed as she looked around the room for a long-sleeved shirt. "Hi. How are you?" She found one, pulled it over her head, and sat on the edge of the bed, legs tightly crossed.

"You coming by the store today?"

Are you kidding?

"Uh. Sorry. I'm busy." She bit her lip. "And, by the way, how'd you get my number?"

"Your registration. We keep them here at the store in case we have to check up on anyone."

I don't need you checking up on me.

Ellie stood. "Look. I've got to go. There are people at the door."

"Yeah. Catch you later then."

"Bye."

Ellie threw the phone on the bed and wiped her hand on the sheets as though she'd just touched something dirty.

A car honked. She pulled apart the heavy venetian blinds. Palm fronds blocked her view. More honking accompanied her frantic dressing. She ran in bare feet across the lawn and tiptoed across the vines to the gate.

A young man leaned against it, smiling. She read the name of the landscaping company on his shirt through the iron bamboo fronds.

"Sorry. I forgot you were coming." She looked down and fiddled with the key in the lock.

I've got my shirt on inside out. Sweet.

"Mahalo." The young man waved his thumb and pinkie at her and climbed into a black pickup. A caravan of three trucks and two trailers with machinery drove through. Ellie waved at the muscular youths inside.

What did Celine say about my not being lonely?

She picked her way back across the vines toward the house as a burly, gray-haired man with a kind face approached. Six men fanned out across the property behind him. Ellie signed the proffered paperwork and handed the foreman a spare gate key. She skipped up the porch stairs and had her hand on the door when renewed crunching of tires sounded from the drive. A white van pulled up behind the trucks.

The cleaners.

Ellie gave the crew of four Asian women a quick tour of the house. Then she retreated to her bedroom to change. But a knock caught her in the act of raising her t-shirt. She pulled it down and answered the door.

"Man at door. Say you want to buy apply ants."

Ellie laughed. "Apply ants? What are those?"

The young woman nodded seriously, stepped to the side, and motioned for Ellie to go to the door.

"Got it. I'll just change."

The young woman shook her head and tugged Ellie's sleeve.

"Okay. Ants first. Changing for hot studs later."

The woman's brow wrinkled. "Excuse?"

Ellie grinned. "Never mind."

A warm morning breeze blew down the hall. Strands of hair drifted across Ellie's face and she brushed them out of the way, feeling tangles tug at her fingers.

Celine would not approve of the first impressions I'm making.

The middle-aged Caucasian at the door looked as though he belonged in Iowa. His skin was pale and his plaid button-down short-sleeved shirt was tucked into khaki shorts secured with a web belt that looked like it had come from an army surplus store.

"Mrs. Atherton?"

Ellie glanced at his serious face and bit back a laugh.

"Kind of."

"You called. Said you wanted to buy some appliances. You wanted…" He checked a computer printout. "An estimate for a refrigerator, stove, microwave, dishwasher, and disposal."

"I want to buy *apply-ant*-ces. I get it."

A weed whacker revved to a screeching start in the garden, followed closely by the roar of two rider mowers.

Ellie sighed and nodded. "You might as well come in."

Two hours passed before she re-entered her bedroom suite. There, the shining bathroom floor, glittering mirror, and sparkling chrome made her grab her purse and run.

"Wait." She beckoned to the women in the white van backing cautiously around the gardeners' trucks. The driver lowered her window.

"House okay?" Her glance at Ellie betrayed an anxiety to please.

"House is fantastic. Amazing. You did an awesome job." She gave a thumbs up.

The woman showed a row of brilliantly white teeth.

"Here." Ellie fished five twenties from her wallet. "A tip."

The woman's seat belt constrained her attempt at a bow. "Mahalo."

Ellie inclined her head. "Mahalo to you." She stepped back. The women in the back of the van beamed at her.

She waved and spoke softly to herself. "I think Viv's never going to forgive you, though, when he figures out you cleaned up all his dead roaches."

Ellie strolled toward the house and suddenly stopped.

The vines are gone.

The entire driveway, previously choked with green tangles, was now bare. Its cracked, dingy asphalt and crushed gravel lay exposed, a dull charcoal gray. Sharply manicured grass edged its sides. Ellie closed her eyes and inhaled air tinged with the scent of freshly mowed lawn. Her shoulders relaxed. Then a leaf blower exploded into life, driving her back into the house.

Before noon, the kitchen overflowed with dirty bowls and spoons. White flour dusted the counters. The air smelled of baking cookies. Viv lay on the windowsill, blinking at Ellie who flung open cabinet after cabinet.

"Where'd I put that stupid serving tray?" She stood still, hands on hips. "What's the logical place for that?"

She scanned the enormous room. "Who needs fifty cabinets in a kitchen? This isn't a freaking hotel."

She finally found it over the oven and piled it high with warm chocolate chip cookies. After hesitating, she removed a few and put them on a plate.

"No point in giving away *all* of them." She bit into one and peeked at herself in the shiny surface of the large but defective refrigerator.

Hair brushed. Bikini on. Sarong tied provocatively. Celine would be happy.

Outside, she stepped carefully while investigating the uneven ground for stumbling hazards and simultaneously watched the tray for signs it might topple. Gardeners clustered near their trucks eating lunch. They ignored her until she came close, when one of the young men caught her eye.

"These are for you." Ellie proffered the tray, which tipped dangerously.

The man jumped to his feet and relieved her of the load.

"Wow. Thanks." His accent indicated he wasn't a local. He brought the food back to his co-workers. Ellie she fended off a volley of *thank yous* with a wave of her hand and a smile.

The youth sauntered up to her again, amid some muted whistling from his friends. He munched a cookie and held two extra.

"We're going to devour that." He jerked his head back at the others. "I thought you might want some yourself."

Ellie declined.

The youth looked hurt. "My hands are clean. I used hand sanitizer before I touched them."

Ellie blushed. "It's not that. I dropped a whole sheet of them on the floor earlier. I didn't have as many as I'd planned, so I took some from your tray before I brought it out."

"Bummer about the accident."

"You're telling me."

The youth blinked in the sunshine and shielded his eyes.

He looks like a high schooler. Can't be more than twenty-one.

Ellie pulled her sarong higher, covering her cleavage. "Can you show me what you've done so far?"

"Sure." He stuffed another cookie in his mouth. "I'm just part-time. But I know what everyone's up to."

"Great. I just want to get an overview, so I can tell the owner."

"Sure." The final cookie disappeared with remarkable speed. "I'm Brandon." He held out his hand.

She shook it. "I'm Ellie."

Brandon strolled over to the fountain on the ragged lawn. "Here's what I'm doing. We don't know if we can get this to work." He pointed to a concealed pipe and on-off handle. Will probably take a plumber. But I'm in charge of rebuilding the wall." He kicked some loose lava rocks. "Got to take most of it apart first. There's vines all in it."

Ellie looked at the fountain's immobile dancer, framed by the ocean. "From here she looks like she's standing on the water."

Brandon cocked his head. "Yeah. And giving us Molokini."

Ellie pointed. "That's the little island? What's the big one?"

"Kaho'olawe."

Ellie narrowed her eyes. "Really? Say that slowly."

"Ka-ho-o-la-vey. Hawaiian words sound like they're spelled."

"That doesn't help. I couldn't spell that to save my life."

Brandon laughed. "You've heard of the state fish, right?"

"No."

He winked. "Humuhumunukunukuapua'a."

Ellie burst out laughing. "What's that in English?"

"Triggerfish."

"That's the reason I speak only English. I don't want to break my tongue."

Brandon nodded his chin toward the bushes at the edge of the property. "Want me to show you what we've been doing over there?"

***

Late that afternoon, Ellie clicked shut her laptop and responded to a knock at the front door. She squinted out the long living room windows into sun and noticed the gardening crew packing up. She waved at Brandon.

A backlit figure leaned against the open door. Her eyes adjusted. She stepped back as Noa stepped into the house.

"Hey, Ellie. Though I'd stop by."

Ellie's toes curled in her flip-flops. She crossed her arms but didn't say anything.

"I've been thinking of you." Noa smiled and stepped closer.

Ellie brushed past him onto the porch. She spoke slowly. "I don't remember inviting you."

"No problem." Noa made a noncommittal gesture with his head. "The gate was open."

Ellie looked at the trucks in the driveway. Brandon was loading hedge trimmers into the bed of a pickup. "I don't see your car."

Noa moved closer and obstructed her view. He tried to catch her eye. "I parked on the road. Didn't want to block the workers when they leave."

Ellie avoided his gaze, backed into the deck chair, and scooted around it.

"Look. No offence. But I don't like people just showing up."

Noa's face registered genuine surprise. "Even me?"

Ellie's lips tightened. "What do you mean?"

"I thought I'd be welcome any time, babe."

Noa moved around the chair. Ellie spun it. The armrest caught his knee.

"Shit." He bent and rubbed the spot. "That fucking hurt." He raised his head with a blackened look. "What's up with you?"

Ellie forced herself to look him in the eyes. "Please leave."

"I don't have to."

"Yes, actually, you do." The man's voice made both Noa and Ellie turn. Brandon stood at the top of the stairs with his arms at his side, fingers loosely curled. Ellie shot him a look of gratitude.

Noa stared at him. "Who the hell are you?"

"Brandon. Ellie's friend."

"*I'm* Ellie's friend." Noa tried to put a possessive arm around Ellie. She trotted from behind the chair to Brandon's side. Noa dropped his arm. "She never told me about you."

Brandon looked at Ellie. "You want him to go?"

Ellie gave a slight nod.

"Look." He stepped toward Noa. "I'm sure you've got other things to do." He pointed to the trucks. "My friends are over there. We just want to go home at the end of a long day." He opened his arms wide.

Noa held his ground. "So go. Why the fuck you interfering, brah? She's my lady. Not yours."

At those words, Ellie backed behind Brandon and spoke in a tone she hoped only he could hear. "I hardly know this guy."

Brandon nodded. "How about it, dude?" He motioned toward the stairs.

An instant later, he danced sideways and Noa's punch shot through open air. Brandon grabbed Noa's fist and twisted it behind his back. Ellie saw the other gardeners drop their machinery and advance as one being toward the porch.

Brandon pushed Noa gently down the steps and let him stumble to standing.

Noa looked from the group moving toward him to Brandon and Ellie.

"You two-timing bitch. I knew you'd turn out to be like all the others. Fucking sleeping around behind my back."

The pack advanced. Noa fled, limping, across the lawn.

"You have a house alarm?" Brandon's eyes flicked at the door and windows.

Ellie held back tears, her whole body trembling. "No."

"Lock everything up at night. I think he's harmless. But it's better to be safe."

"You don't have to tell me. I'm pushing furniture against the doors tonight."

Brandon removed a cell phone from his pocket. "What's your number?"

Ellie told him.

"I'm texting you. If you have a problem, call the police. But if I can help, you have my number."

Ellie locked the door behind her and strode around the house closing the windows. Viv followed her, dejected.

"Sorry, Viv." Ellie fastened the final latch. "New rule for inside. No more creepy crawlies."

CHAPTER 8

Jacqui flipped into a yoga headstand, her legs stretched toward the bright blue morning sky, her toes pointing at a lonely cloud drifting toward Molokini. Ellie wiggled her toes in the sand, still partly shadowed by the enormous hotel at their backs. She studied the other women waiting for Jacqui to return to an upright position. Athleticism was the predominant feature of the group, evidenced by little arm flab, tight tummies, and solid derrieres. Ellie tugged her tank top over her Lycra swim bottoms.

Wish I hadn't eaten that second malasada.

Jacqui's feet plopped to the sand. Her spine undulated like a cobra, rolling until she stood upright and faced the group. Her face glowed in the pink morning light.

"Aloha and welcome to Motivating Monday yoga."

The small crowd murmured, "Aloha."

Ellie stretched unobtrusively.

Wish I could sit down.

"You're here because you are beautiful, inside and out. You want to embrace all that Maui has to offer. This class will set you on the right path for today and, if you want, for the rest of your life."

There was light clapping.

Ellie suppressed a yawn.

Wish Denver were here. Her gaze picked a spot on the sand a few feet in front of her. *Watching him would motivate me.*

"We'll start with pigeon pose."

Ellie's mouth fell open as she watched Jacqui drape herself flat over one bent leg. The women near her collapsed onto their mats and beach towels, racing to imitate the instructor, who gave melodious directions without raising her head.

Ellie pulled her towel to the back of the group and kneeled. She pulled one leg forward, bracing herself with both hands. With effort, she maneuvered a foreleg to the ground. But her body refused to relax on top of it.

Jacqui moved among the participants, adjusting an arm here, massaging a back there.

Ellie twisted her neck and looked up at her friend. "My body's not meant to do this."

Jacqui's eyes sparkled. "It can do anything you want it to."

Ellie lowered her voice. "You really believe that?"

Jacqui's hands tugged at Ellie's legs and massaged her shoulders. "It's my job to believe it. But ask me again after quitting time."

Ellie closed her eyes and willed herself to be flexible. "I don't think this pose looks like a pigeon." She inspected the group. "We look like dying monkeys."

"Wait till you see what we're doing next."

"Oh, joy." With a dramatic sigh, Ellie dropped over her bent leg. "Hey, I'm doing it. Jacqui, it worked."

Her friend patted her on the head. "See. Anything's possible."

After class and a quick shower, Jacqui and Ellie strolled to the hotel entrance. Ellie rolled her head and rubbed her biceps.

"You do that every morning?"

Jacqui greeted porters and hotel guests as they passed, emanating a radiance and self-confidence Ellie admired.

"Five mornings a week."

"And do you really believe anybody can do all that stuff. Downward donkey and squirming swan?"

Jacqui looped her arm through Ellie's and laughed. "You keep me real, sister."

They passed one of the hotel's huge exotic flower bouquets, a delightful explosion of pinks, whites, greens, and purples. Jacqui disengaged from Ellie, reached in a fluid motion for a hibiscus blossom, broke it off, and put it behind her own ear.

"It's okay to do that?" Ellie looked over her shoulder at the display as they kept walking.

"Everything's possible, remember?" Jacqui's long fingers adjusted the ornament in her short hair. "Besides, I've got some gray coming in on that side. This covers it up."

***

Near noon that day, Brandon stood outside a small café on the corner peering at his phone. Ellie tapped him on the shoulder.

"Hey." He stuffed the phone in his shorts. "See you found it."

"Google maps." Ellie followed him into the dark interior of the tiny restaurant. "I parked up the street a bit. I wanted to walk along the shore."

Brandon nodded. "Feel you. Couldn't get over the palm trees and the water at first either."

Ellie looked at a menu written on boards hanging from the wall. "I'm glad there's not a lot of traffic. Sometimes I'm watching the beach instead of the road."

"It'll get worse. Visitors start coming after Thanksgiving. The roads fill up."

They ordered and Ellie waved aside Brandon's offer to pay for himself.

"This is an appreciation lunch, remember? You saved me from Noa."

He ruffled his hair. "I didn't do much."

"You did plenty."

Stools lined white tile counters under an awning. Ellie regarded the brown mound on her plate. Her nose wrinkled.

"Trust me." Brandon stuck his fork into an identical heap in front of him. "It's better than it looks."

Thick gravy oozed over a fried egg that cloaked a hamburger patty stacked atop a dense pile of rice. Ellie dipped her fork into the gravy.

Brandon grinned. "Loco moco's local. You've got to say you tried it."

"It's not bad." She chopped at the egg. "Heart attack on a plate. But tasty."

Stand up paddlers in rash guard tops hauled boards and paddles in and out of the water at the park across the street, where palm trees shaded public bathrooms and gazebos. Cars crawled intermittently by, maintaining the twenty miles per hour speed limit. Sun burned tourists ambled along the sidewalks, with their heads turned toward the ocean.

Brandon pushed his clean plate from him. "Hate to ask. No more problems with the jerk, right?"

Ellie shook her head. "I blocked his number."

"Good. I know too many like him."

Ellie looked at him over her half-eaten burger. "You do?"

Brandon twisted his napkin around his little finger. "Not here. Back in Seattle."

"I thought Seattle was all high tech geeks."

"Didn't hang out with those dudes. My crowd was…tougher."

Brandon rubbed his biceps.

"Is that tattoo from then?" A dark green leaf peeked from the bottom of his sleeve.

Brandon lifted the arm of his t-shirt.

Ellie laughed. "Oh, I thought it was a marijuana leaf."

"Not impossible. But I got this one later. It's a kind of maple. Reminds me of home."

She grinned. "You're turning over a new leaf?" Her fork sliced the remaining egg.

Brandon's eyebrows sunk over his brown eyes. "Trying. Maui's making it hard. It's so fricking expensive. I'm working six days a week. It's only part-time, sure. But I didn't think it would be like this. Rent's killing me. Dude here told me Hawaii rent's, like, more than double the national average. Wish I'd known that before I arrived."

Ellie bit her lip. "I never thought of that. I've been so busy pretending I'm rich."

"It's cool. I didn't mean anything about you. I'd jump at the chance to pretend like that." The napkin tore and he threw it on his plate. "It's just my girlfriend's coming out. And I got to tell her she'd better find a job soon. I used to take care of her. Some ways at least."

"Bring her over to the house. I'd like to meet her." Ellie covered her plate with her napkin. "Now I can't eat another bite. This—"

Brandon scowled. "Shit."

"No." She smiled. "It was really pretty good. I'm just—"

Brandon interrupted. "He's back." He pointed to the street.

Ellie swiveled from her stool just as Noa turned the corner in his truck. He made an illegal U-turn and stopped abruptly across from the café.

Brandon pulled Ellie's elbow as she flung money on the table. "Come on. Let's go." He held his hand flat to stop approaching cars. They jogged across the street.

"What you running for, brah?" Noa's voice carried over the honks that accompanied his own dash through the sparse traffic.

Brandon shoved Ellie under a tree. "You stay here." He strolled in Noa's direction, arms swinging, head to one side. "Hey, Noa. Howzit?"

The surf on the nearby beach drowned out most of the details of the two men's conversation, but Ellie strained to hear.

"...saw you two...kill her." Noa thrashed his arms wildly, as though fending off bees.

Brandon stayed still, head still cocked, his gaze even. "Take it easy..."

The thrashing slowed. "...throwing me over."

Brandon's voice was low and even-tempered. "...all good, dude...just friends."

"You can have her..." Noa jerked his middle finger at Ellie.

She shuddered.

"...don't push it." Brandon maneuvered Noa away from Ellie and turned them both to the road. He strode at his side, one hand behind Noa's back, not quite touching him.

Ellie watched them part at the curb. Noa wove unsteadily among the cars, climbed into his pickup, gunned the engine, and roared north along the quiet street.

Ellie threw her arms around Brandon when he approached. "What would have happened if you hadn't been there?"

Brandon squeezed her and let go. "Not much. A lot of noise. He was too wasted."

Ellie shuddered. "Is he stalking me?"

"He was driving by and saw us. It was just bad luck."

Ellie tramped to a picnic table and sat on her shaking hands. "Was he drunk?"

"High."

She raised her eyebrows. "Really?"

"Trust me. I know what it looks like."

Ellie shook her head. "A few days ago my biggest problems were geckos and roaches. Now I feel like I should call the police."

Brandon perched himself on the table with his legs on the bench. "You can. But I think he's full of shit."

Palm tree fronds rustled overhead, sounding like gentle rain. Waves cascaded against the beige sand. Children screeched, chasing each other across the rough grass. Surfers hosed their boards at a public faucet.

"This is paradise?" Ellie fought a rising nausea.

"Yep." Brandon yanked her from the bench.

"What are you doing?"

He schlepped her across the grass. She dragged after him, her sandals slapping a reluctant beat on the turf.

"Where are we going?"

He slowed at the sand but kept running. The blue water splashed as he leapt through the shallows. Ellie stumbled after him, giggling.

"I don't have a suit on."

Brandon splashed water at her with his free hand. "Who cares?"

A wave rose behind him. She tugged to get away. His grip held her firmly in place.

"Dive into it." He suddenly let go and plunged, arms stretched forward, into the body of the wave. Ellie screeched and followed close behind. They emerged farther out, shaking water from their heads and laughing. People on shore clapped.

103

CHRISTINE HARTMAN

Ellie rubbed sparkling water droplets from her eyelashes. "I'm going to get you for this, Brandon." She sprung toward him with an enormous smile.

"Have to catch me first." He kicked away on his back, his sneakered feet visible through the clear water, his t-shirt billowing around him like a gently rising balloon.

***

Construction on the house began in earnest early the following week. Ellie and Viv retreated frequently to the bedroom suite, farthest from the noise. Viv sulked in a cat basket in the closet. Ellie worked on her computer from a pile of pillows on the bed.

"You must have seen this coming." Devora's image surveyed Ellie from the screen.

"*All* white? Seriously? The kitchen cabinets are practically new."

"You met Dr. Lovejoy. She likes surgical sterility."

Ellie sighed. "If that kitchen's all white, I'll never be able to cook again. Did I tell you I dropped a tray of cookies on the floor? Can you imagine what that would do to a white floor?"

Devora snickered. "What makes you think Dr. Lovejoy eats cookies? Or even thinks about cookies?"

Ellie snickered. "Everybody thinks about cookies."

"Right. Everybody but one. Now let's go over it. Lanai sanded."

"Hold on." Ellie raised her hand. "What's the lanai again?"

"The porch."

"Got it. Go on."

Devora read from a long list and put it down. "I'll email you the details. You have authority to prioritize. But the house always comes first. Leave everything to do with the ohana until later."

Ellie raised her hand again.

Devora squinted one eye. "Right. Ohana is guesthouse. Want to use the card to pay for some Hawaiian lessons?"

Ellie stuck her tongue out at the screen.

That evening, Ellie worked on a .gif for Denver.

Ellie: Made this for u.

The animated clip showed Ellie repeatedly spilling coffee on a white floor.

Denver: Childhood fears?

Ellie: Adult horror.

Denver: Dated someone once like that.

Ellie: Clumsy?

Denver: Very neat.

Ellie flipped onto her stomach.

Ellie: I'm not. Neat. Am clumsy.

Denver: I like that.

Ellie sat up and leaned against the pillows. She hesitated, and then typed.

Ellie: Want to video chat?

Denver: Love to. But can't. Boarding flight.

Ellie slid down the pillows. She held the phone high and zoomed it around her head like an airplane.

Denver: Sorry.

Ellie: No prob.

Denver: Do it soon.

She nestled the phone against her breast.

Ellie: Holding u 2 that.

***

Ellie declined Jacqui's invitation to attend the Fantastic Friday yoga class. Instead, she made Belgian waffles with fresh pineapple and maple syrup. She carried a full plate, a cup of coffee, and Celine to the lanai.

"Watch out, girl. You're going to drop one of us."

"Don't care." Ellie bumped open the front door

with her hip. "The floors will be all white in a few months. Whatever I do to these now won't matter."

"Wish I could do that."

Ellie balanced the plate on the deck chair's armrest and put her coffee on the floor.

"What? Drop stuff?"

"Have enough money to rip out something I don't like the color of."

Ellie spoke through a mouth full of waffle. "You would never do that."

"Why not?"

"Because you care too much about other people. If you had that kind of money, you'd set up a foundation to get kids clean drinking water. I'm the mercenary who ditched school to take this job."

"All for the greater good, sister. That way I can keep my high morals *and* have a free place to stay on Maui over fall break."

The gardeners' arrival cut short the phone conversation. As the men unloaded equipment, Brandon walked up to the house with a young woman. Ellie shoveled down the last of her breakfast.

"Hope you weren't kidding when you said I could bring Olivia."

Ellie wiped her mouth with a paper towel. "I wasn't." She turned to Olivia. "Having only hot guys around gets old."

Olivia laughed. "I'm Olivia. Mattingly. Guess you heard about me from Brandon." She kissed him on the mouth and he returned to the trucks.

Ellie observed Olivia's thin figure, her pale face, and the dark circles under her eyes. "Want to come inside? We can sit in the kitchen. I've got tons of leftover breakfast."

She settled Olivia on a stool by the counter and pushed a full plate in front of her. Olivia looped her pageboy cut over her ears and dug in.

Are those two not getting enough to eat?

Olivia noticed Ellie looking at her. Ellie busied herself with cleaning up.

"Do you need some help?" Olivia pushed a pineapple chunk through the syrup.

"You finish first." Ellie skimmed a sponge across the countertops. "After that, you can keep me company. I'm not saying help. Just moral support. I've spent the morning cleaning gecko poop out of suitcases."

Olivia put down her fork. "Gross."

"Sorry. No graphic details. But life in this house isn't all it was cracked up to be."

Olivia brightened. "I like cleaning."

Ellie flung the sponge into the sink with a disgusted look. "You're kidding."

"No." Olivia brought her plate to the sink and washed it. "I enjoy the process. Ask Brandon. Before I arrived, I think he messed up the apartment on purpose, just to cheer me up."

"You weren't happy when you got to paradise?" Ellie looked into Olivia's face. "You're too young to have serious troubles."

Olivia blinked and turned away. "I'm twenty-one, same as Brandon." She pulled a clip from her pocket and pinched hair back from her face. "Now where's the dirt?"

Olivia followed Ellie into the spare bedroom,

where two suitcases lay open on the floor. Ellie picked up a spray bottle, some rags, and a package of disposable kitchen gloves.

"So, how did you and Brandon meet?"

Olivia reached for a spare pair of gloves, tugging them from Ellie's grasp when Ellie held on. "We both went to the University of Washington. Same chemistry class freshman year."

Ellie lugged a third case from the closet.

"I think the problem is I didn't zipper them closed. I thought they should air out. Who knew the little reptiles would think I opened a public restroom?"

Olivia's mouth twitched. "First thing I'll do when I get home is tape ours shut."

The scent of lemon and bleach pervaded the air as Ellie started on the new bag. "Did you major in chemistry?"

Olivia scrubbed at a stain on the lining. "I didn't finish school. Neither did Brandon."

"Oh."

"It's fine. We got sidetracked. Well, he did. And I thought I could help."

"Look. Tell me when to shut up. I don't mean to pry."

Olivia flipped the suitcase over. "You're not." The locks beat a rhythmic tapping against the floor as she rubbed. "Believe it or not, I went to prep school. I even got into Harvard. But *that* seemed like a straight shot right down my father's scary, narrow alley. So I ran in the other direction."

A sudden gust blew the room door shut. Viv's plaintive meow sounded from the hall.

Olivia's eyes twinkled. "You have a cat?"

"Viv. Want to meet him?"

"I love cats."

Ellie opened the door and Viv ambushed her legs, embracing them with his paws. When he registered Olivia, he dropped his behind and busied himself licking his tail.

"He's embarrassed you caught him acting silly. Come here, Viv." Ellie snapped her fingers. "Meet Olivia."

Viv sidled up to her.

"Oh, you cutie." Olivia swept him into her arms where he snuggled, tummy up, like a baby.

"Now that's unusual. His mother told me he doesn't usually like strangers. But he likes Devora. He likes Celine and me. Now he likes you."

Olivia buried her face amid the black spots. Viv arched his back with contentment. "Maybe he didn't like his mother?"

Ellie snapped her rag in the air. "Funny you should say that."

Brandon yelled down the hallway a few hours later. "Olivia? We've got to go. The guys are packing up."

Ellie hurried to the front. "She'll be here in a second." She handed Brandon a red Target bag. "Take this."

"What is it?"

"I got way too much stuff this weekend. You know how Costco is. Too much of everything. I should get a grip and not go."

Brandon's expression was uncertain. He looked in the sack.

110

"Seriously. Take it. My mom raised me not to waste food. Please?"

Brandon's face relaxed. "Okay. Cool. We can help you get rid of it." He dropped his voice. "No sign of Noa?"

"No. I don't know what you told him, but he hasn't come around. I'm still locking everything at night though."

"Should be fine. He's moved on to something else by now."

Olivia appeared and Brandon almost dropped the bag. "Dude, you look so much better."

Olivia beamed. "Ellie's got a cat."

Ellie looked toward the kitchen. *And food.* "It was great to hang out together today. I'll text you about sushi with Jacqui."

Olivia gave her a quick squeeze. "Thanks, Ellie."

"Thank *you*. I'm not the one who crawled under the sink to find Viv's dead roach supply."

Brandon grinned. "Ah. Cleaning. *That* explains her good mood."

CHAPTER 9

Ellie returned to the counter at the sushi bar and sat between Jacqui and Olivia, fanning her hands in the air. "The bathroom dryer's broken." She glanced at Jacqui. "What's she gotten you into?"

Jacqui chuckled. "Who me?"

The chef at the sushi bar placed two pieces of a gelatinous orange mass on a rectangle of rice and wrapped it with paper-like seaweed. Jacqui's eyes sparkled as she watched. Olivia appeared to cringe.

"I know you well enough by now to understand you've got a big streak of mischief."

Jacqui took a sip of sake. "I aim to broaden people's world views."

Ellie turned to Olivia. "Don't let her bully you into anything just because she's older."

Jacqui put her elbow on the counter, forearm up. "Who are you calling old?"

Ellie shook her head. "Uh-uh. I'm not testing you. I've seen your muscles in yoga class."

The chef placed two jiggling orange pieces in front of Olivia with a slight bow. Olivia groaned.

"You're going to love this, honey." Jacqui poured more soy sauce into Olivia's small container. "Sea urchin's one of my favorites. The perfect way to end a long meal."

Olivia lifted her beer and sipped. "I'm not sure. I'm a California roll kind of girl."

"You've known me for…what?" Jacqui peeped at her phone. "Over two hours. Don't you trust me by now?"

Olivia grinned over her glass. "Maybe?"

"Nobody's forcing you." Ellie patted her hand. Jacqui leered over Ellie's shoulder. "I got you two together because you're my only girlfriends on the island." Ellie flashed Jacqui a mockingly stern look. "I didn't think about the consequences."

Olivia gulped the remainder of her beer. She shot Jacqui a defiant look, grasped a piece with chopsticks, dunked it in the soy sauce, and plopped it in her mouth, closing her eyes as she chewed.

Ellie followed Olivia's movements. Jacqui poured herself more sake.

Olivia's eyes popped open. "I like it."

"See?" Jacqui turned to the chef. "Two more *uni*, please. For my other friend here."

Ellie laughed and shook her head to negate the order. "No, I'm good. We just need the check."

"Spoil sport."

Outside, Ellie scanned the dark streets. The sidewalks were bare. Only an occasional car rolled by. "It's only nine o'clock. Where is everybody?"

"Nine p.m. is the new two a.m., Maui time." Jacqui's flowing tunic fluttered gracefully in the soft night air.

Ellie directed them to her car. "Good thing we're heading to *my* house to continue this party. I operate on California time."

Olivia tottered slightly. "How does California help?"

"Never mind." Ellie opened the door for her. "This designated driver needs a drink."

The moon shone low in the sky above the unlit street. Ellie pulled in front of her gate and climbed out. Her bright blue dress radiated in the glow of the headlights against her long, dark hair. She bent and tilted her purse toward the light. After a long search, she got into the front seat and reversed the car onto the road.

Olivia hummed to herself in the back. Jacqui turned in the passenger seat. "Forget the gate key?"

"Yep."

"Uh-huh." She waited for Ellie to park on the side of the street. "Got the house key?"

Ellie pursed her lips. "Nope. But I think the house is open. If we can get over the gate, we're in."

In front of the gate, the three of them stared at the tall metal bamboo shoots. Olivia reached her hand to the top. "Looks smaller when you're in a car."

Jacqui stepped forward and interlaced her fingers. "Step in here."

Neither Olivia nor Ellie moved.

Jacqui pointed at Ellie. "You. I'll boost you over. Then Olivia."

"And what about you?"

"I'm a yoga instructor, remember?"

Ellie hopped one foot in Jacqui's sling, pulled herself over the gate's large hinge, and jumped to the ground on the other side.

"Wait here. I'll run in and get the key." She dashed to the house.

When she emerged through the front door, gate key in hand, Olivia and Jacqui were sitting on the front steps.

"How'd you get here so fast?"

Jacqui looked smug. "I helped the twenty-one-year old over. Then I jumped it alone."

Olivia stared with alcohol-blurred eyes at Jacqui. "I hope I have your muscles when I'm in my thirties."

"Yoga, clean living, and lots of sex."

Olivia blushed up to her forehead as Ellie led them inside.

***

Four hours later, Jacqui took a key from Ellie and inserted it in the lock for the driveway gate. She heaved the heavy metal to the side with a flip of her arm.

"Wow. Okay." Ellie watched the gate collide with the shrubbery. "I have to shove it with my shoulder to move it. Maybe I should come to your yoga classes more, after all?"

Jacqui grinned. "Just saying. If you don't use it, you lose it." She gently put her hands on Olivia's shoulders to steer her down the drive and to Jacqui's car. "Honey, I'm taking you home." She winked at Ellie, who followed them. "Drive safe."

Ellie laughed. "Very funny. I just have to move my car up to the front of the house. You're the one behind the wheel for the next hour."

"I've lived Upcountry fifteen years now. Could do it in my sleep." Jacqui protected Olivia's head as she flopped into the passenger seat of the Civic.

Ellie waved them off and sat behind the wheel of her Sentra.

What's that?

She rubbed her eyes and got out. The driver's side wiper pinned a piece of notebook paper to the windshield. She removed it and read the untidy print.

Know what you're up to. Bitch.

Ellie shuddered, suddenly cold. She scanned the dark street, ripped the note in quarters, and jogged to her garbage can, which stood waiting for the next morning's pickup at the edge of the street. She lifted the lid and threw the note in.

"Disgusting."

Once inside, she texted Brandon.

Ellie: Olivia's on her way home. Noa left a note on my car. It was outside my gate for a few hours.

As she locked the living room windows for the night, she studied the metal bamboo blocking the driveway exit.

Jacqui thought it was nothing to climb over it...

But in bed the alcohol helped Ellie drift away

116

despite images of Noa leaping from the shadows. She was fast asleep when her phone pinged.

Brandon: Keep the note. You might need it for the police.

***

Ellie awoke to the clattering of a garbage truck. She pulled a pillow over her head.

Damn Maui sunshine.

The truck rattled down the street. Viv pawed at her arm.

She mumbled from under the sheets. "Go away."

Her phone pinged. The unmistakable sound of Viv knocking it to the floor followed.

"I give up."

She stretched her legs under the sheets and massaged her temples.

What was that yoga pose for headaches again? Warrior Twenty-five?

She crawled out of bed. With her back to the window, she wiggled one bent knee forward and extended the other leg behind.

I can hear Jacqui now. Breathe in freshness. Expel toxins with your exhalation. She coughed, lost her balance, and tried again. *Doubt this'll work. Don't think ancient yogis knew about hangovers.*

The phone pinged from the corner, where Viv played, ricocheting it off the wall.

Ellie ignored the noise and concentrated on steadying her wobbly posture.

Inhale the Maui magic.

117

The phone rang. Viv jumped back. Ellie untangled herself and picked it up without looking at the screen.

"Hello?"

"Hi, Ellie. It's Denver."

Oh, crap.

She contemplated her reflection in the full-length mirror. Tousled hair. Streaked make-up. A pink 'smile if you love Hello Kitty' nightshirt.

Please, please don't ask me to video chat.

"Ellie?"

"Sorry. I'm just waking up."

"Want me to call back?"

"No." Her chin dropped to her chest.

Just tell him.

"But I'm not exactly ready for prime time video."

"I'm sure you look great."

She fingered a hole in a shoulder seam. "Don't be so sure."

"Well…maybe you can work yourself up to seeing me in person?"

Ellie bounced on her toes. "Are you coming back to Maui?"

"I'll be back tomorrow. I was thinking maybe we could get together on Tuesday?"

Ellie gripped the phone between her chin and shoulder and did a quick 'Single Ladies' dance in front of the mirror.

"Ellie?"

"Sorry. That's awesome. I'd love it."

Calm it down a bit, Ellie.

"Have you had loco moco yet? There's a great

place in Wailuku."

What is it with guys and that stuff?

"I had some in Kihei. But I'm willing to compare."

"I could pick you up."

A vision of his arriving early and finding her without makeup flashed through her mind.

"How about if I meet you there?"

"Okay. Let me give you the address."

After they made the arrangements, Ellie hung up and immediately dialed Jacqui.

"Quick. I need the name of a salon that's open tomorrow."

"You don't even let a girl finish her morning yoga routine."

In the bathroom, Ellie put the phone on speaker and splashed water on her face. "I did my yoga already. Now I need help."

"I'm impressed with your dedication. So I'll help. The salon in the hotel should be open Mondays. If they say they can't get you in, talk to Heather. Tell her I sent you."

Ellie toweled her face dry. "Bless you. My hair looks like something out of Planet of the Apes."

"Let me guess. Mr. Snorkel Rescue called."

"Yes. And he wants to get together on Tuesday."

"Way to go."

Ellie closed her eyes. "What if he doesn't like me in person?"

"Ellie, honey, he met you in person already. And he liked you."

Ellie shrugged. "I was the damsel in distress. Maybe he won't like the independent me."

"Breathe in some of that Maui confidence, darling. Men like women who believe in themselves. Trust yourself. Trust him. Now...tell me about your yoga poses."

***

Ellie maneuvered her car into a space at the back of the restaurant, taking in the pickups, police cars, and shiny sedans parked around her.

He has his own business. Which car is his? She eyed a Porsche convertible nestled between two SUVs. *Probably that one.*

Her heart pounded more than she wanted as she rounded the front corner of the building. Denver, in a muted Aloha shirt, tan shorts, and beach sandals, glanced up and smiled.

Awesome. I'm over dressed.

She brushed the front of her short, white skirt and pulled at her silk blouse. Denver held out his arms and kissed her on the cheek.

"You look great."

A jolt of adrenaline propelled her heart into overdrive and she suddenly didn't know what to do with her arms. He pulled open the door and, with his hand on her back, ushered her inside, where he stepped forward to talk with the hostess. Watching his athletic back, he struck Ellie as the kind of person who would age elegantly, the type who would go skiing and horseback riding with his grandkids, who'd whisk his white-haired wife around the dance floor on their fortieth wedding anniversary.

The lightly air-conditioned room smelled of burgers, fries, and something vaguely Asian. The interior reminded Ellie of an old-fashioned diner. At a long counter, customers in black t-shirts and work boots sat on round silver stools next to police officers in uniform. Families with young children chatted at long communal tables in the back.

But the conversations near them paused as they were ushered to a booth. Ellie noticed she and Denver were the only *haole* in the restaurant.

She glanced at the waitress, who beamed at them.

"First time here, yeah? Welcome."

Ellie scanned the menu, avoiding Denver's eyes. *What are we going to talk about?*

"They serve breakfast all day if you're not in the mood for loco moco." He pointed to the top of a page. She could tell he was trying to make eye contact, but she buried her head behind the plastic menu. The swiftness of the waitress's return surprised her.

"Ready to order?"

Ellie chose banana pancakes, Denver the loco moco.

"I can't help it. I always get the same thing. My parents used to take me here when I was a kid."

Ellie stared at the mound a heavy-set man was attacking at a neighboring table. "You finished all that as a kid?"

"I think maybe they gave me a small portion. But, yeah, I remember cleaning my plate."

"You didn't live on Maui, did you? I looked you up online. Your parents have an avionics company in Seattle, right?"

"I'm flattered you looked me up."

Ellie blushed.

If he only knew how many hours I spent.

"My parents had a small house here. A vacation place. We used to come at Christmas. Maybe a week in the summer. They rented it out the rest of the time."

"Was Maui the same back then?"

"You mean way back in the 1990s?" Denver's face relaxed into a grin that emphasized his deep brown eyes and sparkling teeth.

Ellie leaned back. *I could get used to looking at those eyes.*

"I mostly remember the beaches. Driving around dirt roads in the sugar cane fields. There were fewer people around, that's for sure. And fewer hotels. More places like this." He nodded at the older Asian couple in the booth next to them. "More places where people knew each other. I hate the box stores you see here now."

Ellie cringed. "You mean Target? I'm a loyal customer at the Kahului branch."

Denver laughed. "Of course you are. It's probably not fair, anyway, my saying what should be here and what shouldn't. That's for the locals to choose."

Halfway through the large stack of pancakes, Ellie noticed she was no longer tense. By the time Denver had polished his bowl clean, they were laughing.

"So if *Aliens* is your favorite movie and *Love Actually*'s mine, what's that say about us?" Ellie spun her spoon absentmindedly on the laminated wood.

"Our second date shouldn't be a movie?"

Ellie flicked the spoon and it flew into Denver's lap.

She closed one eye and pulled up the corner of her mouth. "Sorry."

He held onto the spoon. "Okay, next topic. Your most embarrassing moment."

She covered her face with her hands. "Anything but that."

"No way. Come on. Give."

She stared into his eyes. "This one."

He lifted his eyebrows and peered at the spoon.

"Not the spoon. That I have to tell you my most embarrassing moment."

"I don't get it."

"I don't have just one moment, Denver. I have a list. It starts in kindergarten and gets longer every day. And that's only what I can remember myself. My parents say it started before they took me home from the hospital."

"I don't believe it." Denver's face registered genuine puzzlement. "You've got poise. Some kind of natural…energy."

"Misdirected energy. Normally described as clumsy." Ellie hiccupped and covered her mouth, blushing red to her hairline. "Want an example? How about the eighth grade musical. I can't carry a tune, but they needed someone flexible to play a rabbit. A non-speaking role. I was supposed to hop across the stage. Not difficult. I did fine in the dress rehearsal."

She leaned toward Denver and lowered her voice.

"Then the custodians waxed the stage before the main performance. I took one hop in my fuzzy outfit and slid on my pink butt across the floor into the orchestra pit. That was before YouTube, luckily. But I broke most of the flutes in the wind section. They had to do a special fundraiser to replace them before football season."

Denver slid partly under the table, holding his sides as he laughed.

"Oh, it gets better. How about my senior year on the volleyball team? I dove for a save during a game and hit my head on the net pole. Knocked myself out. In mid-air. That was in the early days of YouTube. It went viral."

Denver gasped. People in the neighboring booths stared at him.

"Stop. I believe you." He wiped his eyes and focused on her.

Ellie sat back, arms crossed.

His face dropped its smile. "I'm sorry. I shouldn't laugh. That must have been really hard."

Ellie grinned. "Stop biting your lip. I know I'm my own best comedy channel."

"No. Really." He reached his hand across the counter, palm up.

She hesitated, and then put her hand in his. His fingers closed around hers in a tight squeeze. "I want to laugh *with* people. Not *at* people. That first time I saw you in the water, you were scared. It could have looked funny to someone else. But it didn't to me."

Ellie stared. "Nobody's ever said *that* before."

Denver's unblinking eyes held her gaze for what seemed like Ellie to be hours.

"You never met *me* before."

***

At Kanaha Beach Park, the deep green folds of the West Maui range created a mystical backdrop to the brilliant blue ocean and tan sand. Wind surfers shot across the water, bouncing on the rough surface whipped up by the strong northerly blast. Ellie held her hair in her hand, sand blowing against her bare legs. She and Denver meandered along the shore. Eventually, the hot sun drove them to the shade of a *hau* tree, where gusts of warm, moist ocean air fluttered the heart-shaped leaves.

"Wait here." Denver held up his hand and jogged back to his Ford Escape.

Ellie watched. He was handsome, she thought, the way a stallion is handsome, overflowing with graceful power, built for speed and hard work, yet also unexpectedly silken and alluring.

He returned carrying a beach blanket and a mini cooler.

Ellie's eyes narrowed. "So this wasn't an impromptu side trip after all?"

Denver presented her a bottle of cold water.

"My parents are pilots. I'm always prepared for an emergency landing."

Denver sat cross-legged. Ellie fidgeted.

Why'd I wear a skirt? Can't cross my legs. Kneeling's stupid. Sideways gets old.

She finally apologized and stretched out, supporting her head on her arm, looking into the boughs above.

"If you're going down, I am too." Denver stretched himself beside her at a respectable distance.

Ellie closed her eyes. "Hawaii's amazing if you pay attention."

"There's no place like it."

"My friend Jacqui says it can bring out the worst in people. She says she sees visitors who spend their whole vacation seething with resentment."

"Because it's so beautiful?"

The ocean breeze whirled through the overhead leaves. "Because their own home *isn't* beautiful. They're pissed they have to go back."

"So they never really arrive."

Ellie rolled to face him. "I guess so. I don't want to do that."

Denver turned on his side. "Are you afraid you will?"

"Maybe." Ellie squinted at him. "Do you have something you'd do over again if you could?"

Denver dropped a hand to the blanket with a thump. "Sure. I wouldn't have gone into business for myself. I'd have joined my parents' company." He rolled onto his back again and stared at the sky.

"I'm not complaining. I like my company. Drones are cool. We're on the cutting edge of a lot of things. But there's a lot of pressure. It would have been easier to learn the ropes from my parents first. Now I feel like can't go back and ask them questions all the time."

"Are things going well?"

"RED's doing…okay. There's a lot of demand. Drones for non-military purposes is what we do. China's a big market with a lot of possibilities. But my partner and I are the only front-office employees. It sometimes feels…overwhelming."

Waves crashed against the sand in the distance. Near the parking lot two homeless men scuffled about rights to a bench.

"A lot of pressure?"

"It's fine. I worry too much." Denver shifted back to face her. "What about you?"

Ellie brushed hair back from her forehead. "Worry?"

"No. What would you do over?"

Ellie pursed her lips and examined the hem of her skirt. "I would go to Stanford instead of the University of Delaware."

"You got into Stanford and didn't go?"

"My parents teach at the U of D. It's a good school." Her momentary smile faded. "But I stayed in Delaware for such a basic reason. To be with my boyfriend, Elliot. The same jerk who dumped me after we moved together to San Francisco."

Denver skidded abruptly across the blanket. Her heart skipped a beat and she held her breath as he enfolded her face in his hands. She closed her eyes, waiting and wishing for what might come next.

Still, when his lips bore down on hers, the intensity made her shiver. She stared at him. His unblinking eyes told her exactly what he thought of the loser who had let her go. Time and space telescoped for her to that one instant. The roar of waves filled her ears, a light breeze caressed her body, and the scents of sunscreen, sea, and Denver's aftershave made her head spin. She clutched his hands to anchor her, afraid she would float away.

Denver explored her mouth and neck, bearing down insistently, nibbling at her as though he could not get enough. Ellie melted into his embrace, borne along on the tide of his passion. His hands rubbed her back. His lips pulled her earlobes. His rough cheeks rubbed against hers.

His desire staggered her. It felt like a strong tide washing her out to an ocean she had never explored, had never even known to exist. Her participation in their entwined fervor came in spurts, as she rose to the surface and gulped for air, pressing back against his lips, gripping his smooth back with her fingers. Then he pressed himself against her again and she dove under, submerged by the waves, letting him lead, floating, blissful, in his arms.

She expected him to stop or to push her too quickly to a place she wasn't quite ready to go. But instead he rode the wave of her desire perfectly, matching the rhythm it beat against his shore. When he did pull away, seemingly hours later, it was at the exact moment she thought she would need to resurface for air.

She lay breathless in his arms, heart-shaped shadows playing across her chest.

***

Keep your mind on the job at hand, Ellie.

Her car followed the reflective road stripes of Mokulele Highway in the early evening dark. But her thoughts floated constantly back to the blanket under the tree, the insistence of his kiss, the hour that magically disappeared from her day in the space of what felt like a few minutes.

It was only kissing. No big deal.

Her lips still tingled from his last embrace in the parking lot. Her body still throbbed from the way his chest rubbed against her breasts.

Snap out of it.

A car behind her honked, jerking her mind back to the road. She could still make out the taillights of Denver's SUV in front of her. She sped up to keep them in sight.

Traffic thinned as the highway transformed into the wide, tree-lined main street of Wailea.

No way. He lives near me?

She watched his car turn left at a traffic light. She raced through the yellow signal.

I'll follow him home.

She felt a faint twinge of guilt at the idea and dismissed it. The road snaked past grand hotels, gated communities, and a golf course. Her foot eased on the accelerator.

Ellie stared. Denver's turn signal flashed. He veered carefully down a side road. *Her* road. She braked and waited a few seconds before following. When she rounded the corner, the street was empty. She drove slowly past her neighbors' homes, peering down driveways right and left. In one she finally caught a glimpse of the Escape's brake lights disappearing behind a solid metal gate.

Ellie's mouth hung open. She pulled in front of her own metal bamboo fence.

He lives next door.

CHAPTER 10

The house seemed strangely empty after the date with Denver, and after changing into more casual clothes, she retreated to the front steps. Residual heat from the mid-day sun still emanated from the sculptured cement, warming her legs as she sat. Viv, on a leash, explored the grass for critters.

Geckos chirped, shrill and insistent, like young birds waiting to be fed. The evening air was motionless, the rhythmic crashing of waves growing louder the longer Ellie listened. She gazed at the shrubbery that separated her yard from Denver's.

Her phone pinged.

Denver: Miss u already.

Her heart jumped. She squinted toward the bushes.
No light. Where is he?

Ellie: Did u see me follow u?

He'll think I'm a stalker.
Delete.

Ellie: Craziest thing. I live next door.

TMI after just one date. Way awkward if this doesn't go anywhere.
Delete.

Ellie: Had gr8 time.

Denver: What r u doing tomorrow night?

A party song boomed to life in her head. *He wants me.* Her shoulders wiggled in time with the music.

Ellie: Nothing. Want to get together?

Wait. A colder part of her brain flipped off the dance music. *Don't jump in headfirst. Take it easy.*
Delete.
She pursed her lips.

Ellie: Sorry. Busy.

Denver: This weekend?

Damn. This time I really am *busy.*

Ellie: My friend's coming from CA on Sun.

Denver: Sat? U been to Maui's swap meet?

Ellie grinned.

Ellie: No.

Denver: U'll love it.

Ellie: Love thinking about going with u.

She shook her head.
Get a grip.
Delete.

Ellie: Looking forward to it. Sleep tight.

She kissed the phone lightly.

Denver: U2.

"Come on, Viv." Ellie kept her voice low and tugged the cat's leash. Viv braced his feet against the steps, arched his back, and resisted with every ounce of his nine pounds.

"What's so great out here?"

Everything, his body seemed to say.

"Be sensible. Bad creatures could eat you." She reached under his belly and hoisted him into her arms, where he hung limp and dejected. "You can't always do what your heart says, you know. Sometimes you have to use your brain."

***

The following morning Ellie heard the gardeners

pull into the driveway just after breakfast. She
yanked a towel from the bathroom rod and wrapped
it around her head, dug in the kitchen drawers for
her beach sunglasses, and threw her San Francisco
Giants windbreaker over her sarong before she
stepped outside to greet them.

"You look like you're trying to avoid paparazzi."
Celine laughed at her later from the corner of the
laptop, which Ellie had perched near the living
room windows.

"What would you do in my position?"

"Act normal."

Ellie pushed the drooping headdress from her
forehead. "Normal?"

"Sure. He doesn't know you followed him home.
If he notices you next door, you can act surprised."

Ellie made a face. "Are you kidding? How good
am I at acting?"

"Bad."

"Right. I think my plan's better. Wear disguises.
Hope he doesn't notice. And figure out a way to
bring it up casually later. If there *is* a later."

Celine rolled her eyes. "He asked you out again,
didn't he?"

Ellie maneuvered her little finger inside the
turban and scratched. "He doesn't know what he's
getting into."

"Believe me. He knows. That was no speed date
you went on."

"No." Ellie's eyes glittered. "But I came here to
get away from all that."

"Remind me what your plan was again?"

"To avoid the dating grind. The broken heart

crap."

Celine nodded slowly. "Ah. I see. That kind of stuff that's only possible in San Francisco."

"I'm starting fresh."

"You told your next door neighbor you're keeping it casual?"

Ellie shook her head. Baby blue terry cascaded across her face. She forced an opening through the folds. "Got to go work on my disguise."

"See you later, Double-Oh-Seven."

In the afternoon, Ellie drove to a tourist outlet before heading to Jacqui's hotel. She flicked through hangers of garishly colored sundresses, choosing ones two sizes larger than what she usually wore. A floppy woven leaf hat and oversized sunglasses joined the pile on the counter while Don Ho music drifted on the air-conditioned breeze.

Jacqui met her at the hotel spa check in desk. She dragged Ellie quickly behind the counter. "You bring yoga clothes?"

"No. All I've got is spy clothes."

Jacqui's eyebrows shot up. "I'll ask you about that later. But right now I'm in a pinch. I'll lone you something."

Jacqui strode past glass brick walls and gleaming marble counters with Ellie jogging to keep up. Pink flowers overflowed from baskets hung overhead with invisible wires, creating the sensation of walking under a cascade of blossoms. Harp music filtered from screened speakers. The air smelled of lavender and musk. Jacqui veered into a dark hallway behind a door discretely marked

'*Personnel Only*'. Ellie followed. They stepped into a white locker room. Jacqui flung open a locker door and rummaged through the contents. She handed Ellie a crumpled black bundle.

Ellie held tiny Lycra pants at eye level. "You think I can fit into these?"

Jacqui eyed her. "You're not any bigger than me. They stretch." She tugged off her shirt and Ellie turned away as Jacqui undid her bra.

"I've got a class to teach and only one student showed up. You have to help me out." She handed Ellie the still warm bra and tank top.

Ellie averted her eyes, mouth wrinkled. "I have to wear these?"

"Unless you want to wear this?" Jacqui turned around and displayed a skin-tight leopard pattern exercise top.

"Uh, no." Ellie looked around for a changing booth.

"Just do it here." Jacqui fiddled her bra into place. "I've got to put on some make-up. Nobody comes in here at this time of day."

When Jacqui disappeared, Ellie removed her street clothes and struggled with the Lycra bottoms. *I've put on jeans with more give than this.* She heaved the hem above her hips with a two-handed tug. It snapped into place.

"Ow."

"You okay back there?" Jacqui craned her neck in the mirror.

Ellie rubbed her backside. "I don't think I'm quite as thin as you think I am."

"Doesn't matter how you look."

136

"Says who?" Ellie waved Jacqui's bra in the air and sniffed carefully. *At least it's not stinky.* When she had it on, she looked down with dismay, seeing that her breasts hardly filled the cups.

Jacqui rounded the corner of the lockers. "You look great."

Ellie beheld herself in a mirror. "You don't have a single bump of fat, and you're falling out of that bra. I look like I snuck into my mother's closet."

"Nobody will be looking. Follow me."

Ellie traipsed after her. "Why exactly am I taking your class again?"

Jacqui pushed her out the door back into the guest area. "Because it looks bad if I don't have at least two people. You said you wanted to be a spy. Here's your chance to go incognito. For the next two hours, you're a rich hotel guest from Washington State. Now follow the signs for the yoga studio."

Jacqui pulled the door closed behind her.

Ellie pulled at her sagging bra and sighed. "Two hours?"

Two and a half hours later, the friends sat at the hotel bar by the Maui-shaped swimming pool. Couples held hushed conversations around them. Muffled Miles Davis mingled with the splashing of the pool's waterfall.

Ellie raised her Blue Hawaii with a groan, one hand supporting the other. "I'm never going to be able to lift my arms again."

Jacqui pushed aside a half finished gin and tonic and stared at the waterfall. "You're building muscle."

"I have no muscle. That's why I kept falling over."

Jacqui glanced at her phone. "Keep the big picture in mind—moving with grace though the universe."

Ellie folded her arms on the bar and flopped her head to rest. Jacqui instinctively whisked Ellie's drink out of harm's way.

Jacqui held up her phone again. "I just got another text."

Ellie opened one eye and peeped at her. "Something serious?"

Jacqui shook her head. "Don't know. It's just a rumor. But it's going viral."

Something in the tone of Jacqui's voice brought Ellie to a sitting position. "What happened?"

"They say someone was killed on the hotel grounds last night." Jacqui inspected the pool in front of them. "Here."

Ellie drew her legs up in disgust. "Eew. In the water?"

"I think so. Nobody's sure. And management apparently isn't talking." She lowered her voice and grinned. "Look at all those couples in the pool. You think they'd be swimming if they thought a body had been floating there last night?"

Ellie lowered her legs and took another sip. "I don't think it can be true. Why aren't there cops everywhere?"

"They say it was late. Could have been all cleaned up by morning."

"I don't know."

Jacqui shoved the phone in the waistband of her

floral Capri leggings. "You're right. No point in worrying about it. Now, tell me about your date."

The level of the blue liquid in Ellie's glass lowered rapidly as she told Jacqui about Denver.

"I thought you were on Maui to play the field?"

Ellie blinked. "My field's got only one player right now. You know any others?"

"What about the hot stud gardeners?"

Ellie laughed. "Brandon's the best of the bunch."

Jacqui motioned to the bartender for another round. "Then Olivia's lucky."

"Seriously. I texted to ask if she wanted to join us later. But she didn't answer. Brandon didn't show up for work today, so they must be doing something." Ellie bent over with another groan and pulled her phone from her purse. "Oh. She texted back. She wants me to call her."

Jacqui hopped off the bar stool and carried their glasses to an empty table. They sat. "So call. I've got some classes I can set up."

Ellie dialed and watched a young man in the pool hoist his girlfriend onto his hips and fling her backward into the water with a splash.

"Olivia? It's…hey. Hold on. What? Speak slower. I can't understand you."

Jacqui frowned at her and put down her phone.

Color drained from Ellie's face. A sound like rushing water enveloped her, and the world began to sway.

Jacqui nudged her chair closer to Ellie's and motioned for Ellie to put the phone on speaker. Ellie, eyes large, handed her the phone. Jacqui pushed the button.

"...police came over. I can't believe it. Brandon."

"Olivia, honey, this is Jacqui. Is somebody there with you?"

"No." The voice sounded empty, an infinitesimal rasp in the long silence that followed it.

Jacqui pushed back her chair and waved signals at the bartender who waved back. "You stay put, Olivia." She motioned for Ellie to head to the exit. "Make yourself a cup of coffee. Ellie will talk to you. We're on our way."

Before handing the phone to Ellie, she covered the microphone with her hand. "What happened?"

Ellie nodded. "It's totally crazy. Brandon's dead. She says they found him in a pool."

Recognition dawned on both of them at once and the two women stared at the blue water in front of them.

"Oh, God." Ellie closed her eyes. "I didn't even remember he worked here."

A cool breeze carried the scent of seaweed and decaying fish from the nearby ocean.

Jacqui pulled her arm. "Come on. Keep her talking. I'll drive."

***

Jacqui tromped the wooden stairs to Olivia's apartment two at a time. The boards creaked disquietingly as Ellie followed. The door was leaned opened. Inside, the shades were drawn.

"I should have told her to turn on the light." Ellie flipped a switch to the right of the door. "Olivia?"

Olivia lay face down on a bamboo frame sofa, the phone still clutched in her hands.

She turned her head, as though the effort cost her a great deal. "You came." Her voice barely reached them.

Ellie squatted by her head. "I told you we were downstairs, silly."

Olivia wiped her eyes with the back of her hand. Her face was blotchy and wet. "I didn't believe you."

Jacqui returned from the galley kitchen with a towel. "Here, honey, wipe your face with this." She glided her arms under Olivia's neck and legs and swung her expertly to a sitting position.

"Go look for some chocolate or cookies or something, Ellie. She needs a little kick to her system. And bring water."

Jacqui sat next to Olivia and put her arm around her shoulders. Olivia slumped against her, her body convulsing with sobs.

Three chocolates and fifteen minutes later, Olivia began to talk, speaking a torrent of words that poured out of her like a stream plunging over a rocky river bed. Phrases bumped and jolted, swerved and halted, spinning and tumbling over one another. Ellie sat with her arms around her legs, willing herself not to cry. Jacqui stroked Olivia's tousled hair as a mother would a child's.

The police, Olivia said, had knocked on the apartment door before dawn. Brandon didn't usually get home from his maintenance job at the hotel until two or three in the morning, but she was surprised he wasn't there. The police told her

141

Brandon had been found dead in a hotel pool with a blow to the head. It looked as if someone had hit him and then pushed him in. They said whatever happened took place between ten-thirty and eleven at night.

Olivia told the police she had been at Target until the store closed at eleven. She was certain the clerk would remember her. They'd had a long discussion about the respective merits of Target and Walmart. When she'd gotten home, she'd gone to bed. She hadn't been worried. Brandon was always there when she woke up in the morning.

When she finished, she began to shake in rapid vibrations over which she seemed to have no control. Jacqui looked around the room for a sweater. "Honey, you need to get away from here. We're driving you down to Ellie's house tonight."

They bundled her into Jacqui's car. The long, mostly silent drive back to sea level gave Ellie time to think.

Who would kill Brandon? Was he involved in something illicit? Was he selling drugs or something?

She thought back over their interactions, all she knew about him.

Something was going on in Seattle before he came here. Probably the same reason he and Olivia dropped out of school. It must've made him able to handle Noa. And it must be why he had that tattoo.

At her house, they ensconced Olivia in the guest bedroom, where she fell almost immediately into a sleep that looked more like unconsciousness than slumber. Her fetal-position ball formed an incongruous and lonely bump under the yellow and orange plumeria comforter Ellie had purchased for Celine's arrival.

After Jacqui left, Ellie prowled the kitchen between the two bedrooms, Viv pacing at her side as though sensing unrest in the house. She spoke quietly on the phone with Celine.

"You freaked?"

Ellie shuddered. "Totally. It's got nothing to do with me, but I *knew* him. I *liked* him. I can't believe he's dead."

"What do you think happened?"

Ellie opened the front door and sat on the lanai steps. "No clue. But if I had to guess, I'd say it was his past catching up with him. He was super nice, but there was something he wasn't saying. Olivia too. Their life in Seattle wasn't all Starbucks lattes and trips to the Space Needle."

"Shit."

"You're telling me." The moon shone bright above the ocean, creating a light yellow reflection on the waves that extended like a searchlight to the shore. Ellie circled her arms around her knees. "If it were at a hotel miles from here and I didn't know the guy, I wouldn't think twice. But this is practically next door. It's not like I'm next on the list. But it does mean a murderer's wandering around."

"The underside of paradise. That ice-witch boss of yours willing to pay for a security system?"

Ellie nodded. "I texted Devora already. She said she'd wave the word murder in front of Vivyenne. Told me to go ahead and call some companies in the morning."

There was a pause. Ellie heard a drawn-out intake of breath that sounded like Celine pulling on a cigarette. Only Celine didn't smoke. "Maybe a man in the house right now wouldn't be a bad idea. Have you thought about calling Denver?"

Ellie smiled. "Beat you to it. I called twice already. But he doesn't pick up."

"You could go over and knock."

Ellie laughed. "I'm a mess. I wouldn't want him seeing me like this." Ellie tromped through the house, flipping on light switches as she moved through the rooms. "You still sure you want to come on Sunday?"

"Hell, yeah. Seems like a girlfriend from the 'hood will fit right in."

Ellie smirked. "You grew up in Oak Park. That isn't the 'hood, remember?"

"A minor technicality."

CHAPTER 11

The next morning before Olivia got up, Ellie began calling alarm companies. She sat cross-legged on a stool at the kitchen island, her laptop in front of her, a cup of black coffee placed strategically to one side.

"That's right. The best system you've got. And I want signs. Huge ones. All over the yard. For the windows and doors too."

She typed notes on the computer.

"Is that the fastest you can get it installed? I'll pay extra if you'll rush."

A shape darkened the kitchen door. She motioned for Olivia to come in and pour herself a cup of coffee.

"I'm going to need an hour or so to think about it. Can you pencil me in and I'll call you back? Thanks."

She hopped from the stool and gave Olivia a hug.

"How are you doing?"

Olivia stared at her with haunted, dark-circled

eyes.

"Stupid question. I heard you throwing up last night. You feel like shit, of course." Ellie pulled eggs and milk from the new refrigerator. "Let's have waffles. After that, I can drive you home if you want. Jacqui and I got my car back here this morning while you were still sleeping."

Olivia suspended an egg over a bowl, looking out the window. After waiting a moment, Ellie took the egg from her hand and guided her to the counter. "You sit. I'll make the waffles."

"I don't want to go back." Olivia's voice broke through Ellie's whisking.

"Back to the apartment?" The waffle iron sizzled as the batter oozed slowly among the raised iron squares.

"Uh huh."

"Then stay here. No problem. I've got more furniture arriving today. White sofas. You can help me decorate." She peeked at Olivia through the steam from the waffle iron. Her skin looked as pale and brittle as an eggshell. "Or just watch me do it."

After breakfast, Ellie installed Olivia in the guest bedroom again with "Men in Black" playing on her iPad. She resumed calls to alarm companies.

She'd narrowed the field when the timer on her phone reminded her Olivia's movie was finished. She stretched and went to the living room to get Viv.

"Enough fun in the sun." She picked up the warm creature. "You've got work to do today."

She knocked on Olivia's door and nudged it open when she didn't get a response. Olivia lay on her side, the pad propped against the comforter. She hardly looked up when Ellie entered, but her face brightened slightly at the sight of Viv.

"I brought you some company." The cat hopped onto the bed and pranced toward Olivia's outstretched hand. "He told me he really wants to watch *Men in Black II* with you."

Ellie perched on the edge of the bed as she queued the movie. Viv rubbed enthusiastically against Olivia's cheeks.

"Did you find an alarm company?"

"Yep. They'll be out in the next few days to get started."

No point mentioning they won't be finished for weeks. Hawaii doesn't do 'rush.'

"You're all set." The introductory music played. Ellie drew the curtains.

Olivia used Viv's paw to tap the pause and play button. "He's so cute."

Ellie rolled her eyes. "He's my little bundle of joy."

Olivia dropped the furry arm and Ellie saw a tear edge down her cheek.

Ellie fingered the curtains. "I don't want to...but yesterday you said not to let your parents know. Do you still feel that way? I could call them for you."

Olivia shook her head and met Ellie's eyes. "You don't understand. I haven't talked with my parents in a long time. Not...since...well, right after I dropped out of college."

Ellie's gaze wandered from Olivia's grief-stricken face to the plumeria photos on the walls. "My parents don't always approve of what I do

147

either. They weren't thrilled about my coming here. But I can rely on them in an emergency."

Olivia hit the play button and spoke in a voice barely audible over the music. "Mine are different. I can't."

An hour later, in the middle of Ellie's preparing peanut butter and liliquoi jelly sandwiches for lunch, Olivia walked into the kitchen clutching her phone.

"The police just called."

Ellie dropped the knife. "What'd they say?"

"Good news. They don't think I did it." Olivia attempted a smile.

"They could have called me for that answer." Ellie finished making a sandwich and thrust it at Olivia, who pushed the plate away and then picked it up when Ellie shot her a listen-to-your-elders look.

"They think it might be drug-related."

Ellie parked herself at the counter. "What? Brandon using drugs?" She tried to sound surprised.

"They're wrong."

Ellie thought back to her conversation with Jacqui that morning and the rumors flying at the hotel. Drugs topped the list of suspected reasons for the murder of a part-time maintenance employee.

"Are you sure?"

"There's no way he was doing drugs." Color rose to Olivia's face, blotchy red streaks that only emphasized her overall pallor. "No fucking way."

"I believe you. But maybe his murderer was involved in drugs?"

"They didn't say anything about that." Olivia bit

into the sandwich. "They don't even know for sure that someone tried to kill him. It could have been an accident."

"That's right." Ellie shrugged. "We don't know anything. Brandon could have been with anyone that night."

Olivia rounded on her, eyes flashing. "Brandon wasn't hanging out with users."

Ellie sat back, stunned. "Chill, Olivia. I didn't mean that. I'm just trying to help."

Olivia slammed the counter. "Not if you say things like that."

What's going on with her?

Ellie leaned forward. "Look, I'm sorry. I really like Brandon."

"Liked. He's dead." Olivia threw the remainder of the sandwich on the counter. "And drugs had nothing to do with it." She stomped from the room.

Ellie followed. "What are you doing?"

Olivia picked her sweater up from the floor. "Going home."

Ellie settled on the bed, arms crossed.

Tears rolled freely down Olivia's cheeks. She petted Viv and looked up taxi companies on her phone. "I'm freaked."

Ellie uncrossed her arms and gestured for Olivia to sit next to her. "I'll drive you back."

Olivia shook her head, spoke to a dispatcher, and hung up. "They'll be here in ten minutes. I'll wait outside."

Ellie rose. "I'll go with you."

"No." Olivia looked around the room. "I'll go by myself." She strode into the hallway and turned around. "Ellie, just fucking forgive me, okay? My whole life...I feel like I can't breathe."

Ellie's shoulders slumped and tightness wrapped itself around her chest.

I can't believe he's dead either. So how must you feel?

Ellie waved at the back of Olivia's taxi. Her phone rang. Jacqui listed sympathetically to the story of Olivia's departure.

"Forgive her, honey. She just lost her boyfriend and doesn't know which end is up."

"Of course I will. But why'd she go ballistic? Now I feel like if I mention anything I'm wondering about, I'll be stepping on a landmine." Ellie lay stretched on the floor of the lanai, her hand shading her face.

"Why don't you call Denver? He'll take your mind off it."

Ellie stared at a set of overhead fans she'd never noticed before.

Explains that mystery switch near the front door.

Ellie sighed. "He texted me this morning. Mr. Drone Company has some kind of stupid conference in LA. He won't be back until tomorrow night."

"Honey, I'm sorry, but I have to go teach serenity to stressed out visitors. What about some retail therapy after?"

"The white furniture's supposed to arrive any minute now. I'll be stuck here for hours."

"I'll call you later. In the meantime, spill some coffee on the sofa when the movers leave. It'll make you feel better."

Ellie grinned. "Sick idea. I'll go make a pot."

***

The next day, a text interrupted Ellie's impromptu testing of the new living room furniture. When the phone pinged, she jumped guiltily from the white sofa as though Vivyenne had just walked into the room.

Olivia: Sorry 4 yesterday.

Ellie: All's good. How r u holding up?

Olivia: Throwing up.

Poor thing.

Ellie: Want me to bring soup?

Olivia: Don't think I could keep it down.

Viv eyed the new sofa and reached out a paw to touch it. Ellie scooted a cardboard cat scratcher in front of him. "Don't get any ideas." Viv hopped on the scratcher and wriggled in the catnip.

Ellie: Need company?

Olivia: Thx. Brandon's friends r coming over soon. Just wanted to say sorry.

Ellie: No need. Big hug.

Ellie added an emoji of a smiling face blowing a kiss.

She walked into the strong morning sun and texted Celine.

Ellie: Can't wait for u to get here.

Celine: Liar. Ur only thinking about tomorrow with Denver.

Ellie laughed.

Ellie: That too.

Celine: U still in disguise?

Ellie shook her head, enjoying the breeze in her hair.

Ellie: He's in LA till tonite. So I'm plainclothes today.

Celine: If you spend the night at his house tomorrow, text me. I'll take a cab from the airport.

Ellie: Not happening.

Celine: Just saying.

Ellie turned off her screen and skipped across the grass into the ocean. Warm water caressed her calves. Small white fish flitted in the shallows, casting gray shadows on the sand. She squatted for a closer look, cupping her hands around her face to shield herself from the glare. Her yellow sundress billowed, reminding her of another day she'd submerged herself in the water fully clothed.

She lay back, suddenly sensing the emptiness of the space around her. Buoyed by the ocean, she let tears for Brandon mix with the infinity of the salty water.

***

At seven Saturday morning, the Kahului Whole Foods parking lot was nearly empty. Ellie parked under a tree she hoped would provide shade for most of the day and sat on the hood.

A black Nissan Altima pulled in the slot next to her and honked. Ellie frowned at the shape behind the tinted driver's side window. It lowered to reveal Denver's sparkling eyes and dashing grin.

"You going my way, lady?" He turned off the engine and stepped out.

Ellie hopped down and Denver embraced her. His athletic arms seemed to wring the fear and anxiety of the past days from her soul. Myna birds squawked in the trees overhead. Sparrows tweeted in the grassy medians. A crisp ocean breeze lifted the hem of her shorts. The morning seemed suddenly fresh and bright, her chest and shoulders free, her heart light.

His lips found hers and she melted against them, her tongue entwining with his. Their dance made her think of sex, of lying together naked in Denver's car, in her car, even on the empty pavement. One leg wrapped involuntarily around his, pushing his hips into hers. Denver's laugh broke their embrace.

"I take it you missed me."

Ellie blushed. "Not really."

His fingers ran possessively through her hair, pulling it back from her face. "I missed you too. And I'm sorry I've been so busy. Work's been kind of crazy."

Ellie took his hand. "You're here now." She looked at the black sedan. "I thought you had a green Escape."

Denver chuckled. "You stalking me?"

Color rose from Ellie's chest to her forehead. "Who me? Stalking?"

"Just kidding. It's a rental."

"You don't have your own car? I thought with a house and all…"

Denver opened the passenger side door. "In you pop."

A smiling woman took the swap meet's fifty-cent fee at an entrance to a fenced enclosure on the University of Hawaii Maui College campus. She beamed at Ellie and Denver. "Honeymoon?"

Denver winked at Ellie, who coughed into her hand.

"Wait." The woman reached into a bag at her feet and handed them each a star fruit. "From my neighbor's tree. You enjoy."

They strolled among the first stalls. Ellie tried shoving the odd yellow fruit into a pocket of her shorts and then handed it to Denver. "I feel bad I took it."

"We made her happy." He pushed one fruit into his front pocket.

Ellie shook her head. "I'm not going to say what that looks like from here. But you have to take it out or you'll get expelled for indecency."

"I should have brought a bag."

"*I* should have brought one. I have, like, a lifetime supply of Target bags back at the house."

A soft mist fell from the clouds hovering over the nearby mountains and wafted intermittently across the fenced grounds, providing a cooling alternative to the rapidly rising sun. Vendors displayed coconut shell art, t-shirts, hand crafted soap, cut flowers, original paintings and photography, and ceramics. Ellie and Denver wandered hand in hand among the fruit and vegetable stalls. They bought ripe apple bananas and fresh bread. They washed it down with rainbow shave ice. They talked about her family and his. Ellie felt the same intrinsic comfort in his presence as she had the first day at the beach. The horror of Olivia's situation slipped into the past. Her present telescoped, focused on their laughter, his hand in hers, the fresh Maui air, and a pleasant feeling of anticipation mingled with contentment. Before she knew it, almost two hours had passed and they were headed back to his car.

"Get me to the trail before this sugar high wears off." Ellie bounced in the passenger seat as they wound up a narrow road on the northwest side of the island. Dilapidated wooden houses clung to the steep mountainside. Dark blue ocean stretched wide to the horizon on their right. Green folds of West

Maui peaks soared above them to the left.

Denver turned at a Boy Scout camp sign. The sedan crawled and bumped up a steep trail at ten miles an hour.

Ellie looked around. "You sure you know where you're going?"

"Trust me." An empty dirt parking lot with one other car opened up to the right across from a field of black cattle. On the backs of a number of them perched thin white egrets, balanced like precarious porcelain statues.

A few steps into the hike, a cow ambled across the trail. Ellie hung back. "I haven't seen this part of Maui before. I didn't know they had cows."

Denver laughed. "Cows don't bite."

"I don't like the look of those horns." She bent to try and look at the cow's underside. "Are you sure these aren't bulls?"

"Where'd you grow up again?" Denver took her hand and pulled her past a lowing animal.

"Delaware." Ellie broke free and sprinted up the steep trail.

Denver jogged on muscular legs and easily overtook her. "They don't have cows in Delaware?"

"Not that I noticed."

Well past the grazing area, Ellie stopped, panting, at an overlook. Before them the grassy verge pitched straight down for miles into a steep valley where the faintest echo of a waterfall rose from the depths. Beyond the gorge, the mountain folded in upon itself again and again, an undulating fabric worn by water and time. In the distance, the buildings of Kahului harbor glistened as the morning sun reflected off countless windows. Heavy surf broke across nearby reefs, creating a frothy white contrast in the cobalt sea.

Ellie rocked on her heels. "For the record, they don't have views like this in Delaware either."

"I'm glad you're not in Delaware any longer." Denver pulled her against him, urgent and determined.

In his embrace, she again lost track of her surroundings and of time. Where he led, she followed, letting her hands roam over his body in equal proportion to the way his explored hers. His lips nuzzled her ear. She ran her tongue along the contour of his earlobe. He cupped her face in his hands and slowly ran his fingers through her hair, letting it cascade down her back like a trail of silken threads. She gripped his short wavy hair and tousled it, massaging his scalp with her fingernails. Her heart thumped when his fingers brushed across her breasts. She flitted her palms across his chest, rising against him as he pressed firmly into her.

Their progress to the top was hindered by periodic kissing sessions: beneath banyan trees, while gazing at the ocean, after eating fallen guava fruit, and before retying a shoelace. But the trek rewarded their perseverance.

At the trail's end the ridge continued before them. A sign warning of abrupt drop offs, complete with a visual of someone plummeting off a cliff, marked the end of the recommended passage on foot. Helicopters giving guided tours of the island flew overhead, hovering deep in the valleys below and then streaking up the mountainsides.

"You couldn't pay me to ride in one of those." Ellie leaned back against Denver.

"Scared of heights?"

"Scared of falling."

His arms encircled her. "I'd be happy to be your seat belt."

On the way down, Ellie's head swam with primal energy. She capered along the slippery clay path, enjoying the sight of Denver's broad shoulders bouncing in front of her. No man she had ever known had buried his way into her heart in such a short time the way Denver had.

Something sparked for me that first moment on the beach.

As a teenager, she'd dreamt of love at first sight. But she had only participated in love as a gradual and awkward transition from friendship to lust to something more.

What is it that draws me in now so completely?

Preoccupied with her assessment, she forgot to watch the path at her feet. An exposed tree root caught her foot. She stumbled. Suddenly, the green brushy hillside rushed toward her. As she sailed through the air, she marveled at the calm thought that flashed in a millisecond through her mind.

This could be worse than initially anticipated. Better let him know where I've gone.

"Denver." She sailed over the edge of the trail. Her voice betrayed only a glimmer of anxiety. Hips flew over her head. She summersaulted backward down the steep ravine.

Grab something.

Thick spongy tangles of brush broke her fall. She

158

flipped twice before a tree caught her legs and she slithered to a halt.

Denver's anxious face peered down at her from a surprisingly far distance.

"Hang on. I'll come get you." He threw a leg over the side.

"No. Stay there. I can get back up." Ellie clung to vines and shrubbery and heaved herself up the cliff. At the top, she brushed herself off.

Denver's face was pale. He took her hands.

"Are you hurt?"

Ellie laughed. "Not unless you took a video."

"No, really. You're okay?"

"Let me prove it to you." She snuggled against him and showered his neck with kisses.

On the drive back to her own car, Ellie fought an internal battle.

Go home with him? Don't go home with him? What her body wanted and what her mind told her were too different to reach any compromise. When she thought one side had the upper hand, the other pushed back.

Denver's hand rested on her knee. She traced the outline of his knuckles with her index finger. In the now crowded parking lot, Denver searched for a space.

"You know." He squeezed her hand. "It might be easier to leave your car here." He glanced at her as a Range Rover backed into the lane. "You have to be back in Kahului to pick Celine up tomorrow, don't you?"

See? I knew he was going to ask.

Ellie bit her lip.

"You could come back home with me. I could bring you here tomorrow before her flight."

Heart or brain. Why is this so damned hard?

Denver redirected his gaze. "I'm not pushing you. I'll be here all week. When's Celine leaving?"

"Wednesday afternoon."

He shrugged. "We could make a date for Thursday."

Ellie mentally kicked herself for her indecision. "This isn't easy for me. It's just that I'm so…"

Scared.

"…busy. I've got so much work to do…"

On myself.

"…at the house. There are so many…

Relationship issues in my past.

"…workers coming every day. And I'm not even…"

Telling you the truth about everything.

"…ready for Celine's arrival."

Denver ran his fingers through her hair with one hand and pushed the emergency flasher button on the dash with the other. He turned to face her.

"I get it. My neighbors are having construction done while they're somewhere else too. It's noisy from dawn until after dark. I hide all day in the guest cottage with earplugs just to do my work."

Tell him you're the neighbor. Go home with him.

Ellie tugged the door handle. "If I don't leave now…"

I'll never leave.

"…I'll be up all night preparing."

He drew her to him. "One more kiss isn't going to make a difference."

A few minutes later, Ellie slumped at the steering wheel of her car. She watched his black sedan pull out of the lot.

One more kiss almost *had* made the difference. But not quite.

CHAPTER 12

Denver's body throbbed with thoughts of Ellie. He maneuvered the car into the slower of the two lanes that ran between the red dirt fields where the last sugar cane had already been harvested. He let the eager tourists rush past him in their search for the perfect Saturday afternoon in paradise. He focused on the taillights of the car in front of him and put his driving on autopilot while his mind relived the morning with Ellie.

Throughout, his phone vibrated incessantly in his pocket, tickling his thigh, a welcome distraction from the strong sensations his body was experiencing elsewhere. But the more it wiggled, the more the intoxication of the last few hours waned. When he pulled into his driveway and shut off the engine, one glance at the phone screen popped the few remaining bubbles of joy. The sensations left over from the outing floated up, out of reach, through the palm fronds, and into the clear blue sky. His feet dragged along the concrete pathway to the guesthouse. He called the number that had left five voicemails in the past hour.

"What's up?…Sorry. I couldn't get to the phone. Bad reception…Do I want to hear this?…Christ."

Denver let himself into the small guest bungalow. The venetian blinds were closed against the strong sun, but shafts of brilliant light streamed through the cracks, illuminating the open floor-plan room. A laptop swam in a sea of computer printouts of graphic designs on a dining table that separated the living space from the kitchen. Cereal bowls and coffee mugs rose in towers from the sink basin. The large king-sized bed in the far corner was unmade, its cover sheet and pillows crumpled into mounds.

"Fucking China. Idiots write stories about it being the biggest break small companies ever had. But how can we keep up when the have a new regulation every week?…I'll see what I can do…Yeah, you don't have to remind me. I know what's at stake."

He tossed the phone on the table and sunk into the one armchair, running his fingers through his hair. The phone pinged with a text message. Denver's chin fell to his chest. He rubbed his shoulders.

He remained seated for a long time, ignoring the periodic beeps from the table. Then he heaved himself determinedly to his feet, searched for a contact on the phone, and hit the call button.

"Mom?" He covered his eyes with his free hand. "You free for a minute? I could use your advice."

Half an hour later, he perched on a stool at the kitchen bar, chin resting on his hand, phone still to his ear.

"No. I'm not giving up. But this isn't what I had in mind for the business."

He spun a spoon on the counter with his fingers.

"In retrospect we should have waited. Teaches me not to be so greedy…No. I'm okay. I've still got a little money in my personal account."

He laughed. "Yeah, thank the Kirkpatricks for me when you see them. Using this guesthouse has been a godsend. I wasn't getting anything done at the Seattle office with people coming through the door every five minutes. Here the only way to get me is email or phone. At least I have some control over that."

He kicked absentmindedly at the chair rungs. "Is that why you and Dad had that place here?…Yeah. It was great. Too bad you sold it…Yep. I check on the main house here now and then. You can tell them everything's fine."

His spine stiffened.

"Bad idea, Mom. We're not together anymore. You know that…Sure. She's got a lot of business experience. But knowing her, she'd laugh and then try to buy me out…Yeah. I'll start packing. See you soon…Me too."

Denver laid the phone face down on the counter. He pulled a carry-on suitcase from under the bed, opened it onto a chair by the table, and propelled the mass of papers into it with several sweeps of his arm. He shoved the laptop into a side pocket and zippered it shut.

Half an hour later, a pile of dishes lay drying in a rack as he locked the guest cottage door and wandered, suitcase in hand, through the afternoon sun toward his car. A gust of warm air from the south emphasized the drilling noises from his next door neighbor's lanai.

Denver shot a resentful glance at the barrier of hedges and palm trees that separated him from the workers. "At least I'm not going to miss *that*."

***

Returning from her date with Denver, Ellie bounded across the lawn and up the steps to her house. Inside, she nearly collided with a man in white overalls.

"Careful. I almost speared you with this." The worker held up a drill.

"No problem." She skipped a step down the hallway and turned around. "I know I'm supposed to know, but there are so many jobs going on right now. What are you guys doing again?"

"Putting in new doors." He pointed to the front door.

"Oh." She cocked her head. "It kind of looks the same to me."

The man gave her a funny look. "That's because we haven't replaced it yet. We've got the new one in the truck. We'll get you the new set of keys when we're done."

"Right."

The man eyed her. "In case you're wondering, the crew with blue t-shirts is here about replacing the floors. They're in the kitchen, I think."

"Thanks. Those are the people I want to talk to." Ellie meandered to the back of the house, taking a short run and sliding now and then across the dark wooden floorboards. She sang softly as she glided along the smooth surface.

Her phone rang before she reached the workers.

"Jacqui, darling." Ellie tossed the phone gently in her hand. "What's up?"

"You haven't heard?"

Ellie skidded to a stop. "Heard what?"

"There was another murder."

Ellie veered into her bedroom and closed the door. "What?"

"This never happens on Maui. I mean *never*. There's a lot of domestic violence. And visitors die of heart attacks while snorkeling. But not this."

Ellie dropped onto the bed. "Who was it?"

"The boyfriend of Noa's ex-girlfriend. Noa's the prime suspect. But they can't find him."

Ellie lay back, stunned. A muffled meow issued from beneath her and Viv scuttled out from under the comforter.

"Sorry, Viv."

"What?"

"Nothing. The cat." She screwed her eyes shut. *This can't be happening.*

"The boyfriend apparently went out night fishing, alone. Was supposed to go with his buddy, but the guy got sick or something. Anyway, it looks like Noa swam up to the boat and ambushed him. They found his body and the boat two days ago. It was on the news before, but I don't always watch."

"I don't get it. How do they know it was Noa?"

"Beats me. But the ex-girlfriend had a restraining order out against him."

Ellie slid off the bed and sat with her back against the wall.

"Is there some kind of seedy underworld here on the island I didn't know about?"

"Honey, I don't know. I got all this from the local evening news. Nightline it ain't. We're seriously lacking for in-depth reporting."

Viv crouched on his stomach and wiggled his behind, preparing to pounce on the window curtain.

"I can't really wrap my head around this."

"Have you talked to Olivia?"

"I talked to her on my drive home. She didn't say anything."

"Drive home? Oh, right. Your date. How'd it go?"

Ellie's face relaxed as she thought of Denver's arms around her. "Okay."

"Ha. Your mouth says okay but your voice says awesome."

"I could use some motherly advice, actually."

"Motherly? Hear that noise? That's me hanging up on you."

Ellie threw a sock at Viv, who was considering climbing up the curtain. "I just mean advice from someone older."

"Click."

"More…enlightened?"

"Keep talking."

"I really like him."

"And that's a problem because?"

"Because I don't really trust myself." Ellie wiggled her toes. Viv ignored her in favor of batting the sock across the wooden floor. "Or maybe I don't trust him."

"I think those two are related."

"Oh. I never thought about it that way."

"Come to yoga class tomorrow. It'll clear your mind."

"Don't you mean it'll wear me out?"

"Once again, those two things are related."

That evening before going to sleep, Ellie moved Viv's water bowl and litter box to her bathroom. She pushed a white armchair from the living room into her bedroom. Then she turned on every light in the house. Once she and Viv were ready for bed, she shoved the armchair against the closed bedroom door and sat in it.

"This is as close to a safe room as we're getting, buddy."

Viv tromped across her pillows, kneading them into his desired consistency.

She dialed Denver.

"Hope I'm not calling too late."

"Nope." His voice sounded exhausted. "Just working."

"In the guest cottage?"

"Um. No. Actually…"

Ellie grinned to herself. "Phew. Glad your neighbors are finally giving you some peace and quiet. What's the point of owning a house on Maui if you can never use it, right?"

"Well…."

"I mean, you're running a company and making lots of money. You deserve to enjoy your own house."

"I guess. But let me…"

Take the plunge, Ellie.

"I'm looking forward to seeing your place on Thursday."

Her stomach tensed as seconds passed without a response.

"I mean, if you want me to."

"Ellie…"

"Look, never mind. I just like thinking of you nearby. It's…"

Comforting.

"Comforting."

"I like thinking of you too. Now look, I'm really sorry, but I have to get some stuff done before I go to bed."

A strange feeling rose in her chest.

"Everything okay?"

"It's fine, Ellie. I'll text you in the morning before you pick up Celine. Sleep tight."

She curled into a ball next to Viv and looked at the phone's dark screen.

Everything went so well today. Why do I feel like disaster's right around the corner?

***

She noticed an unusual rattling the next morning as she lay in bed stretching after the alarm. It resembled the rustling of palm fronds, but more intense. She drew the phone to her.

Is someone out there?

She lifted a corner of the curtain.

Rain?

By the time she pulled on her Giants

169

windbreaker and donned the new floppy hat, the rain shower had moved out to sea, hovering over Molokini in the distance. Ellie tiptoed in bare feet along the wet grass, leaving a dark trail. She shivered in the uncharacteristically cool air.

A movement by the house caught the corner of her eye and she spun around. The garden didn't stir.

Is somebody here?

Phone in hand, she roamed the perimeter, looking for something out of place.

I'm just freaked because of that murder.

The guesthouse stood lonely and dark, like an unwanted stepchild.

Maybe somebody's in there?

She grabbed a lava rock from the pile near the fountain and crept to the door, ready to defend herself but preferring the thought that the stone might buy her time to flee. Heart beating, she tried the door.

It's locked.

She rattled the handle and laughed at herself.

Okay, Ellie. Get a grip.

On the way back in, she texted Devora.

Ellie: What's up with the ohana?

Devora: House not big enough for u?

Ellie: Very funny. Just tried door. It's locked.

Devora: Should be same key as house.

Oh, great.

Ellie: Got Vivyenne's new doors installed yesterday. Threw old keys in trash so I wouldn't get confused.

Devora: Dumpster dive?

Ellie: Garbage picked up this morning.

Devora: Right. Locksmith. But if u can't get in, nobody else can either. Just leave it.

Ellie: K. U hear about the murder?

Devora: Fifty per day in the US. Which one?

Ellie flung herself on the white living room sofa and jumped off again as though she'd been shocked. She wiped furiously at the stain her grassy feet had left. The bright green spread across the material like a film of algae.

Ellie: Never mind. Got a cleaning emergency.

Devora: Don't want to know what's no longer white. Say hi to Viv.

CHAPTER 13

Later that morning, Ellie left an hour early in case of traffic problems and spent forty minutes waiting in her car in the Kahului airport lot. She rolled down the windows and put her feet on the dash.

In San Francisco I'd have been late. Here I'm way too mainland.

She re-read her morning exchange with Denver.

Denver: Thinking of u. Have fun w Celine. Lots to do on my end before Thurs. Drowning in work. Can't wait to see u.

Ellie: Don't work too hard. It'd take my whole life to do half of what u've accomplished already. Ur amazing.

Denver: I may not be all u think I am.

Ellie: No. Ur more!

She appended a smiley face.

Poor guy. So busy. Serious cheering up in order Thursday. She smiled at thoughts of what cheering Denver up might entail.

Ellie: At least we're both on Maui. Maybe Celine & I will see u.

Denver: I'd love that. But don't count on it.

When re-reading texts grew boring, she re-read everything she could find about Denver and his family on the Internet, scrolling through open tabs from prior searches and adding ones about Denver and Maui. But the new efforts only resulted in a record of a house sale his parents had made in the early 2000s.

Probably bought his own house in a company name.

After that, she switched to collecting screen shots of Denver's online photos and saving them in a folder. She signed up for his company newsletter and looked at RED's Twitter feed and Facebook profile.

When Celine finally texted that her plane had landed, she had fallen asleep with her legs on the dash. She walked across the small parking area to the open-air baggage claim. Birds fluttered here and there and picked crumbs left near the coffee shop. Tourists in suits and long pants, blinking in the strong light and sweating in the warm, moist air, tugged massive suitcases from conveyor belts and rolled them over the bumpy pavement.

A pink orchid lei hung over Ellie's arm. She scanned the clumps of new visitors entering from both sides of the lobby. Celine's tall, slim figure stood out among the families with small children tromping in.

Ellie gave her a one-armed hug and draped the lei over her head.

Celine sniffed the flowers. "What's good, Miss Snorkel Queen 2016? Thanks for letting me bust in on your romantic getaway."

A corner of Ellie's mouth twitched upward.

"I see I'm right." Celine grinned.

"I cyberstalked him while I was waiting for you."

"Ah. Now I know you're in love."

Ellie pulled the carry-on from her friend's grasp. "Is this all you brought?"

"Lift it. Then you won't be so impressed."

Ellie pulled the lurching roller bag across the sidewalk. Celine jerked to a stop and squinted at the West Maui mountains. She shielded her eyes while she fished a pair of sunglasses from her purse. "*That's* what you have to put up with every day? Must be rough, girlfriend."

Ellie laughed. "Remember, I work every day."

"Sure. Hard work. Like taking care of a nine-pound cat. I feel you."

Ellie threw the suitcase in the trunk and they got in the car.

"Like locking up the house at night and pushing a chair in front of my bedroom door."

Celine stared at her as the car joined the short exit line.

"You serious?"

Ellie shrugged. "I did it last night." She handed the aloha-shirted attendant her credit card. "I woke up feeling totally paranoid. But it's worn off. I looked around the yard. No one's out there."

"Who, exactly, would be out there in the first place?"

"Don't exactly know." Ellie pulled into the lane of slow moving cars across from Costco. At the light she glanced at Celine. "But the police think Noa killed someone."

"Your snorkeling instructor? A murderer? You got some luck."

The cars edged their way toward the left turn. "They think he killed the boyfriend of his ex-girlfriend."

"Ex-girlfriend because she's dead too?"

Ellie laughed. "No. At least that's a bright side. She was together with another guy and had a restraining order out against Noa. They found that other guy dead in his boat. The police suspect Noa did it."

Two surf shops flitted past Celine's window in rapid succession. Celine looked around as though lost. "Another murder? Where am I again? Downtown L.A.?"

"Right?"

"You got bolts on the doors?"

Weeds in the former cane fields swayed on either side of the highway as they drove past. "Better. Vivyenne had me order new doors and they were put in yesterday. Get this. They have a steel core. I got to love Vivyenne sometimes. She's crazy. But she's thorough."

Celine bent for a better glimpse of the Haleakala volcano out Ellie's window. "Still safer here than Hunters Point, San Francisco. And prettier."

A few hours later, Celine bobbed in the ocean at Polo Beach, her arms wrapped around a long blue Styrofoam noodle. Ellie floated next to her on an inflatable ring with a mask in her lap.

"Remind me again why I didn't shove you out of the way for this 'job' of yours?" Celine's fingers drew quotation marks in the air.

Ellie splashed her. "You thought Viv looked like a leopard."

"I take it all back. That cat's your fairy godfather."

At the shore, children built elaborate sand castles using buckets and upside down Frisbees. Serious swimmers stroked from the northern rocks to the southern shore, their hand paddles sending arcs of droplets into the air. Umbrellas and tents dotted the beach, vying for space with beach chairs positioned to enable their occupants to take maximum advantage of the sun.

"Imagine having so much money that you'd pay someone to take your place in paradise. Vivyenne must have some wicked other houses."

Ellie pulled the mask on her face and flipped over. Almost immediately she ripped it off and threw it at Celine.

"Quick. Put it on. There's a turtle swimming by."

Celine drew her legs in. "They bite?"

"No. Hurry."

Celine pulled the mask over her tight curls and paddled backward toward the shore as she put her head under the water. After a few seconds, she reversed direction, kicking to keep up with the shadow just visible below the surface. Ellie propelled herself alongside. Celine surfaced and submerged repeatedly. Her full head finally reappeared as they approached the south side of the beach.

"Awesome. That thing was almost as big as me. And so graceful." She flapped her arms lazily in imitation. "Like gliding."

"Told you."

"To think I was freezing my butt off in computer class Friday afternoon."

Ellie slid off the ring into the water to cool off.

"Am I missing a lot?"

"That hot young professor who used to work for HubSpot? Monday there was some kind of total electrical failure. They brought in this big easel for him to use, but the guy couldn't spell. His handwriting sucked. He cancelled class halfway through."

"Maybe he shouldn't have switched careers. There are no big bucks in academia."

"Not always big bucks in tech either. You should ask Mr. Drone how he makes his millions."

"I don't know if I'd want to be in his shoes. He's working, like, all the time."

Celine scrutinized Ellie's face.

"Trouble in paradise?"

"Not really. He's amazing. And I want to be supportive."

The tide tugged them gently toward the ocean. They kicked against it to stay in place.

"What's he think about your murderer snorkeling instructor?"

"Haven't told him."

"Got it. Too busy playing tonsil hockey."

Ellie jumped off her ring, yanked Celine's noodle from under her arms, and dunked her in the waist-high water.

***

Late that night, Ellie stood over Celine's bed. She tapped her friend's shoulder and stood back.

"Did you hear that?" She tapped Celine again, and then tugged on the hem of her new black and white Hello Kitty tank. Light streamed into the darkened guest room from the hall.

Celine rubbed her eyes. "What?"

"I heard something."

Celine mimed throwing a pillow at her. "If I'd known you were going to wake me in two hours, I wouldn't have had that third Mai Tai."

Ellie plucked nervously at Celine's comforter. "Something woke me up," she said. "I went to the window. I saw someone in the garden."

"You're hearing things." Celine rolled over.

"No." Ellie sat on the bed. "I was thinking about it. Noa's girlfriend breaks up with him. He goes after her. She gets a restraining order."

"Go back to bed." Celine pulled a pillow over her head, but Ellie tugged it back.

"Listen. He can't go after her, so he goes after

the boyfriend."

"Whatever."

"Remember how Noa texted me and then came over? I think he had some crazy idea he and I were a couple. Then he saw me with Brandon and went ballistic. He went after his girlfriend when she was with someone else. Maybe he tried to come after me. Remember the note on my car?"

Celine rolled over and looked at Ellie. "Go on."

"He couldn't get me. So he went after Brandon. And now he's coming after me again."

Celine sat up.

"You call the police?"

"No."

Celine pushed herself up on her elbows. "You got your priorities backwards, girl. With a theory like that, you call the cops *before* you wake up your friend."

Ellie stood.

"Go. Call."

"I've never called 9-1-1 before."

Celine yawned. "You push 9-1-1."

Tears welled in Ellie's eyes.

"Shoot. Get your phone. We'll put it on speaker. But I didn't see anything, so you'll have to do the talking."

The Maui Police officer who arrived twenty minutes later struck Ellie as the kind of person you'd want around in an emergency. The band on his cap reflected the lights that shone under the lanai and his eyes blazed with trustworthiness and energy. He was no taller than Celine but built like a tree trunk, with biceps that filled his short-sleeved shirt and thigh muscles that stretched his dark pants. His round face was inquisitive, intelligent, and inviting.

The officer, who introduced himself as Sergeant Rao, focused immediately on Celine. She stood in a pink cardigan and gray sweat pants with crossed arms, defiant yet compliant, daring him to question the authenticity of Ellie's night prowler. Ellie marveled how Celine could project fierce protectiveness while simultaneously maintaining a respectful demeanor, even sexy, demeanor. Ellie rested against the wall, shaken and quiet. Celine explained the situation. The officer listened, maintaining constant eye contact and nodding at intervals.

When he returned from a patrol of the garden, Celine and Ellie sat on the living room sofa. The room was a contrast of light and dark, furniture and floor, inside and outside, Ellie's frightened, pale face and Celine's composed one.

Officer Rao sat on an oversized ottoman. He aimed his attention at Celine.

"I searched the perimeter. I didn't see anything."

She cocked her head and raised an eyebrow but didn't say a word. The officer smiled.

"I'm not saying Ms. Atherton didn't see anybody. But you know there's a public access path to the beach just south of your property, yeah? It's likely somebody took a wrong turn or wanted to explore a little. It happens."

"She told you about Noa and the note."

"I'm interested in that." He swiveled with seeming reluctance away from Celine to face Ellie.

"It's a shame you threw it out."

"Tell me about it. Do you have any idea where Noa is?"

"We're following some leads. We're considering him armed and dangerous. But you haven't had any contact with him since the note. And the note wasn't signed, yeah?"

Celine stiffened. "Who else do you imagine would be calling her 'bitch' when she just got to the island? Does she look like the kind of person who makes enemies right and left?"

Rao held up his hand and grinned. "Whoa. I hear you. But we can't do much without evidence." He rose, keeping his eyes on Celine. "My advice is to get an alarm system installed. A woman living alone should have one."

Ellie nodded eagerly. "Believe me, I'm getting one."

Rao nodded. "Get in touch if you hear anything from Noa. I can see myself out." The look he flashed Celine from the doorway mixed equal parts amusement, respect, and invitation.

Celine followed him into the hall. "I'll lock up behind you."

Ellie listened from the sofa to the murmur of their voices. Minutes later, Celine entered the room spinning a business card between her thumb and forefinger.

"What's that?"

"K-Rao gave me his card." She plunked next to Ellie, humming under her breath. Her cheeks betrayed a slight flush.

"K-Rao?"

"Uh huh. Keli'i Rao. Goes by K-Rao. Says so right here." Celine flicked the card. It spiraled through the air and landed on the ottoman.

Ellie shook her head. "You're the only person I know who can turn a police investigation into a speed date."

"When you got it, girl, you got it." Celine patted her leg in time with the song in her head.

"You got it. I'd just like to know *where* you get it."

Late the following morning, Ellie was only slightly surprised to respond to the wind chime doorbell and find Officer Rao on the steps, out of uniform and looking sheepish.

"Come on in. I'll get the one you want."

K-Rao stepped methodically over the threshold but refused to go past the entrance hall until Celine appeared in a short flowing sundress. He followed her into the living room. Ellie pantomimed taking a shower behind K-Rao's back. Celine gave her a nod.

After the shower, a long discussion with the owner of the contracted flooring company, an inspection of the prototype kitchen cabinets, and a peanut butter sandwich, Ellie tiptoed to the living room. She peered around the corner, but the sofa was empty. She texted Celine.

Ellie: Where ru?

Celine: Beach.

Ellie: Alone?

182

An emoji with its tongue sticking out laughed up at her in response.

Ellie: I have to run to tile store.

Celine: B up in minute.

Ellie leaned against a pillar on the lanai and waved at K-Rao, who parted from Celine and strode toward the driveway with firm steps. Celine sauntered up to her.

"Girl, you're not going to believe this."

Ellie put her hands on her hips. "Try me."

"We're going up to Haleakala to watch the stars."

Ellie plunked onto the deck chair. "Now?"

"He says it takes almost two hours to get there." Celine's eyes sparkled with enthusiasm, but she sat on the floor next to Ellie. "You know I've got to do this, don't you?"

"I can see it in your face. You really like him."

"I didn't think I'd ever feel like this, after Kenji." Celine ruffled her short curls. "Hell, I don't really know what *this* is. But I know I'm jumping in with both feet."

Ellie inhaled the sweet floral scent wafting from the garden. "I'm giving you a key. The house will be locked tighter than a can of spam when you get home."

That evening, the house felt lonelier than it had since the first night Ellie arrived. She called Denver, but he didn't answer. She texted Jacqui, but she was in the middle of a date and couldn't talk. Olivia was morose and monosyllabic. And Ellie's mind returned again and again to Celine and her fearless step into the unknown of a sudden relationship.

Why is it so easy for her and so hard for me?

***

The next afternoon, Ellie realized with a pang that it felt comfortable to have a man in the kitchen. It wasn't *her* man, but K-Rao was all man, even though he exuded a different aura from Denver. Where Denver was smooth, K-Rao was rough around the edges. Where Denver was soft, K-Rao was playful. Where Denver was alluring, K-Rao was bashful. But Ellie could see clearly what drew Celine to him. And as he unpacked the shopping bags and loaded the counter with ingredients for his mother's special spaghetti, Ellie relaxed.

No matter what happens, he'll do right by Celine.

He quickly chased the women out of his 'staging area' with a beer for each of them. "Get out there and enjoy the Maui sunshine. I'll call you when it's ready."

Ellie glanced back at the noodle, tomato sauce, soy sauce, tabasco, and spam containers next to the bags of peppers, mushrooms, and green onions.

"How many people does he think he's cooking for?"

"He's got four brothers, I think." Celine pushed the front door open with her foot. "If he got the recipe from his mother, we're in trouble."

They took the drinks to the shore and sat on lava

rocks with their toes in the clear water. Ellie broke the silence.

"How are you doing?"

"You mean because I go back to San Fran tomorrow?"

"No. Because the Giants are starting a losing season."

Celine smiled. The sun beat on them from over the distant island of Lanai. She splashed water up her legs. "I'm surprisingly good. Having way too much fun to worry."

"But you're worried?"

"Girl, you do enough worrying for both of us."

Ellie waded in up to her knees. She tipped the bottle, gulped the dregs, and tossed the empty to Celine.

"I'm worried Denver's going to be mad when I tell him I've been next door the whole time."

"That's why you're out here without a disguise? Tempting fate?"

"Maybe." Ellie undid her ponytail and retied it. "I think I took it too far. Now he'll think I'm deceitful."

Celine joined her in the water, walking in figure eights in the shallows. "That's a strong word for something he'll probably just laugh off."

"I don't know. He's so honest and open about everything." Ellie let the small waves lap at the hem of her shorts. "Like when I asked him about what he'd do over in life. How many twenty-nine-year-olds would admit they should have gone into business with their parents?"

"Maybe more than you think."

"Would K-Rao?"

"His father's a cop. So I guess they're in the same business." Celine caught Ellie's gaze. "You just miss him, girl. It'll all feel better on Thursday. You'll spend the day in bed and see the world through rose colored glasses."

Ellie blushed. "What about you two?"

"I got no glasses in my future."

"He's not spending the night?"

Celine stretched, her long, lean body describing an arc toward the sky. "We talked about it. But I haven't hooked up with somebody since Kenji. It would too much like doing it just to do it before I go. I can't." She shrugged. "He understood."

"Wow, Celine. You hardly ever talk like that."

"Blame it on paradise." She jerked her head back to the house. "Now I think we should get back in there. Did you see how many cans of spam he had?"

The next afternoon, Ellie stood near the TSA line with Celine, who took a final selfie of them with West Maui in the background.

"This outdoor airport thing is killin' it."

Ellie gave her a hug.

"Thanks for coming."

Celine laughed. "My pleasure."

"You'd better…"

A man's voice interrupted them. "Celine?"

They turned to see K-Rao. He stood in uniform just outside the roofed area. Celine dropped her ticket. A gust picked it up and the three of them chased the fluttering paper across the floor. Ellie snatched it and handed it to Celine.

"I'll go back and watch your bag." From a short

distance, Ellie saw K-Rao remove his watch and listened to his explanation.

"Got this from my pa when I was sixteen." K-Rao dangled the band from his fingers. "Had some links taken out this morning. I want you to have it."

A tear rolled down Celine's cheek and she thrust the watch back at him. Her words tumbled out together in an intensifying stream. "I can't take it. It's too much. I can't commit like that. Not here. Not now."

He took her forearm gently in his. He slid the watch over her thin wrist and clasped it shut. His gaze never left hers. "I know. But take part of me with you to the mainland, yeah? Even if it just reminds you of me now and then. Even if…" He fingered the watch face. "If all I ever get from you is this small place in your heart."

He held out his arms. Celine paused longer than Ellie imagined was possible before falling into his embrace.

Ellie brushed away tears that choked her. She looked at the ground for a long time before she saw K-Rao and Celine's shadows approaching.

"You keep that watch safe, yeah." He jerked his head at Celine with a smile.

"I'll keep it on forever." Celine smiled as she pulled her carry-on behind her into the line. She flung her last words over her shoulder. "Or at least until I get to the TSA check."

K-Rao shook his head. "That woman. She's got no fear."

"No. She's got fear." Ellie stared at her friend. "She just doesn't listen to it."

CHAPTER 14

The late afternoon noises outside seemed louder than usual as Ellie cleaned after Celine's departure. Birds rustled in bushes, trade winds shook palm fronds, and something scampered across the rooftop.

Guess it's back to the chair in front of the bedroom door tonight.

The sun sunk closer to the horizon, suffusing puffy clouds over the ocean with shades of pink, orange, and red. Ellie imagined visitors all over the island flocking to shores, sitting in beach chairs, hoisting plastic wine glasses, ready to search for the mythical green flash as the sun disappeared.

Maybe disappearing is what I should do.

Before sunset, she called Jacqui.

"Would you mind some house guests for a little while?"

Jacqui laughed. "Your mansion in Wailea getting too small for you?"

"Too freaky."

"Honey, I told you nobody *ever* gets killed on

Maui."

Ellie pulled Viv to her lap. "Except people I know. And now I've got a strange feeling it's all closer to home than I want." She described her theory about Noa, his misunderstanding of her relationship with Brandon, and how she feared he could end up on her doorstep.

"Hmm."

"That's a first. I've never heard you at a loss for words."

"I didn't know about the police coming to your house."

Ellie dropped Viv to the floor and pulled a carry-on suitcase from the closet. "Can I take that as a yes?"

"Sure. This place will be a step down for you. But I think Viv might like the Upcountry creepy crawlies."

Ellie threw pajamas into the bag. "Anything I can get on my way up?"

"Better make a Costco run. I've had some tummy trouble. Running low on toilet paper."

"Eew. T-M-I."

"Just keeping it real. I'll call Olivia and invite her over for dinner. I've got a feeling that girl's not eating well."

"Great." Ellie paused. "Thanks, Jacqui."

"What are friends for?"

Later, Jacqui, Olivia, and Ellie sat together on an old leather sofa, feet on a rickety coffee table, plates of pizza balanced on their laps, watching the evening news about the manhunt for Noa. Ellie could feel Olivia shivering. Ellie nudged Jacqui and mouthed the words, "Let's turn it off."

"I think we've had enough of that." Jacqui stretched and hit the remote's off button. "How about dessert? Ellie picked up some apple pie."

Olivia shook her head. Jacqui dumped crusts into the take out box.

"Why does everything have to have a drug connection?" Olivia stood up and hunted for Viv, hand outstretched, making beguiling "puss, puss" sounds. She looked under the sofa. "Can't the police think of other motives?"

Ellie watched Olivia crawl across the floor. "I'm sure they're looking into all kinds of things."

Jacqui walked back in from the kitchen with the pie and shot Ellie a "what's up?" glance.

Ellie took a plate and tossed her chin to indicate a change in subject. "I talked with Celine on the way up here. She told me K-Rao said the police haven't found any connection between Brandon and Noa."

Olivia dragged Viv from under a colorful pile of yoga mats in the corner and cuddled him against her. "See? I told you there wasn't. But nobody would believe me."

Jacqui patted the sofa. "Bring Mr. Lovebug over here and have some pie, Olivia."

Olivia finished the large piece in four bites, seemingly unaware of anything except Viv on her lap.

Jacqui wordlessly slipped into the kitchen to get her another piece. Ellie followed.

"You're right." Jacqui slid half the remaining pie onto Olivia's plate. "I don't know her well, but there's something going on with that girl. She can't let go of the drug thing."

"Seriously." Ellie licked goo from the aluminum pan. "We shouldn't have watched the news. I thought she'd feel better since the police told her Brandon's death was an accident." Ellie poured coffee into three cracked mugs. "I know *I* do. I had to stop myself from jumping up and down when she told us."

Jacqui raised an eyebrow.

"That came out wrong." Ellie rolled her eyes at herself. "I am *not* jumping up and down because Brandon slipped cleaning the hotel waterfall and hit his head. But I'm *so* glad nobody killed him. Olivia should be too."

"Give her time. It's early days yet."

Olivia downed the second piece of pie almost as quickly as the first. Jacqui and Ellie watched, astounded. Olivia looked up when she'd finished.

"You guys think I'm nuts, don't you?"

Ellie and Jacqui wiped the flashes of surprise and guilt from their faces and responded simultaneously.

"No."

"Yes, you do. I'm going on about dealers and drugs and whatnot." She kissed Viv on the head to hide the tear that streaked from beneath her lashes. "Well, there's a reason."

Olivia looked from Ellie to Jacqui, a cloud of defiance on her face. Ellie held her breath.

"Brandon was dealing in Seattle. Heavy duty. He had people working for him. He made a lot of money." She brushed her uncombed hair from her face. "It's why he got kicked out of school. It's why I tried to help him."

"Did you tell the police?" The words escaped Ellie's mouth before she could stop them.

Olivia's eyes flashed in anger. "No, I didn't tell the cops. Not then, and not now. There was no reason."

Jacqui scooted forward so she could look Olivia in the eyes. "Honey, I'm so glad you told us. We're not judging you or Brandon. But it's good to tell your friends the truth."

Olivia peered at Ellie from downcast eyes.

Ellie let out a breath she felt like she'd been holding a long time. "What she said. It makes me like Brandon all the more, that he got away from that. It must have been crazy hard."

Olivia nodded. "I wouldn't have come here if he hadn't been clean. He gave it all up before he moved to Maui. That was the whole plan. To start a new life."

Ellie put her arm around Olivia's shoulders and gave them a squeeze. "Do you feel a little better now?"

Olivia's face was pale. "Actually, I think I'm going to throw up."

Jacqui and Ellie stood in the kitchen, Ellie handing Jacqui rinsed dishes for the dishwasher. The running faucet almost obscured the sounds coming from the bathroom.

Ellie paused, mug in midair. "Think it was the pie?"

Jacqui shook her head. "I'm betting it was the subject."

***

What's holding you back, Ellie?

Ellie drove downhill from Jacqui's house, through a few remaining cane fields and past the soon-to-be obsolete sugar mill, toward Wailuku.

Celine jumped into whatever she's got with K-Rao. Olivia's come clean about Brandon's past.

A picnic lunch of peanut butter sandwiches, pineapple chunks, and a slice of apple pie sat in a Target bag at her side. Air rushed from the rolled down windows, whipping across her face, clearing her head, buoying her confidence.

I'm going to tell him.

She thought back on her texts and their phone conversations in the past days. She had done her utmost to present her most desirable, funny, supportive features. She had felt supported, wanted, and even admired in return. The way she felt talking with Denver lifted her mood so much that she hadn't wanted to ruin it by divulging her night prowler concerns. Or by coming clean about being his next door neighbor.

But in the morning her heart and mind were, for once, in agreement. *Today I'll do it.*

Later, in Denver's air-conditioned sedan, Ellie's confidence seeped away without her being able to stop it. The farther his car climbed up the winding road into a jungle-like Maui she'd not seen before, the more the huge green leaves encroached on the path, the more the mountain folds towered above, the less eager she was to bare her soul. Denver seemed different, more reserved, and less passionate. His kiss at the now familiar parking lot had been brief, almost perfunctory. Rather than sweeping her out to sea on a tide of desire, it left her beached and confused.

His hand rested on her knee, but she didn't know what to do with her own. She moved it from his arm to her stomach to the armrest. Conversation was spotty. Ellie was grateful for the changing scenery that occupied her attention. When Denver paid the five dollars and pulled into one of the few remaining spots in Iao Valley Park's lot, Ellie felt her heart pounding not from excitement but from nervousness.

This isn't going the way I'd imagined it.

Around them tourists from Japan, China, and India snapped photos. Ellie read the informational sign at the beginning of the path while Denver took her photo with his phone. He stowed it and led the way, hands in pockets, Ellie's bag slung over one shoulder. Ellie lagged a little behind as they climbed the asphalt path between lush monstera plants.

"There's what all the excitement's about." Denver pointed beyond a short bridge to a thin mountain fold. "The Iao Needle. It's actually not a needle from the side, obviously. Just looks that way from here."

Ellie stared at the narrow peak, worn and smooth, like a finger pointing to heaven. "Maui's mountains seem so soft and inviting compared to what I've seen in California."

Denver's eyes twinkled for the first time since he'd picked her up. "How about compared to what you saw in Delaware?"

Ellie relaxed at the joke. "Very funny. In Delaware we get excited about anything higher than sea level."

He took her hand and led her across the bridge. Then he urged her under a set of green railings and down a narrow path into the shrubbery. When they were out of sight of the tourists on the bridge, Ellie pulled him back.

"The sign said to keep to the designated walkways."

He pointed to the worn trail. "Looks pretty designated to me." He kissed her lightly on the lips. "Really. People do this all the time. And it's so worth it."

The track roughly followed the Kinihapai Stream that cascaded over large and small boulders to their right. The chatter of visitors faded quickly behind them. They clambered over lava rocks, holding on to smooth, thin multi-colored trunks of young rainbow eucalyptus trees. Ellie recognized the shapes of leaves she pushed out of the way, but not their size. The air was pungent with the scent of rotting fruit. She saw Denver stoop now and then to pick something from the ground and put it in her bag.

These look like office plants on steroids.

She brushed sweat from her face. In the increasing heat of the sun, she was grateful for the shade of their path. They climbed gently upward, Denver stopping to help her over particularly steep sections of trail. The river to the right looked increasingly inviting.

No one met them as they continued their journey. Ellie began to pant. Sweat dripped off her nose. The rushing stream taunted her with its clear water and cool breeze.

What's the plan, Denver? Do I get to take a breather?

But she felt uncomfortable asking.

He's worn out. Probably needs a workout to get the job stress out of his system.

When Denver veered toward the small river, Ellie lifted her eyes toward the sky.

Thank goodness. I'm about to faint.

"That was awesome." She beamed at him. "Now what?"

He pointed to a pool nestled behind some large boulders. "Care for a swim?"

A master designer could have crafted the scene. An enclosure of large and small rocks created a natural pool lined with a pebble floor. The stream gushed into it from a two-foot high waterfall on the left and poured out down a similar one on the far right. Between lay a clear, smooth expanse of water about twenty feet in diameter, cool and irresistible.

Why didn't I bring a swimsuit?

"I don't have a suit."

Denver grinned and raised his eyebrows. "Neither do I."

He helped her to a smooth rock partly sheltered from the sun by an overhang of trees. He stripped off his damp t-shirt. Ellie peeked at the chest she had been dreaming about for days.

Wow. He does not disappoint.

Denver stepped over his shirt, leaned over, and

kissed her, in one instant unleashing the longing she had thought was forgotten. She felt him undo the buttons of her blouse, his fingers cupping her breasts through her bra. Ellie pulled down her shorts, suddenly eager and warm. She stood in front of him, naked except for the strips of white lace surrounding her torso and thighs.

"You're beautiful."

Denver scooped her into his arms. She laughed as he carried her into the water.

The pool was surprisingly deep, rising past his shorts. He laid her onto the cool surface, supporting her with a hand under her hips and upper back.

"Relax. I've got you."

Ellie closed her eyes. She let her head float, feeling her hair drifting around her like a comforting halo. The chill water refreshed her mind. Her legs bobbed with the gentle undulations of the rippling stream. She heard the surges of the waterfalls.

I never want this to end.

His hands caressed her from underneath, massaging her neck and slipping down across her buttocks. He bent and kissed her again, not with the demanding passion of the times before but with a loving tenderness that brought a sparkle to her eyes. His lips pulled gently at hers as she arched up to meet him, her mouth pushing back, her body aware of every sensation. Instead of being washed away, she felt her senses heighten, her pulse quickening.

I trust you, Denver. Take it further.

As though reading her mind, his arm glided between her legs, parting areas already awash with moisture. His fingers reached and stroked her, releasing a yearning moan from her lips. His mouth moved to her breasts, still supporting her from underneath. He pulled the thin fabric aside with his teeth and fondled her nipples with his tongue. Ellie's face and lips throbbed with desire. Her body writhed.

Wait. Not yet. It's my turn first.

She reached her hand around his neck and swung herself upright, silencing his protest with a long, deep kiss.

"Now me."

Her hands roamed beneath the surface of the water, tugging at his shorts, squeezing the evidence of his desire. She pushed him backward to the edge of the pool and dove under, letting her head rub between his legs as she lifted one foot then the other. She emerged with his shorts and her underwear in one hand.

Now it's both our turns.

"Wait. Give me those." He held out his hand for his shorts and dug in the pocket.

She blushed as he put on a condom.

"Sorry." He drew her onto his chest. "I know it's unromantic."

She shook her head. "It's all part of the most romantic day a guy has ever created for me."

Her mouth covered his with grateful kisses as her hands maneuvered herself onto him. He let out a moan. She clasped him around the neck, encircling his torso with her legs. They rocked in unison, first gently, then with an ever-increasing passion until the empty valley echoed with the cries of their desire.

***

In the sun on the rock, cuddled against his chest, her face dripping with the sticky juice of ripe guavas, Ellie felt the words pour out effortlessly.

"I followed you home that first night after the beach."

Denver grazed her face with his fingertips and twined a lock of her long hair around them. "You did?"

"Yes. I'll admit it. I'm a stalker."

"I love that you stalk me." He engulfed her nose in a gentle bite.

"Then you're going to love what I found out even more." She caught his eyes and raised her eyebrows.

"Yes?" He propped himself up on his elbows.

"We're neighbors."

"Seriously?"

"Next door neighbors. You know that family you've been complaining about? The one that makes all the noise? That's me."

Denver sat up. "You live next door?"

"I do."

"Why didn't you tell me?"

Ellie shrugged, but with none of the timidity she'd felt before. "I was embarrassed I'd followed you. And it never seemed like the right time to bring it up." She reached her face up and kissed his nose. "You know how it is when you get yourself into a situation where you're not being honest? It's not that you want to lie. You just can't figure out how to tell the truth."

Denver looked at the stream. "I know what that's like."

"You must get into those situations at work."

He gazed at her. "I'm in one of those situations now."

"Well, I know how to take your mind off that." Ellie slid down the rock and nestled her head between his legs.

That night in the bathroom of Vivyenne's house, Ellie texted Jacqui.

Ellie: Not coming home. Staying in Wailea. At my house. With Denver.

Jacqui: Don't waste time texting me!

Ellie: Will u feed Viv?

Jacqui: No. He's full on geckos and cockroaches. Now get back to what you were doing.

A lewd emoji accompanied her text.

Early the next morning, just before dawn, Ellie hummed as she prepared a breakfast of waffles and fruit. Denver emerged from the bedroom in a towel, his hair still dripping from a shower. He encircled her waist and rubbed his hips against her from behind.

"Hey, we've got to eat." She shoved him gently away with her elbows. "I don't know about you, but

I'm starving. That lunch on the rocks seems like days ago."

Denver sat at a stool at the counter, using a kitchen towel to dry his hair. "Need help?"

Ellie poured batter onto the hot griddle. "I'm good."

Denver looked around. "Where's the cat you told me about? Your bread and butter? Did I scare him off?"

"No. He's Upcountry feasting on bugs."

"What? Like at a cat spa?"

Ellie laughed. "It's a long story. But the short of it is that I was getting a little freaked out in this house by myself. So Viv and I moved Upcountry for a few weeks."

Denver abruptly stopped toweling his head. "Viv?"

"Yeah. Strange name for a cat. But his owner's named Vivyenne. Go figure."

Denver stepped forward. Ellie paused, one hand on the open waffle iron.

He spoke slowly. "You're not talking about Vivyenne Lovejoy, are you? It can't be."

Ellie let the iron close again. "It is." The look on his face made her hold her breath.

Calm down, Ellie.

"Christ."

She walked around the counter and took his hand, trying to connect with his eyes. "What's up? You know Vivyenne? It's one of those small world things, right?"

"I heard she'd bought a house on Maui, but I had no idea..." He met Ellie's gaze. "Look, Ellie, I *do*

201

know Vivyenne. We…" He let out a big breath and shook his head. "Why does it always have to be so hard with you?"

Ellie frowned. "Hard?"

Denver tugged her toward him. "I don't mean it that way. But you're not going to like this. Vivyenne and I used to be a couple."

Smoke from behind her drew Ellie's attention to the waffle iron. She opened it and stabbed a blackened mass with a fork, throwing it into the sink and running water on it until it stopped sputtering. She unplugged the iron and took a seat on the opposite side of the counter.

"'Fess up."

"We've known each other for years. We have mutual friends. The Kirkpatricks. That's actually, now that I think about it, probably how she heard about this house. Anyway, we only went out for a few months. And it's been over for…I don't know." He rested his hand on the counter. "It petered out months ago. It's just been an occasional email since then. It wasn't much more than that to begin with. It was convenient, that's all."

Ellie pulled a banana from the basket on the counter and peeled it slowly. "So what was last night with me? Convenient?"

"Last night was the beginning of something special, Ellie. Believe me. Vivyenne's nothing." He held out his hands.

Ellie put down the banana and put her hands in his. "I want to believe you.…" She fixed her eyes on his.

"Let me tell you something else…"

She shook her head. "No. It's okay. I'm with Celine on this one. I'm jumping in with both feet." She brought his palms to her lips and kissed them. "I have this thing about trust. Here you are, good looking, intelligent, rich, kind. It seems too good to be true. But you're true and you're good and I'm going with it." She laughed.

Denver walked around the counter and laid his head on Ellie's shoulder. "Oh, God, Ellie." He squeezed her so tightly she caught her breath. After a moment, she pushed him away.

"We're good. Let me take a shower now. Can you handle breakfast?"

Denver nodded. Ellie spun from the chair and skipped toward the bedroom.

When she returned, Denver presented her with a plate of fruit and waffles. His phone lay next to her fork.

"What's this?"

"Read the email."

She read a short email from Denver to Vivyenne. It indicated he'd met someone special and he wanted to make sure Vivyenne understood that from his perspective their relationship had been over a long time.

"You didn't need to show me. But I appreciate it." Ellie picked up her plate. "Let's eat outside. I love watching the sun light up West Maui and the ocean."

Later, the morning rays lit up more than just the ocean as Ellie and Denver lay naked and entwined on the boards of the lanai.

"Can you come over tonight?" Denver spooned

her from behind and ran his fingers along the contour of her hips. "I'll make us dinner."

So this is what jumping in with both feet feels like.

Ellie smiled into the distance. "I'll be there, neighbor."

***

Denver felt cloaked in euphoria as he strode into his one-room guesthouse. He'd left Ellie getting hurriedly dressed for the morning's workers. She'd shooed him out with a kiss and a wave. He'd sauntered across the lawn and pushed his way through the bushes, ignoring the scratches on his arms and legs.

I'll tell her everything tonight. Get it all off my chest. It'll be good.

He grinned, remembering the day before at the mountain stream. He pulled a pad of sticky notes from under the printouts spread across the dining table and began a shopping list for dinner.

Maybe I can get her to stay here with me instead of Upcountry.

He looked through the cabinets, whistling an off-key Andy Grammer tune. When his phone beeped, he picked it up more out of habit than interest. The text message stopped him short. He put down the note pad and dialed.

"No, you're not bothering me." He twisted open a mayonnaise jar from the refrigerator with one hand and sniffed cautiously.

"Sure." He frowned and threw the jar in the

trash.

"What do you mean no one else showed up? Nobody?"

He stopped walking and stared out the window. "No paychecks. And you're the only one who showed up at work? Where's Eddie?" He jammed his free hand in his pocket. "Look. Cut the bullshit. What do you think happened?"

Minutes passed while he listened, mostly silently, to the person on the other end of the line. Then he fished in his backpack.

"Hold on." He jerked out a white tangle of wires. "I'm plugging in my headset. I want to pack."

He slammed a suitcase onto the bed. "Now give me the details. All I heard was that my fucking company's going under. My partner apparently took off. And the company accounts have no money. I know there's more to it than that."

Two hours later, in the last row of the economy section of an airplane bound for Seattle, Denver bit his lip and texted Ellie.

Denver: Forgive me. Work emergency. On plane back to Seattle. Rain check for dinner?

Ellie: Oh.

Denver: I know. It's killing me.

Ellie: It's all good. Work comes first.

Denver groaned audibly. The matronly woman next to him looked askance and edged to the far side

205

of her narrow seat.

Denver: Not much longer. I'm getting out of this mess as fast as I can.

Ellie: I'll be waiting. When will u be back?

Denver fastened his seatbelt.

Denver: Don't know yet. Might have to go to China.

Ellie: Glad we told each other everything.

Denver slapped his hand over his eyes.
Dammit. After a long pause, he stifled another groan and slowly typed his reply.

Denver: Me too.

CHAPTER 15

Late afternoon the following Monday, near quitting time for the workers, Ellie roamed through the house, inspecting progress, documenting, texting Devora updates. Most of the current work focused on the kitchen. Half the existing cabinets had been torn from the walls, leaving gaping holes in the paint. Exposed cement board contrasted with the smooth silver lines of the new stainless steel appliances. Cabinet door samples in twenty shades of white lined the kitchen counter. Buckets of paint and piles of drop cloths occupied a corner near the back door.

Devora: Take another picture. Make sure the color's accurate.

Ellie sighed and positioned her phone over a door sample for another shot.

Ellie: How's this?

Devora: Doesn't match.

Ellie sent her an emoji with its tongue sticking out.

Devora: Seriously. I'm saving your butt. Vivyenne will go crazy.

It's white. Doesn't all white match?

Ellie: Hold on.

She pulled one of the workers aside, an older man with a gray crew cut and dark tan.

"Can you take help me? I need an opinion on colors. Are these two shades of white the same?"

The man plucked a pair of brown reading glasses from his pants pocket and brought the customized cast concrete and cabinet samples to the window. He held them in the light and shook his head.

Ellie bit her lip. "You sure? They look kind of the same to me."

The man smiled. "Is it your house?"

"No. I'm supervising."

"And they want this whole place white, yeah?"

Ellie nodded.

"Then you're in for a hard time. I'm a painter. Trust me. Of all the colors, white's the hardest to match. So many variations."

Ellie's shoulders slumped. What motivated the owner of a surgical instrument company to design homes that would remind her of an operating room? Ever since Ellie had discovered the jumbo size crayon box as a child, she had loved colors. The more, the better. Celine had called her room in their apartment 'the botanical garden,' referring to the floral colored pillows, rainbow hued bedspread, and Scandinavian designer knock-off sheets. Ellie's dream Hawaii house would've reflected the state's tropical wonderland. Vivyenne's ideal, Ellie thought, resembled the arrival of the next ice age.

Ellie: You're right. Doesn't match.

Devora: Right.

Ellie: What next?

Devora: Get to the store before they place the order.

Ellie called the showroom, grabbed the cabinet installation foreman, and raced to his truck.

"Get us to Kahului before they close and I'll buy you a shave ice."

The foreman smiled and sped out the drive.

They returned after dark. Ellie hopped out and waved. The truck made a U-turn in her driveway and headed back north. She dropped the new samples in the kitchen. Outside, it was already getting dark. She flipped the lights off quickly, locked the house, and jogged to her car. When she pulled into the street to drive to Jacqui's, the steering wheel tugged strangely to one side. The car listed to the left. She got out, then bent and examined the rear tire. It was flat.

Oh, great. Just what I need tonight.

It took the rental agency only fifteen minutes to show up with a replacement car. Ellie transferred her personal belongings to the new vehicle while the mechanic jacked up the rear end to put a spare on the old one. She was about to drive off when he waved and gave her a funny look. She rolled down the window.

"You know your tire was slashed?"

Ellie turned off the engine. "Slashed?"

"Yeah. Big gash in the side. Doesn't usually happen around here." He glanced at the large houses. "People carjack." He winked. "Lots of nice cars to choose from. But there's not much vandalism. Bad luck."

Ellie shuddered involuntarily.

"You know anyone with grudge against you?"

"No."

"Just kidding." The man chuckled. "Your gate open today?"

Ellie nodded.

"Probably just some punk. Keep it locked."

Ellie nodded again.

"Let the police know. File a report. Won't do nothing, but it's good to keep them in the loop. In case more happens later."

Ellie swallowed. "What do you mean by *more*?"

"Just more car vandalism. Not likely in this neighborhood. But might happen."

Ellie's hands shook as she drove the dark back roads Upcountry.

What's going on? Bad luck? Or... She couldn't bear to finish the thought. She plugged in her

210

headset and called Denver. His voicemail picked up.

"Hey, Denver. It's me. Ellie. I was thinking of you. I wanted to leave a message. So here I am. Duh. I miss hearing from you. But I know you're busy. I've just had kind of a shitty day. Crazy Vivyenne stuff. I don't mean to dis her. She's just really picky. I guess you know that. Or maybe you didn't see that side of her? Anyway, after all that, my car tire got slashed. So I'm kind of freaked. Did I tell you about Noa? I don't think so. I was going to at the dinner we didn't have. Oh, I'm out of time. Call me. Or text. I miss you. Don't work too hard."

Ellie massaged her temple with one hand.

That was the single worst message I've left in my life. W-T-F, Ellie?

The new car's engine revved as she navigated the steep Kula hills.

Why couldn't Denver have stayed just one more night? I could have told him about Noa. He could help me think this through. Now he's super busy. And I don't want to depress him. But I hate having to deal with this without him.

She could still see his sparkling eyes, sense his smooth body, feel his warm hands on her shoulders, her breasts, and her thighs. She could still hear his voice and remember every detail of their nighttime conversations, when she shared her hopes for what her future could hold. He seemed sometimes distracted but never absent. His presence felt at once like a comforting blanket and an electrifying jolt. Both were addictive. Both seemed increasingly necessary to her future.

Faint solar lights on stakes illuminated Jacqui's driveway. Ellie pulled in and parked next to the Civic.

One thing's for sure. Without Denver next door, I'm not staying down there after dark. Not until after the alarm system's up and running.

***

A few nights later, Ellie sat in Jacqui's living room alone, talking with Celine.

"She's out with a real estate agent?" Celine smiled at Ellie from the laptop. "I pictured Jacqui with a surfer."

"She met him online."

"Athletes hang out online."

Ellie grinned. "I think he might have misrepresented himself."

"From what you tell me, Jacqui won't let him get away with that for long."

Celine reached for a cup off-screen.

Ellie snapped her fingers. Viv flashed her a sheepish look and dropped his gecko, which scuttled under the sofa. "How's K-Rao?"

A smile stretched across Celine's long face. "Awesome. That man's got style. He actually sent me snail mail. Can you believe it? A real letter. He says his grandmother wrote letters to his grandfather while they were separated in World War II."

Ellie's gaze drifted to the ceiling. "I don't know anyone our age who ever sent me a letter."

"Seriously. I don't even know how much a

stamp costs. My mother's going to love the dude."

"Is he flying there to see you?"

"At Thanksgiving. I hope. We're still working it out."

Viv stalked back and forth across Ellie's lap, his tail swishing at the screen like an insistent flag. She stroked his back and he stretched across her lap.

Ellie leaned back. "Any police gossip?"

"K-Rao told me there's no sign of Noa on Maui. He said they think he might have gotten a boat to take him somewhere. K-Rao said maybe the Big Island." Celine cocked her head. "That's Hawaii, right?"

"Right."

"Why'd they name the state after one of the islands? Wicked confusing."

Ellie laughed. "Anyway…"

"Anyway, K-Rao says if he went off the grid, it'll be basically impossible to find him. He says people do it all the time."

The furrows on Ellie's brow deepened. "Just disappear?"

"It's different in Hawaii, he says. Not like San Francisco. If you've got your own food and water and never go into a town, there's no way to track you."

"I'd love to think Noa disappeared. But who slashed my tire if he's on the Big Island?"

"Maybe it *was* some punk, like the mechanic said."

Ellie's face brightened. "Yeah. Maybe it doesn't have to be connected to Noa. Brandon's death wasn't. Maybe this isn't either."

"What's Mr. Drone say?"

A momentary cloud passed across Ellie's face. "I haven't explained it all. Haven't had the chance. He's swamped at work. But if K-Rao's right, then maybe there's nothing to explain."

"Absolutely. Go with the simple answer."

"Right. No more conspiracy theories."

Ellie lifted Viv to the screen and moved his paw as though he were blowing Celine kisses. Celine blew one back at him.

"Thanks for cheering me up."

"Anytime, girl."

***

A week later, Ellie looked out Jacqui's living room window at a two-foot long electric green iguana clutching a tree branch. The creature's back was covered in spines and a long flap of skin hung from its jowls, like a reptilian beard.

"Crazy. Olivia, check this out."

The two women stood at the window. Jacqui glanced over their shoulders. "A male. There should be two of them. See?" She pointed at a second one higher in the branches.

Olivia moved back to the couch. "Yuck. Aren't you afraid of them?"

Jacqui brought a bowl of potato chips to the coffee table. "It works the other way around, honey. They're afraid of us."

"Speaking of scary males…" Ellie plopped on the sofa next to Olivia. "What about your real estate guy?

"He's so last week. Turns out he never went near a beach except to try to sell it to some developer." Jacqui refilled Ellie's wine glass. "Sure you don't want any, Olivia? Your cheeks could really use the color." She held the half empty bottle of red against the last rays of the sun that filtered through her gauze curtains.

"I'm good." Olivia opened another can of passion fruit sparkling water. "I've got to make a Target run before I go to bed tonight."

"Suit yourself." Jacqui topped off her own glass and curled her legs under her in the papasan chair opposite the sofa.

Ellie took a sip of the wine. "So if it wasn't the realtor, who was the guy from last night?"

Jacqui winked at Ellie and Olivia in turn. "A car dealer."

Olivia choked on her drink. "No way."

"Yoga instructor's oath. I met him paddle boarding by the hotel. He was checking me out, so I flashed him. He capsized. I took it as a big compliment."

Ellie stared. "You're amazing."

Jacqui inclined her head coquettishly. "I'm a current-era devotee of the ideas from the Sixties. Spread the love around."

Ellie nudged Olivia. "But a car dealer?"

"Don't say another word." Jacqui handed them her phone. Ellie and Olivia gazed at the photo of a gorgeous man with his arm around Jacqui's waist.

Olivia put a hand to her chest. "He's killin' it."

Jacqui took the phone back. "Yes. But he's like the view of Niihau from Kauai. Distant and unattainable."

"You mean he's full of dark secrets?" Ellie deposited her glass on the table where it rocked unsteadily until Jacqui balanced it with her foot.

"More like he doesn't talk much."

"With a face like that, who needs talking?" Ellie rummaged in her purse, which had emitted brief, muffled music.

Jacqui rolled her eyes. "I know that text tone."

Ellie fished out her phone. Her heart sank.

Olivia turned to her. "What's up?"

"Denver's on his way to China."

"Did you say he might have to go?"

Ellie walked to the window and tapped distractedly at the iguanas. "Yep. But his flight went through Honolulu today. And he never let me know."

Jacqui tipped the remainder of the bottle into Ellie's glass and brought it to her. "He probably didn't have much of a layover."

"He had four hours. And it's a forty-minute flight to Honolulu. I would have gone to see him for four hours." She felt hurt. "Hell, I would have gone to see him for four minutes."

Jacqui massaged Ellie's shoulders and directed her back to the sofa. "Don't be so hard on him. He probably didn't have time to think things through."

Olivia nodded. "You need a little faith, Ellie."

The fading sun illuminated the trees outside, coloring them pink. In the dimming light, Ellie tried to conceal her sorrow. "Maybe you're right. He did say he'd make this up to me when he came on island again."

"See?" Jacqui settled back in her chair. "You can't keep looking at what's missing, Ellie. You've got to open your eyes to what you've got."

Ellie rolled her eyes. "What I've got is the creeps. He said someone tried to break into his house too, but the alarm system stopped them."

Olivia straightened her back. "Did they catch the guy?"

"He didn't say. Just asked me to keep an eye on things. Like I'm going to do any good."

Jacqui settled her phone into a docking station and pushed some buttons. A rhythmic Tibetan chant pulsed quietly from small speakers hanging in the corners of the room. She pushed the coffee table and papasan to the walls and draped three yoga mats side by side on the floor.

"Time for your lesson, ladies." She tipped herself upside down on her elbows and arced her legs to the ceiling.

Ellie and Olivia stared. Ellie was the first to speak.

"I thought we were hanging out. Relaxing."

Olivia nodded. "Yeah. I don't want to throw up again."

Jacqui regarded them from the floor. "Off your butts and onto those mats. Relaxing? Just wait until I get through with you."

CHAPTER 16

The second week of November, Ellie received notification that the security system was fully installed at Vivyenne's house. She set up an appointment for that afternoon. The company representative walked her through the set up. It took longer than she thought. She glanced repeatedly at her phone and finally spoke up.

"Look. I have to run back Upcountry to get a few things before tonight. Do you think you could do the final testing without me?"

The young man shrugged. "Sure. I can call you with the code or you can make one up."

Ellie put her hand on the doorknob. "Call me."

In the car, she texted Denver to let him know the news. *I'm going to run over to his place in my undies the second he gets home.*

Jacqui helped carry Ellie's suitcase to the car. Her eyes glinted with mischief and a trace of regret. "Just when I was getting used to you."

Ellie returned to the living room and shoved Viv's reluctant body into the cat carrier. "Things are heating up with Mr. Car Dealer, anyway. You'll be happy to get Viv and me out of your hair."

"I don't know." Jacqui poked her fingers through a gap in the zipper to stroke Viv's cheek. "I still haven't gotten him to do a single yoga pose. It can't last much longer."

Ellie lugged the carrier to the car. "What about tantric yoga?"

"Don't mock it till you've tried it."

Ellie gave Jacqui a squeeze before hopping in the driver's seat. "Thanks, Jacqui. I really owe you. I feel so much better about the Wailea house now. I think I needed some time away."

"You needed a security system. And with Denver due back any day, you'll have two. One electronic. The other electric."

Ellie laughed.

Before she had driven a mile, the alarm company called. Ellie pulled the car onto a grassy verge near a plant nursery.

"The house is armed." The man sounded bored. "You have one minute to enter the code. Any questions?"

Ellie switched to the notes program on her phone.

"Tell me the code again."

She typed it in a second time and confirmed it. A convertible with the top down sped past her.

"What if I mess up?"

"Hit clear and try again. But you only have a minute."

"I'm not good under pressure."

"If you trigger the alarm, we'll call you. Give us

the password, and we'll turn it off."

Ellie triple checked the password. She pulled back onto the road, wondering why security had to be so stressful. The sun fell low in the sky over the ocean, casting the water in shades of orange and pink. The mountains of West Maui loomed dark against the graying sky, their softness flattened into jagged two-dimensional harshness in the fading light. Clouds skimmed the peaks, obscuring their contours. But her hands tapped the steering wheel nervously.

Don't panic. What's the worst that can happen? Embarrassment. Not like that *hasn't happened before.*

Near the sugar mill at the bottom of the slope, her phone rang again. She pulled abruptly onto the side of the road opposite the tiny brown Puunene Post Office, a cloud of red dust rising behind her. When she looked at the screen the name of the alarm company stared up at her. She answered. Her jaw slowly dropped.

"Somebody broke in? Already?" She searched in her purse for her headset. "No. I'm nowhere near the house."

She gave up the hunt and eased the car over the bump onto the pavement, one hand holding the phone.

"Yes, of course, you should call the police. I'll be there in half an hour."

Ellie pushed the accelerator and hit sixty-five, blinking each time she passed a forty-five miles per hour sign. When she neared home, blue flashing lights flickered at the end of her darkened street.

Ellie rolled her car to a stop opposite the house's open gate, in front of which a police car was parked at an angle, as though it had arrived in a hurry. She rolled down her window and listened for the sound of the alarm but heard only the roar of the ocean and an occasional gecko chirp.

"Viv, you stay here." She scratched the top of the carrier in the passenger seat foot well. "I'll be back once I find out what's going on."

K-Rao stood waiting for her at the foot of the front steps. She was tempted to give him a hug, but something in his posture told her to keep things official.

"Is everything okay?" She glanced at his hip and was relieved to see his gun still holstered.

"I'm here to warn you."

Ellie felt her knees weaken and held onto the banister.

"Did you catch someone? Was it Noa? Is there blood?"

"We found someone in the house. But…" K-Rao rubbed his chin. Ellie thought she caught sight of a smile behind his hand. "It's a woman. She says this is her house."

"What?" Incomprehension widened her eyes. Then recognition slowly dawned. "Vivyenne? Here?" Her face sank.

"I thought it would be a shock. That's why I waited for you."

"Shock?" Ellie shook her head. "I'm going to lose my job. I locked my boss out of her house. I didn't give her the alarm code. And I set the police on her."

"You didn't give her the code?"

Ellie put her hand to her head. "The alarm just got installed. I hadn't gotten that far." The house's eerie silence accentuated Ellie's rising panic. She turned to K-Rao, her eyes pleading. "Come in with me. There might be bloodshed."

K-Rao chuckled. "You should have seen her when we arrived. Spitting like an angry mongoose."

Ellie punched his arm as they strode through the front door. "Be serious. I'm in huge trouble."

"Don't worry." K-Rao patted his gun. "I'm ready."

Inside, Ellie peered cautiously around the kitchen doorframe. A female officer leaned against the counter near the refrigerator, arms crossed, with a fed-up expression. Ellie inched her head farther into the room.

Vivyenne stood at the breakfast bar with her back to the door, standing erect, phone to her ear. She wore a long white linen jacket with three-quarter length sleeves. Thin, shapely legs tapered to tan open toed sandals with two-inch heels.

Ellie scanned her own outfit of baggy hiking shorts and a frayed University of Delaware sweatshirt.

Does that woman always look like a fashion model?

K-Rao gave Ellie a gentle shove and she stumbled into the room. Vivyenne turned toward her. She looked at Ellie like an ice sculpture turning on a pedestal.

"It's you." The two words seemed to convey all Vivyenne wanted to say but wouldn't in front of the officers.

Ellie pulled distractedly at her ponytail. "I'm so sorry, Vivyenne. The alarm only got installed today. I was going to text Devora the code when I got here. I've been staying Upcountry."

Vivyenne lowered her phone and turned it off. She radiated confidence, disdain, and, Ellie thought, repugnance.

"So I gathered."

Ellie fidgeted, trying to figure out which one of her excuses Vivyenne had responded to.

"I texted Devora this morning. I told her it was almost installed."

The stare from Vivyenne's dark eyes seemed to look both at Ellie and completely through her into the hallway beyond. Vivyenne jerked her chin at the female officer who, with an unveiled look of disgust, moved toward the kitchen door.

"Devora has the flu." Vivyenne's tone made it sound as though she'd uncovered the depths of Devora's depravity. "She isn't responding to most texts. And when she does, she seems to be delusional."

K-Rao stepped into the kitchen. "If things are set here, we'll be off."

Ellie turned to him, ready to hang on his arm to make him stay. But he winked at her and turned to the hall.

Ellie swiveled back.

Vivyenne put her hands on her hips. "The code."

She searched her empty brain, eager to give Vivyenne what she wanted but unable to make the connection. *What code? The Da Vinci Code? My*

223

ZIP code?

Vivyenne closed her eyes. "The alarm code. Give it to me."

"Oh, gosh, sure." Ellie fumbled with her phone. "Here." She scooted the phone across the counter with an outstretched arm, moving minimally, as though giving money to a bank robber.

Vivyenne typed. Bent over, her jet-black Cleopatra haircut emphasized her uncannily square shoulders.

Looks like a skinny football player in drag.

Vivyenne passed the phone back, touching it only with her fingertips, and looked for the first time directly at Ellie.

"I'm staying here. In the house. I want to inspect the progress and get to know the neighborhood. I booked you a hotel room." She pulled a perfectly folded printout from an invisible jacket pocket and placed it on the counter. Ellie picked it up and read it.

The room's at Jacqui's hotel.

Ellie looked up. "I can stay in the guest room if you'd like." As soon as the words left her mouth, Ellie knew she'd made a mistake. The corners of Vivyenne's mouth wrinkled. Ellie backtracked. "Or I can go back and stay with my friend Upcountry. That way you wouldn't have to pay."

"I've experienced how long it takes you to get here from Upcountry." Vivyenne drew in her breath. "You'll stay at the hotel. Be back here tomorrow morning at seven. We can review what's been done on the house so far, what still needs to be done, and what needs to be done over because it's

224

wrong."

"Yes, ma'am." Ellie's brow wrinkled in surprise. *I've never said that before. To anyone.*

Vivyenne swept past Ellie and marched toward the master bedroom. She turned with her hand on the door. "Where is the cat?"

Ellie blinked. "You mean Viv?"

Vivyenne stared at her, her face a mask of impatience.

"Of course you do. He's in the car. I'll go get him."

Vivyenne pushed open the door. Ellie caught a glimpse of leather luggage standing near the bed.

Thank God I cleaned before I left.

"I'm tired. Bring him in and set up…whatever it is he needs." The door closed behind her.

Ellie exhaled a sigh of relief in the hallway and shook her arms as if flicking an unwanted substance from her hands. She stopped in mid-flail when the bedroom door reopened and Vivyenne's head poked out.

"Turn on the alarm when you leave. Can you handle that?"

The door closed on Ellie's answer.

"Yes, ma'am. Will do."

Ellie screwed her eyes shut and leaned against the wall.

At least I still have a job.

Out in the car, she curled up on the passenger seat with Viv on her lap. The cat purred contentedly. Ellie set her phone alarm for five-thirty the following morning.

Better get here early.

The bedroom lights shone from the house. "That woman's a nightmare." She tickled Viv behind the ear and reclined in the seat. "I don't even know why she wants you back. I should take you to the hotel with me. It's not like she'll really notice if you're there or not."

***

One house to the north, Denver pulled the door of the guesthouse quietly shut behind him. The half moon cast long shadows across the lawn. Lights from Ellie's house blinked through the dense shrubbery.

He rubbed his hands and grinned from ear to ear.

She's back from Upcountry. Luck's finally with me.

He tightened the towel around his waist, looked from the driveway to the bushes and back again, and thrust his way between the areca palms. The fronds scratched his bare chest and arms. The beach naupaka that followed was easier on his skin but more difficult to climb through.

Did I go a different way last time?

He eventually stumbled gratefully onto the trimmed grass on Ellie's side of the vegetation. Her lanai lights shone like beacons from across the garden. He saw a woman's figure in the living room settle onto the couch and felt a responsive pulse from beneath his towel. He closed his eyes.

No more holding back. But before you kiss her. Before you make love. You tell her everything.

He pulled up the random Target beach towel

226

he'd grabbed from the Kirkpatricks' mountainous supply of identical towels in their guest cottage. It had seemed like a good idea back there, when his eagerness to see Ellie had almost overwhelmed him. Now he felt awkward.

What if she thinks I'm assuming too much?

He surveyed the hedge behind him, not eager to retreat through it to put on some clothes. His gaze roamed back to the living room.

I won't touch her. Until I've told her.

He turned his back on the house and undid the long towel, repositioning it so that the gap was at the side and the folds draped over his knees.

I'll say I was going for a swim and saw the lights on.

He crouched low as he dashed across the soft lawn, his bare feet leaving tread marks in the sheen of drops left by the sprinkler system. He leapt the steps two at a time, stood, slightly breathless, at the front door, and tried the handle. It yielded to his touch. He entered noiselessly, leaving it open behind him.

The living room was illuminated by a single stainless steel floor lamp that arced gracefully over the sofa and ended in an elongated oval of blown white glass that glowed with a soft light. He looked at the floor and stepped into the room.

"Ellie."

"Denver?"

He flinched at the sound of the unexpected but familiar voice and stared. It took a few seconds to reconcile the expected image of Ellie with the actual figure of Vivyenne rising from the couch, her black bob cut floating like a period above a fluttering white silk nightgown exclamation mark.

"Vivyenne?"

"What are you doing here?" Their simultaneous questions bounced off one another and echoed in the large room.

Denver advanced, but Vivyenne spoke first.

"I heard from the Kirkpatricks that you sometimes stay next door. Am I correct..." Her eyes contemplated his towel. "That you also sometimes stay *here*?"

Denver yanked his towel farther up his chest. "I was going for a swim. I saw the lights on. I thought..."

"Ellie might like to join you?" Vivyenne lowered herself to the edge of the sofa, her white night gown blending perfectly with the surgical white of the cushion.

"I guess." Denver's hands moved restlessly from hips to arms to thighs and back again.

"Do as you like. But she's not here. I sent her to a hotel." Vivyenne smoothed the front of her gown. "You needn't have sent that email, you know. I have a...relationship...with someone, myself. For more than half a year."

She regarded Denver with a glance that mixed pride with disinterest.

Denver shifted from one bare foot to the other.

How were we ever involved?

"I'm happy for you."

"Yes." The corners of Vivyenne's mouth twitched upward for a second and then relaxed. "We plan to move into this house...together. That's

228

why I'm here." She rose in a smooth movement. "Your timing is good. I can return your cat. Philbert is allergic to animals."

"My cat? Return it?"

Vivyenne's eyebrows arched. "You must remember your own animal?"

I remember all right. He's what's keeping Ellie employed.

Denver shook his head. "I can't take him now. I'm just here for a day. I flew in from China."

Vivyenne gave a slight shrug of her square shoulders. "Send the cat to Seattle and get a sitter. You seem to know how to find them."

Is that a joke? Denver eyed her. *She never jokes.*

"Keep Viv for a while longer, would you? It would really help me out."

Vivyenne's hair bounced slowly back and forth as she shook her head no. "Having him here makes it necessary to keep Ellie. In a few weeks, the house will be in a state where I won't need someone here full-time."

"You're going to fire Ellie?"

Vivyenne's face remained as blank as a morning's fresh expanse of snow.

Denver racked his brain. "I'll pay the expenses."

He watched indecision flash across her face and smiled to himself.

Come on. I know you're a cheapskate at heart.

Vivyenne used her little finger to edge a stray hair on her cheek back into place. "Philbert can't relocate for another few months at the earliest. So...we can come to an arrangement until then." She twisted the tie of her robe around her wrist in a

229

tight loop. "Let's see…You pay Ellie's full salary and I continue to use her for the renovations. It's you who is inconveniencing me, after all."

Always have to come out on top. Some things never change.

Denver exhaled quietly and tried to look frustrated. He clasped his hands behind his back.

"I guess you have me over a barrel. Or a cat box." He smiled while Vivyenne stared at him. "It's a deal. Ellie doesn't need to know."

Vivyenne raised an eyebrow again. "As you like. I'll have Devora let you know about the details." She tossed her head. "When that woman bothers to recover."

To Denver, the air in the room, previously tense and conflicted, smoothed. His shoulders relaxed. He took a deep breath and grinned.

You were never one for change, Vivyenne. Thank goodness I still know how to play you.

He looked around the room, a mixture of the old dark wood floors and new white walls and furniture.

It's good to see you again. It makes things very clear. I want Ellie. Thanks for underscoring that.

He extended his arms. "I'm glad we ran into each other."

Vivyenne eyed him skeptically. Then she shrugged. "Yes. I'm glad too. It's saved me some money."

He pulled her into his arms, laughing.

"I love that you never change, Vivyenne."

At a thump and startled meow, Vivyenne and Denver turned toward the door, arms still around each other.

Viv's red cat carrier lay on its side. Beside it stood Ellie, pale and rigid.

CHAPTER 17

In the hotel, Ellie flung herself onto the king-size linen bedspread. Tears streaked her face. Her chin sunk to her chest. She wrenched a pillow from an enormous pile and crumpled it against her stomach, unable to imagine a moment further into the future. Her only thought was that she'd lost Denver forever.

"Denver."

She sobbed into the pillow.

"You love…Vivyenne."

The words burned her mouth, her brain, and her heart. She had searched on the way to the hotel for other explanations. But none of them fit. The only logical conclusion damned him as a cheat and cast her as an ignorant fool. Ellie curled into a fetal position and pulled a second pillow over her head.

"He never even told me he was back on Maui."

The living room scene at the house mocked her no matter how hard she screwed her eyes shut. Vivyenne's white silk nightgown flowing across her strong shoulders, sculpted chest, and thin waist.

Denver's strong arms, squeezing her to him. Their warm laughter. Vivyenne's eyes glittering with surprise and pleasure. The broad smile bisecting Denver's face. The sound of him telling Vivyenne he loved her.

Through every image, the towel wrapped around Denver's firm stomach glowed like a beacon. It was *her* towel, she was sure. It had to be. It was just like the one she'd bought at Target that first night for her beach adventures. The one she had washed and folded and put in the master bedroom closet before her move to Jacqui's house. Of everything she had seen and heard, the thought of the towel she had bought covering the nakedness he'd obviously been about to share with Vivyenne dug into Ellie's soul.

Why did they think I wouldn't come back in and find them? How long was I out in the car with Viv? Or did they want me to walk in? She screamed frustration and hurt into the fluffy down bolster.

Only now, after he was gone, did she realize how much she had given herself to Denver. How her thoughts over time had become intertwined with his. How she had incorporated his face into her days. How his work trouble slowly became something she thought about at night. How the little joys he shared with her over the phone or in texts lifted her own spirits.

Without conscious effort, she had strung their lives together, weaving one cloth from their two separate skeins. He had seemed so aligned with her. She thought back to their half-formed ideas of how they could build on what they had. Could she finish school and move to Seattle? Could he open a branch office in San Francisco? Maybe her computer skills could help him with his business?

She bit the pillow, reviewing the minutes after she had dropped Viv to the floor. But the scenes were fuzzy, still photos of live action, compiled from the glances she shot toward their feet, the white sofa, the darkened windows facing the garden. She'd wanted to look anywhere but directly at the two perpetrators.

What did he say? That he'd seen the lights and come over? Vivyenne had said something about cat supplies. I said I had to go.

She remembered running back through the gate. Spinning her car violently in the driveway. She'd wanted to return to Jacqui's but couldn't face having anyone see her torn heart. Her head and hands barely held the thing together.

She remembered slapping her car keys into the hand of a bemused valet and stumbling into the women's bathroom near the hotel's front desk. She'd splashed cold water on her face and rubbed away the tear smudges as best she could, making herself presentable enough to check in and get her room key.

She'd fumbled in the bright elevator alone, its lights and mirrors ridiculing her from every angle. The tears in her eyes had made reading numbers difficult. The conveyance had finally whisked her silently to one of the top floors. She'd squinted through her tears at the room numbers, found hers, and slipped the key card into the lock.

After an hour on the bed, Ellie hoisted herself to her feet and shuffled around the room, jerking open cabinets in search of the minibar. When she found it tucked inside a dresser, she loaded small bottles of gin and vodka into her shorts and carried two sodas back to the bed. Half an hour later, empty bottles and cans formed a pile. Ellie lay curled under the covers, staring at the screen of her phone. A white 'delete contact' button hovered over Denver's information.

Fuck you, Denver.

Her finger weaved. She poked randomly at the screen until she hit the button. His information disappeared. Then she navigated with only marginally more adroitness to the calls screen, where Denver's name had fifteen recent calls registered behind it. Tears rolled down her cheeks as she blocked the number. She chucked her phone into the far corner of the bed.

Good riddance.

She sobbed for hours and finally fell asleep.

***

A quacking awoke her the next morning. Her eyes resisted opening, glued shut with the residue of tears, sleep, and too much alcohol. She wrested them open with her fingers and peered, blinking rapidly, around the brightly lit room.

Where am I?

The disaster of the previous evening rushed back at her, crushing her to the mattress. Only the annoying duck sounds from her alarm roused her to action. She found the phone, turned it off, rolled to the floor, and flung her arm over her forehead.

Why did I drink so much?

She rubbed her temples, willing the throbbing in her head to subside. Later, the rainfall shower that cascaded over her head slowly washed away her headache. Underneath lay smoldering anger. Ellie climbed out and stomped around the stone tile floor, manically rubbing her hair dry with an oversized towel.

You want him, bitch? You can have him. And just so you know, I'm quitting your job. I don't need your money.

At twenty to seven, Ellie pulled in front of the house, face firmly set, eyes narrowed and resolute. But it took the next twenty minutes for her to wrestle the conflict that churned within her to the ground.

Just act cool. Get everything arranged. Get back to San Francisco as fast as you can. Then you can surprise her and quit. You don't have to do anything this morning.

At the door, Ellie's gaze shifted from the floor to Vivyenne's immaculate short white skirt and cream top and back again. Vivyenne hardly glanced at her.

"Let's get started. There is a lot you have to fix."

This woman's made of ice. She's acting like last night never even happened. Fine. Two can play that game.

Vivyenne led the way through the house, pointing out defects, design flaws, and do-overs. Ellie took notes on her iPad, eyes boring hatred into Vivyenne's back.

When they entered the master bedroom, Ellie couldn't stop herself from scrutinizing the bed for signs of the previous night's passion. But the crisp sheet and cover looked like they'd just returned from a military barracks. They stretched tightly over the mattress and Ellie was sure a penny would have bounced if she'd thrown one.

Bet she has sex like a robot. Ellie made a face behind Vivyenne's back.

The room itself looked unlived in. The suitcases had disappeared, the towels in the bathroom hung just as Ellie had left them, and there were no toiletries on the sink.

This woman's a freak. How can she not leave a sign of herself anywhere? Ellie pulled a towel to the floor as she exited the room behind Vivyenne.

She expected Vivyenne to be less meticulous about the garden than the house, but she was wrong.

"That bush ruins the sweep of the view." Vivyenne pointed at a magenta bougainvillea plant near the house that Ellie had particularly admired. "It will go."

She marched to the fountain. "And these loose lava stones. Why aren't they in place?" Her foot nudged a stone as carefully as Ellie would nudge a scorpion.

An involuntary band tightened around Ellie's chest. For the first time, she looked at Vivyenne's face, defiant and ready to fight. "The guy who was doing that was Brandon. He passed away. I think the others just haven't had the heart to touch this yet."

Vivyenne's expression registered only consternation. "This needs to be finished. It's been long enough." She shrugged, her straight shoulders moving toward her ears like the inept flap of a bird's wings. "Now this…"

Ellie closed her eyes with a sinking feeling as Vivyenne strode toward the line of shrubs and trees that separated her house from Denver's.

"This set of trees is hardly high enough to serve as a real privacy wall."

Ellie gazed at the ten-foot tall palms.

What kind of privacy are you after? I thought you'd want them to build a gate to his house.

Vivyenne's long fingers fondled a frond. "Find out whose land they're on, mine or the neighbor's."

The neighbors? That's what you call him?

"If they're on my property, they'll need to be cut out. Something else will have to be planted. Something taller."

"Right." Ellie traipsed after her onto the lanai, where Vivyenne turned and stared over Ellie's head as she talked.

"You can move back in here tonight. I've seen what I needed to see. And something at work has come up. I will fly back this afternoon."

Ellie stared. "What about Den…Viv?"

"Who? Oh, the cat." Vivyenne wiped her hands on the sides of her skirt. "He will stay."

Not with me, he won't. Not in the house where you had sex with Denver.

Ellie dropped her iPad onto the deck chair. "Vivyenne…"

"You won't have to take me the airport." Vivyenne swung around to the door, her back bob sweeping around her head, looking for a split second as though it might slice her neck with its sharp corners. "Denver's offered to take me." She paused before stepping across the threshold and spoke to the empty hallway before her. "I think you know Denver. The man from last night."

Ellie stood riveted, jaw sagging toward the floor.

***

Celine's concerned expression stared at Ellie from the laptop that lay propped on her knees.

"He took her to the airport?"

"I guess. I wasn't here. By the time I got back from the hotel, the alarm was set and the house was empty. Except for Viv. Poor guy. I don't think she fed him or anything." Ellie's fingers played absentmindedly with Viv's paws. "They probably went back to San Francisco together. The whole work thing he was telling me about all the time was probably a lie."

Celine's eyes blazed. "If I ever see Denver, girl, he's going to hear some language that will make his eyelashes curl."

A brief smile flickered then died in Ellie's eyes, wet with a sheen of tears. She rubbed her cheeks with the back of her hand.

"What should I do? Should I quit? I was going to this morning." She blew her nose. "Now I don't know. If they're both gone, I might as well stay here and take her money. It's not like I have any other place to go."

"Sure you do. You can come back here. For Thanksgiving at least. Get your mind off this."

Ellie shook her head.

239

"You think you'll feel better feeling sorry for yourself?" Celine tapped the camera to get Ellie to look at her. "K-Rao's coming. Try to get on the same flight as him. He'll keep you entertained."

"I'm so depressed. I'll spoil your Thanksgiving." Ellie lifted Viv and rubbed her face in his stomach. He batted at her head with soft paws.

"I'll have booze and friends waiting for you. Hold on." Celine propped her phone against something and typed for a minute. "There're some first class seats left on K-Rao's flight."

"First class?"

Celine nodded. "Spend some of that bitch's money. And when you get here, we'll call her up. Give her some West Side Chicago attitude. You deserve a raise."

CHAPTER 18

Thumping music from the living room reverberated through Celine's small apartment, making the glassware jiggle. Ellie stood in a crowd of people near the second bedroom. She was telling a story, hands waving wildly, the wine in her half-empty glass sloshing like a mini tsunami. With a particularly violent swing of her arm, the glass itself soared toward the wall. A young man in an untucked flannel shirt and dirty jeans intercepted the flying object before impact.

"Nice throw." He laughed, wiping the white wine from his shirt. "You want a refill?"

"What?" Ellie focused on him with effort. "Sure. Get yourself another glass."

He grinned and began pushing his way through the crowd. Ellie grabbed the tail of his shirt and tugged.

"Get me one too." She looked quizzically at her empty hands. "I must've put mine down somewhere."

K-Rao stepped forward.

"I think you've had enough, yeah?" He grasped Ellie's elbow and steered her skillfully through the dense crowd of twenty-somethings in the hall. "Excuse us, folks. I'm taking this lovely lady for a walk."

At the long living room sofa, he whispered in the ear of a tall youth with long, untidy hair and a torn sweatshirt. The man hopped up and K-Rao settled Ellie in the seat he'd vacated. Ellie stared after him.

"That guy was my professor." She squinted. "Used to work at HubSpot."

K-Rao settled on the sofa's arm. "Wouldn't be surprised. Celine throws a hell of a Thanksgiving party." While Ellie stared at her professor's retreating back, K-Rao pointed at Ellie's head and gave Celine, who was watching him from the kitchen, a thumbs up.

Ellie leaned conspiratorially against K-Rao's shoulder. "You miss Maui?" She had to shout to be heard above the music and surrounding conversation.

"Nope. Maui's not going anywhere. I'm happy to be here."

"I miss it." Ellie burped and put her hand to her mouth, giggling. "I miss Viv."

"You miss the big-ass house." K-Rao punched her lightly in the shoulder. Ellie fell in slow motion, colliding eventually with the woman on her other side.

K-Rao pulled Ellie upright.

"I miss Denver." Ellie slumped toward him again. He propped her against the backrest. "I blocked his number." She groped for her phone and pulled from her back pocket. "See?"

K-Rao looked thoughtfully at the blank screen. "It sucks, Ellie. The guy was a bastard."

"Yeah." Ellie's head bobbed back and forth, knocking repeatedly against the headrest. "Did you know his company was a hot mess? I should have seen it coming. He was a total loser."

"That's right." K-Rao patted her arm and looked through the living room window at the glittering lights of the neighboring high-rises.

"So why do I miss Maui? I met only jerks. Like Noa." She stopped nodding and followed K-Rao's glance out the window. "Anything new about him?"

"Nope. He disappeared. I think you can forget about him, yeah?"

"Not so easy. Jerks stick in your mind."

"Yeah." K-Rao grinned. "What are you planning after you finish your courses? You job hunting yet?"

"Vivyenne. She was another class-A jerk." Ellie poked a finger at her phone. "Treats Devora like shit. And Devora's actually really nice, once you get to know her."

K-Rao scratched his head. "How about your parents? Are they coming to visit?"

Ellie yelled into the phone. "Fuck Vivyenne and her tight-ass surgical white fetish."

He laughed and tried to catch her gaze. "Hey, Ellie. I'm trying to switch the subject."

Ellie smiled to herself. "It's Thanksgiving. You're supposed to be grateful. I'm texting Devora."

"You're in your own little world right now,

aren't you?" K-Rao squeezed her shoulders. "Wave if you need me." He elbowed his way through the throng in the direction of the kitchen.

Ellie turned on her phone.

Ellie: Happy turkey day.

She was putting her phone back in her pants when it jingled. She looked at it with surprise.

Devora: Right. U too.

Ellie: Ur around on T-day? I'm at a party in San Fran.

Devora: Severe FOMO. At my parents'.

Ellie: Aww.

Devora: Not aww. Oww.

Ellie: Come over.

Devora: We're in L.A.

Ellie pursed her lips in thought.
"What the fuck."

Ellie: I want a raise.

Devora: Go for it.

Ellie: And first class ticket back.

244

Devora: Right. Anything else?

Ellie patted her head with both hands.
"Come on, Ellie. Think. What else?"
She scrunched her eyes tightly shut for a second.

Ellie: Got ideas?

Devora: U should have asked for more money from the beginning. I was authorized to give u more.

Ellie: WTF.

Devora: Can tell u more. I'll call u in 5.

Ellie looked up from her phone in bewilderment, as though aware for the first time of the buzz around her. She pretended holding the phone to one ear and plugged the other with her finger.
Can't hear anything but this music.
The mass of young people around her swayed in time to the pulsating beat. Conversations, in-person and virtual, augmented the noise.
Nobody goes home for Thanksgiving anymore?
She stumbled over outstretched legs and people sitting on the floor. The area by the front door was less crowded than elsewhere, but when she reached it she realized why. It served as an echo chamber, all sound reverberating against the close walls. Ellie lurched into the condo's hall. The door closed behind her, cutting the volume by half. She stepped across the narrow strip of carpet to the communal

garbage and recycling area. After the metal door clanged shut, the only reminder of the party across the hall was a faint thump.

She slid down the wall to face a large pile of flattened Amazon boxes. The phone rang.

"Hey." Devora's voice sounded quiet and less confident than Ellie remembered.

"Hey." Ellie listed to one side. "Don't think we've actually talked since I moved to Hawaii."

"Right. Texting's better. But that phone's Vivyenne's. Sometimes I think she monitors my messages."

"Wouldn't surprise me." Ellie kicked the boxes with her foot and they tumbled forward. "Shit."

"What's up?"

"Hold on." Ellie set the phone on the floor and re-assembled the pile. She scooted farther away so she wouldn't be tempted again. "Sorry. I'm in the garbage closet. It's quiet."

"I'd take a garbage closet. I'm at my parents'. It's a nightmare."

Ellie registered the slight slurring in Devora's speech. "You sound drunk."

"So do you."

Ellie laughed. "That's because I *am* drunk."

"Right. Well, here no one officially ever gets beyond tipsy. My grandfather's so tipsy that he's passed out in front of the TV."

"You should really come over. I've never had a Thanksgiving like this. The room's full of people our age who apparently don't need to be home."

"What about you? Why aren't you back in Delaware?"

Ellie closed her eyes and a vision of her family around the mahogany dining room table washed briefly in front of her eyes. "Wish I were. It's fun at Thanksgiving."

"Right. But that's not why you texted."

"Oh, yeah." Ellie's spine straightened against the wall. "You wanted to tell me about the raise."

"Right. Ask for double."

"Double what?"

"Double what you're making right now."

A noticeable amount of wine stopped circulating through Ellie's system. Her head suddenly cleared. "Double?"

"That's right. Doctor Lovejoy's in a good mood. It's rare, so take advantage of it. She just got engaged to some old flame."

She felt as though an Olympic boxer had landed a direct punch to her gut. Her mouth hung open. She dropped the phone, which skidded across the concrete.

"Ellie?" Devora's voice sounded tinny and distant.

She held the phone next to her ashen face. "Shit."

"You okay?"

Ellie rocked back and forth against the wall. "Fuck. Fuck. Fuck."

"What's up? I thought I was doing you a favor."

"You are." Ellie rose, leaning against the wall for support. "Ask that bitch for triple what I make now. And a first class ticket back. And a better car. And…" Ellie wiped her mouth. "I get to have final say over the garden."

247

"You're giving me life here, Ellie. Hold on."

Ellie lay down on the cold concrete. It cooled her throbbing head. She stared at the piles of cardboard, the recycling boxes, the garbage chute.

Denver's marrying Vivyenne. The thought made her gag and she sat up, coughing.

"Hey." Devora's voice sounded excited. "You're *never* going to believe this."

Ellie massaged her temples. "What? She fired me?"

"No. You'll rake in sixty-six thousand dollars from now until the end of January. Basically all she said was, 'Okay. I'm sure Denver would want her to have it.' Whatever that means."

Ellie's voice was flat, defeated. "That means she's feeling guilty."

"Guilty? You don't know the woman. Guilt is not something she wastes time on."

"No." Ellie shook her head. "Probably not. She just hits and runs."

Ellie heard a muffled conversation from Devora's end of the line.

"Hey, I've got to go. I was hiding in my brother's bedroom, but they found me. You have a great Thanksgiving. Have some fun for me, okay?"

Ellie wiped a tear from her cheek. "Sure."

She lay back on the floor and pulled a piece of cardboard over her head.

An hour later, Celine shoved the garbage area door open and screamed. Ellie flung the box from her as though she'd been shocked and sat bolt upright.

"Girl." Celine held her chest. "You scared the

life out of me. What are you doing in here with a box over your head like a homeless person?" She eyed Ellie's face. "You get lost?"

Ellie sat up and hung her head. Tears dripped onto the gray floor, staining it with dark circles. Celine dropped the bag of empty bottles into a bin and squatted beside her friend. "What happened?"

Ellie leaned into her. "Denver's getting married." Her voice cracked as she choked out the last words. "To Vivyenne."

"Oh, Ellie." Celine rocked her gently while she sobbed. "You deserve someone better than that." She whispered to herself. "And he'd better watch out, because I'm siccing K-Rao on his sorry ass."

***

"I thought the money would make me feel better."

Ellie sat with a large mug of coffee at the kitchen table amid the detritus of the prior night's party. K-Rao and Celine reclined, looking the worse for wear, across from her.

"But it doesn't?" Celine raised her eyebrow. "That's some serious cash."

K-Rao elbowed Celine and nodded at Ellie. "But it's tainted money, yeah?"

"That's right." Ellie shuddered. "I'd be taking money from the person who stabbed me in the back. I'd feel like a whore."

Celine walked to the refrigerator, pulled out a pie dish, and stared accusingly at K-Rao. "Who was at my pie last night?" She tipped the pan toward them and Ellie eyed the gouge marks left by spoons and forks. K-Rao looked at the table.

"I might have brought it out. Just at the end. A couple of the guys were really hungry."

"Well, I guess you'll be baking us another one this afternoon, right?" Celine winked, dropped the pie on the table, and fished three forks out of a drawer.

Ellie poked at the crust. "I'm basically screwed. If I go back, I make lots of money but feel horrible. If I stay here, I have no money but feel self-righteous."

Celine shook her head. "That's not the way I see it."

Ellie bit into a tiny piece of pie. "What do you see?"

"I think you're going to feel like shit no matter what you do. So take the money."

K-Rao turned in his chair. "My woman's got no morals." He kissed Celine on the cheek. "What about Ellie's self-esteem?"

"Let's be clear." Celine's gaze flitted between Ellie and K-Rao. "For sixty-six thousand dollars, my self-esteem can go flush itself."

"That's the spirit." K-Rao spewed crumbs onto the table as he talked. "You're a mercenary."

"I'm a pragmatist. What would you do?"

K-Rao swallowed a sip of coffee. "I'd stay in San Francisco."

"That's why you became a cop. You think people should always do the right thing." Celine rolled twinkling eyes at the ceiling. "Scary."

Ellie's fingers played with the end of her

ponytail. "Denver lives right next door."

Celine slapped the table. "Behind a huge palm-tree fence. You'll never see him. You never did before. Take the money, girl."

K-Rao buried his face in his hands and peeped through his fingers, grinning at Celine.

Ellie sat up and slapped the table. "Okay. Screw Denver and Vivyenne. I will."

***

Jacqui met Ellie at baggage claim carrying Viv in his red carrier.

"You said this little guy would be great company while you were gone. *Ha*. He pouted the entire time." She passed the cat to Ellie, who unzipped the carrier and lifted him out.

"Did you miss me?" She snuggled Viv against her face. He tried to climb onto her shoulder. Ellie laughed. "Did you bring his leash?"

"Right here."

She fastened the purple collar around Viv's chest while he purred against her.

Jacqui walked with Ellie and Viv to the on-airport rental car shuttle.

"How was your flight?"

"Amazing. First class is awesome." Ellie's voice lacked conviction. They joined the crowd waiting for the bus.

"But you're not happy to be back?"

"I feel like a slut."

A very pale, heavy-set woman in a floral skirt and sensible shoes peered at Ellie over her

251

sunglasses and moved farther back in the group.

Ellie lowered her voice. "I'm not sure I made the right choice."

Jacqui's mouth twitched up in a teasing smile. "There's hardly ever only *one* right choice, honey. You do the best you can and try not to hurt anybody in the process." She waved as she walked to the outdoor parking lot. "Have fun with your new rental."

In the car rental lot, the engine of Ellie's new Infinity Crossover was barely audible, and only the lights on the dash reassured her that she'd started the motor. She eased the car cautiously onto the main road, worried about tourists distracted by the view, their limited hours in paradise, or their screaming children.

Stay in your lane and don't hit my car.

She gripped the wheel, her foot hovering over the break. Jacqui sped by, waving out the window of her own car. Ellie waved back and tapped the break.

Who knew driving a fancy car would be so stressful?

The house in Wailea seemed familiar but cold. Inside the front door, she unleashed Viv, who scuttled into the living room in search of bugs. Ellie paused, watching him bound over the furniture.

It will get easier. You'll walk by this door twenty times a day. You won't always see the two of them there.

The kitchen still looked like a bomb had gone off. Cabinets of sparkling white with frosted glass doors gleamed next to gaping holes in the wall.

Ellie ran her fingers over the old marble island whose electrical circuitry and plumbing showed evidence of recent tampering.

Brandon sat here. And Olivia...And Vivyenne.

She spun on her heel to the bedroom but jerked to a stop at the entrance.

I can't sleep here.

After half an hour of lugging her belongings from the master bedroom to the guest room, Ellie changed into a bikini and walked into the cool evening air. She willed herself not to look in the direction of Denver's house. But the more she resisted, the more it drew her gaze. Finally, she snuck to the border and peered through the hedges and trees. The main and guesthouse bungalow were dark and silent. She heaved a sigh.

At least he's not here. I hope he stays away. I hope they both stay away.

She approached the fountain and passed by her property's own guesthouse, pushing away thoughts of Brandon. She traipsed toward the shore, hoping the ocean would wash away some of her confusion and loneliness. Instead, the light breeze wafted an odor of rotting fish.

Stinking paradise.

She turned on her heel and marched back into the house. Lying on the guest bed, exhausted and ill tempered, she tried to focus on piles of money. But the image that floated on the backs of her closed eyelids was Denver's face.

CHAPTER 19

Jacqui pulled through Ellie's gate and watched Olivia halt behind her. Olivia hefted a large paper bag from her backseat and lugged it to Jacqui's car.

"I got Mexican takeout, fried chicken, mac and cheese, and ice cream."

Jacqui grimaced. Her short skort and yoga top emphasized her athletic shape as she hoisted a woven basket effortlessly onto her shoulder. "Remind me not to send you shopping alone again."

Olivia's puzzled expression made Jacqui laugh.

"I'm not dissing your choices. It's just the combination. Seems a bit…unusual."

Olivia deposited her bag carefully on the deck chair. "I didn't know what Ellie would consider comfort food. So I tried to cover all the bases."

She peeked inside Jacqui's basket. Jacqui smiled.

"I guess I did that too. I got beer, gin, tonic, whiskey, coke, and wine coolers."

"Wow."

"Okay. Here goes nothing." Jacqui lifted her hand to knock and then let it drop. She turned to

Olivia. "Is it just me, or do you feel like something's off? I don't feel like she gave me the whole story about coming back here. When she left for San Francisco, I honestly didn't think we'd see her again."

A breath of evening air carried the fragrance of flowers and something vaguely fishy. Olivia balanced herself on the deck chair's wide armrest. Her blue tank top stretched tightly across her chest. She crossed her arms.

"I don't know. It kind of makes sense. She said she got a raise."

Jacqui pushed her hands together in a prayer pose and balanced one leg against the other. "But why rub her own face in what happened in this house? How much money would it take for you to do that?"

Olivia studied the porch lights and then surveyed the dark garden. "You could say the same thing about me. Maybe I should leave Maui. But it's kind of comforting to be where Brandon used to be."

"Oh, honey." Jacqui returned her foot to the ground. "Of course it is. But Brandon's death was an accident. He didn't betray you."

Olivia shrugged. "Maybe not intentionally. But I still have to deal with everything. He's gone and I'm on my own."

In the pause that followed, Jacqui raised an eyebrow and studied Olivia's face. "Is there something you're not telling me, honey?"

Olivia hoisted the paper bag onto her hip. "Nope. Let's get in before the tacos melt the ice cream."

***

Later, the women pushed back from the kitchen island that was cluttered with take-out containers and half-empty bottles and cans. Candles flickered on the stovetop and windowsill, their wavering light creating strange shadows of contractors' tools and spare boards that leaned here and there in the unfinished room. Ellie rummaged through the new cabinets.

"Where did they put the bowls?"

Olivia scooped spinach curry onto her plate and dipped a tortilla chip into the green pile. Jacqui shaded her eyes.

"I can't watch you mix and match cuisines anymore. Japanese pickles on the mac and cheese. Fried chicken with kimchee. Now this."

Jacqui's phone rang. "Saved by the bell." She marched into the hallway.

Ellie returned to the counter with three yellow bowls.

"Where's Jacqui?"

Olivia paused with a dripping green chip mid-air and mumbled through a half-eaten mouthful. "Someone called."

"You still want ice cream? I found some chocolate sauce." Ellie held up a glass jar.

"Can I get an amen?" Olivia gave Ellie a fist bump. "Chocolate chocolate-chip with chocolate sauce. Got any whipped cream?"

"You're out of control."

Jacqui strolled back in. She straightened her black Lycra top and hopped onto the counter, her bare, shapely legs swinging against the cabinets underneath. "I have an announcement. That was the car dealer. He's at my place. He wants a yoga lesson."

Ellie stared. "In the middle of the night? I thought you broke up with him."

Olivia's gaze traveled between her two friends while she ladled ice cream into a bowl.

Jacqui held up her phone. "No breakup's ever the end of everything. It's only ten. And the moon's out." She picked up her purse. "Ladies, I hate to leave you, but professional duty calls."

"*Ha.*" Ellie threw a crumpled napkin at her. "I know exactly the kind of lesson he's looking for at ten at night."

Jacqui winked. "There's only one way to find out." She glanced at Olivia busily pouring chocolate sauce. "Ellie, walk me out."

At the door, Jacqui held her arm. "I'm a little worried about our young friend."

"Olivia?" Ellie pushed her hair behind her ear. "She seems okay. She's eating again."

Jacqui rolled her eyes. "You don't have to tell me. But she's holding something back. Keep your ears open."

Ellie saluted with a grin. "Will do."

"And you." Jacqui peered into Ellie's eyes. "You call me if you need me, okay?"

"What? In case I forget how to do downward facing monkey?" Jacqui's serious expression made Ellie stifle her laugh.

"In case you forget that you're better than Denver and he should rot in hell for making you so miserable."

Ellie turned so Jacqui wouldn't see the quick, hot tears that filled her eyes. She shut the door as her friend left.

In the kitchen, mounds of ice cream filled two bowls in front of Olivia. Ellie stopped short. "Is there a football team hiding in the bedroom that I don't know about?" Ellie spun around her serving, observing it from all angles. "Who do you think is going to eat all this?"

Olivia thrust a spoon at her. "You."

"Then I'm going to need some fresh air and a little more vodka first." She poured herself a tumbler, covered her ice cream bowl with plastic wrap, and put it in the freezer. "Want to go out to the beach?"

The two sauntered across the lawn, Ellie with a drink, Olivia carrying her dessert protectively. A half moon illuminated the shore, its reflection an elongated runway of bright yellow on the gently lapping ocean.

Olivia wrinkled her nose. "What's that stink?"

"I wish I knew." Ellie glanced around her. "I never noticed it before. Maybe some dead fish washed up on the beach."

"Eew." Olivia shuffled her feet in the sand before sitting down. "That's gross." The young woman spooned ice cream into her mouth, hardly pausing to chew.

Ellie followed Olivia's movements with an incredulous expression. "Some people might call the current contents of your stomach gross."

"This?" A gob of melted chocolate plopped from

Olivia's spoon back into the bowl. "It's old-fashioned American."

"On top of old-fashioned Southern, Indian, Mexican, Japanese, and Korean."

"I'm multi-ethnic. My mom's Irish and my dad's Egyptian."

"Then I'd understand if you were eating potatoes and fava beans. But where'd you get the taste for what you ate tonight?"

"I'm eating because…" Olivia stopped herself in mid-sentence with another mouthful.

Ellie buried her feet in the sand, wiggling her toes until they were merely convulsing vibrations under the smooth surface. She leaned back on her arms, gazing at the sky.

"Look at all those stars."

Olivia flopped back completely, her empty bowl balanced on her stomach. "Awesome."

Ellie placed her drink on a rock and lay down. Above them whirled spindly clouds through which shone bright planets and stars at the edge of the sky. Ellie recognized the Orion constellation and the Big Dipper. After a few minutes, Olivia sat up.

"I'm hungry."

Ellie propped her head on one arm and stared. "Is that a thing? You can't possibly be hungry."

Olivia rubbed her stomach. "No. Seriously. I am." She lifted her bowl. "Can I go get more?"

"Be my guest." Ellie relaxed onto the sand as Olivia sauntered toward the house.

"Hey. Can you get me another one?" She sat up and lifted her glass. But Olivia was already at the low border of bushes that separated the beach from

259

the main garden. She hadn't heard. Ellie rose and cantered after her.

The moon highlighted the shrubbery and trees, painting them a darker shade where they fell into shadow, brightening areas where its beams reached. To yell in the warm silence of the still night seemed out of place. Instead, Ellie followed Olivia's form across the grass, slowly closing the distance.

Olivia was approaching the fountain when Ellie noticed a movement by the guesthouse. She slowed, turned to look, and froze. The tumbler slipped from her hand and spun to the turf where it landed inaudibly and rolled gently to a stop.

She hadn't thought about him in days, hadn't seen him in over a month, but she recognized the face and the limp even in the dim light. *Noa.*

A chill raced through her from head to foot, making goosebumps pebble on her flesh. Noa slunk next to the guesthouse wall, wearing a tight-fitting camouflage wetsuit. One hand held what looked like a long rod, a bag, and goggles. In the other hand flashed a knife.

Ellie's mouth dried. Her heart pounded in her throat. She whipped her gaze from Noa to Olivia and back again. In a few steps, he would be at the front of the guesthouse with a full view of the garden. He would see both women, illuminated and exposed on the wide expanse of grass.

He's been hiding here. On this property somewhere.

Ideas blazed through her mind in less time than it took to blink. If she turned back, the bushes at the beach offered her protection. But what about

Olivia? She sauntered on, oblivious, exposed, and vulnerable.

Scream to warn her?

Noa advanced. The knife glinted, a fleeting sparkle of silver against the dark of his thigh. If she screamed, he'd see them both. And then neither one of them might get away. Ellie froze for an instant with indecision.

My phone's in the house.

She might be able to sneak past Noa if he saw Olivia. She could run to the house and call the police. But what would he do to Olivia? Ellie shuddered.

Hide at the beach or warn her? She squinted at Noa, who peered into his dangling bag.

Adrenaline pumped in her veins, expanding every moment, slowing time to a crawl.

Warn her? Hide?

She closed her eyes and held her breath for a heartbeat.

Hide.

Ellie opened her eyes and focused. She sped silently across the lawn, faster than she knew her legs could carry her. At the fountain, with both arms outstretched, she shoved her friend with all her might. Olivia stumbled and fell behind the hula dancer, out of sight. In the same instant as she fell, Ellie screamed. She darted away from the water sculpture, waving her arms wildly, yelling, and making a beeline for the illuminated steps of the house.

***

Ellie smelled Noa closing on her before she heard him. The odor of fresh fish, seaweed, and something indescribably awful overwhelmed her before she had covered half the distance to the house. His footsteps pounded unevenly. The stench increased and suddenly a gloved hand clamped over her mouth.

"Shut the fuck up."

The rough fabric tore at her face as Noa dragged her, struggling, back in the direction of the guesthouse. Ellie closed her eyes so she wouldn't look at the fountain.

Olivia, stay put. When he's got me inside, get help. But for God's sake, stay hidden till then.

A wave of calm washed over her as she thought of her friend.

She's safe. And I can fight.

Hard iron blocks on Noa's belt dug into her waist. His left arm hooked firmly under her armpit. Ellie willed her body to relax, to create dead weight and resistance. He surprised her with his wiry strength as he pulled her up the two steps to the front entrance, her feet bouncing on the floorboards. He grunted and shoved his shoulder against her while he fumbled with the door.

The pungent, stinging odor inside made Ellie gag. He dropped her without warning and she crashed to the floor. Her head knocked against the hardwood and for a moment the room's darkness closed in on her with an even deeper blackness.

***

Olivia lay flat behind the fountain. Her knees hurt. Her head spun. Her ears rang. She rubbed her eyes, confused.

What's that noise?

The ringing in her ears sounded increasingly like screaming. Her brow furrowed.

Is that Ellie?

She pushed herself to the fountain rim with effort, wincing at the pain in her knees. Near the house, she saw Ellie fly across the grass. A man charged after her. Olivia held her breath as the man grabbed Ellie from behind and dragged her back across the lawn.

She ducked back behind the fountain and stretched herself flat on the lava stones, hoping the man wouldn't see her. The rocks, still slightly warm from the sun, soothed her face. She stared at the wall inches from her face, torn by loud strings of commands racing in her head.

Sprint to the house. Call the police. Run to the neighbors.

But she couldn't move.

This is just like what happened to Brandon. I saw them pull him into that car. I didn't hear from him for days. They could have killed him.

The fear of those interminable hours that happened years ago washed over her now with undiminished intensity. She had waited then for Brandon, helpless, alone, and frightened. Dread and hopelessness had paralyzed her, weighing her down with as much force as a block of cement. And they did the same now.

"Run," said one voice in her head.

"I can't," said another.

The war raged, with neither faction gaining the upper hand. She laid still, the trampled victim of indecision, rage, and foreboding. Breathing seemed an effort. She concentrated on the lava stones in front of her. The patterns of air holes in the ancient rock, the leaf-like shape of the chiseled lines.

Leaf? Lines?

A new thought cleared her head as effortlessly as a child blows dust from a forgotten toy.

A maple leaf.

Her finger slowly traced the shape.

Brandon's maple leaf. Here in the stone. He carved it. For me to see.

The rough surface seemed to transfer energy to her hand. Strength shot through her arm, animating her limbs. Determination and forcefulness blossomed in her chest, unbidden but welcome.

She peered over the edge of the fountain. The garden was deceptively still, with no obvious sign of the recent deadly chase. Only a faint track of scuffed grass indicated where the man had forced Ellie to the guesthouse.

Hold on, Ellie. I'm getting help.

Olivia dashed for the lanai in a soundless sprint.

***

He'll kill me.

The thought pumped energy through Ellie. She held her hand to her nose and breathed through her mouth as she spied Noa unsheathe the knife from the holster on his calf. In the gloom she could barely discern the outline of a table, two chairs, and galley kitchen.

"What'd you do that for, bitch?"

Ellie cried out as Noa's foot collided with her ribs.

"Nobody ever would have found me."

His guttural laugh made her shiver.

"I've been right under your fucking nose for weeks. The cops even came by, lights flashing. I thought you'd found me out."

He snorted and kicked her again. He wasn't wearing shoes. But the pain made her gasp and she rolled away from him.

"Cops are such losers."

"How'd you get in here?" The sound of her own voice surprised her. It was rough and faint, almost unrecognizable.

"Fucking easy." He kicked her again. "Broke in and put in a new lock at night. Anybody can do that."

No more questions, Ellie. But her voice had a mind of its own.

"What's that smell?"

The collision with her ribs this time lacked the vehemence of before.

"Raw fish. Lobster. What you think I've been living on?" He threw something wet and sticky at her face. Ellie pawed frantically at the substance, willing herself not to think of what it could be.

Noa laughed. "Spearfishing. I'm in the water all day. Nobody bothers me." His voice lowered and Ellie curled into a ball with her hands over her head, dreading the implication of the drop in tone. "Not until now."

He pulled her up by her hair. She rose reluctantly, clutching at the top of her head to minimize the pull. He shoved a chair into the back of her legs. She fell into it, her bottom hitting so hard it knocked the wind out of her.

Her head throbbed. Her stomach pitched a violent fight to empty itself. Her eyes had trouble focusing.

"You slut." The collision with the butt of his knife drew blood from Ellie's lips. The bitter iron taste felt like a relief in the stifling air of the cottage.

"I saw you outside with your boyfriend. Giving him what you should have been giving me."

Ellie racked her brain.

What's he talking about?

Then nostalgic scenes bubbled through her mind's chaos.

Denver. And me. That morning he slept over.

She held her breath.

Noa was watching.

He waved the tip of the blade in front of Ellie's eyes.

"See this?"

Ellie nodded.

"Want me to use it?"

Ellie clamped her hands between her legs and Noa laughed. He swung the knife at her face. Ellie blocked it with her arm just before it connected with her cheek. She screamed as the sharp edge cut deeply.

The pain of the gash crystalized her emotions.

She leapt from the chair with a shout of rage and flailed at Noa, pummeling him with her fists and kicking him with her sandaled feet. Her knee made contact with his groin and he reeled backward, knocking into the table. The knife fell from his grasp.

A sudden voice from outside made them both pause in mid-fight.

"Police. Come out with your hands up."

Noa regained his sense of place an instant before Ellie, long enough to grab her arm and twist her around so that he held her with a chokehold by the throat.

"I've got a hostage," Noa yelled at the door. "Get me a fucking boat."

"Come out and show your hostage."

"Fuck you." Noa screamed into Ellie's ear. "Come in here and find this bitch for yourselves."

He pulled Ellie to the window and wiped her bloody arm across the pane. Ellie shrieked. In the darkness she watched the black smudge weep down the window in long trickles. She felt Noa inhale deeply. His chest rumbled against her back and he released his hold on her slightly as he yelled.

"Think that's my blood? Think I cut myself? Get me a boat, or I'll cut off her hand and throw that out next."

Ellie tucked her chin and bit. She ground her teeth into Noa's arm, his blood mixing with hers as he wrenched his arm back and forth. He punched her face with his free hand but she held on, desperation fueling her grip, her hands protecting herself as much as she could. He finally landed a

267

solid blow to her solar plexus. She gasped and fell to the floor.

From her position, Ellie watched Noa bend.

He's got the knife.

Just before she covered her face with her arms, she caught sight of a pair of feet dashing through the front door. A thud reverberated in the small room. Ellie hoisted herself on the chair back and struggled to her feet. Behind her, two men grunted. Furniture crashed. Ellie staggered through the door.

***

She lurched down the two steps to the grass, where she fell to her knees.

"Ellie."

The woman's voice reached her as if through a long tunnel. Ellie's head spun. The pain in her face and arm seared its way to the surface of her thoughts. She heard sirens in the distance. Then someone stood over her and a warm hand pulled under her good arm.

"Thank God. I thought he'd killed you."

Ellie focused briefly on the face that gazed down at her.

"Olivia?"

Olivia smiled. Then she wrenched Ellie forcefully, pulling them both toward the house. Ellie tottered but Olivia tugged insistently.

"I can't." She fell to the grass.

Olivia hovered over her, pointing to the guesthouse.

Ellie made out two figures, one limping down

the grassy expanse in the direction of the ocean. The other tearing after him. Ellie held her hands in her head. She glanced up at Olivia, who nodded almost imperceptibly and answered Ellie's unasked question.

"That's Denver." Ellie felt a rush of unexpected energy at the thought. Every muscle in her strained to protect him.

Near the shore, Noa turned and slashed at him with his knife. Denver staggered.

Ellie surged to her feet, ready to run after them. Olivia held her back as police cars screeched into the driveway and, almost before the first one stopped moving, an officer sprinted over the grass, gun raised.

Noa plunged into the ocean, the waves reflecting moonlight even so far away. Ellie jerked from Olivia's grasp and followed the men at the shore. She barely noticed the gallop of footsteps that raced close behind her.

As she neared, she saw the officer push Denver aside and stand, legs astride, on the sand. He fired repeatedly into the water after Noa, who splashed farther out to sea and submerged.

The officer threw off his belt and kicked off his shoes. He plunged through the shallows and dove toward the place where Noa had been.

Denver lay on the grass, face pale, chest bleeding. Ellie knelt next to him. She tore off her shirt and pressed it hard against the cuts on his torso. The wound on her arm flowed more freely as she clamped down both fists.

Officers trained lights on the ocean, the brilliant

glare reflecting off the still water.

"There." A female officer pointed. "I saw Rao."

K-Rao? Ellie jerked her head to look.

"Over there."

The beams illumined two heads that shone black and wet in the glittering whiteness around them. They bobbed a foot apart. It was impossible for Ellie to tell who was who. For a moment, she forgot Denver, her arm, the events of the night. Her attention centered on the two men in the water, splashing, fighting for their lives.

One man's head sunk momentarily beneath the surface. Ellie held her breath.

K-Rao?

It reappeared for an instant and vanished again. The second head floated for another moment and then, in a flash, was gone.

Lights skimmed the surface where the two men had been. The water smoothed itself. Gentle waves lapped the shore. The small group clustered on shore, no one speaking, everyone gazing at the spot that had melted into the great expanse of the Pacific as the moon rose higher in the sky.

CHAPTER 20

The following morning, Ellie sat at the kitchen island, a mug of green tea placed far away from her open laptop. Her face sported dark, puffy bruises. The skin on her neck glowed with angry stripes. Thick white bandages wrapped around her left arm, which she propped on the granite, her hand protruding, immobile, like a tan head on a ghost.

She typed, one-handed, into boxes on a web page. The logo of a recruiting firm specializing in non-profit sector hires stared up at her from the screen.

Experience? Got lots, with companies that value corporate profits over public good.

She bit her lip and hesitatingly filled in a text box.

Preferred work location? Hmm…

Olivia slouched into the kitchen carrying a chisel in one hand and a large wooden mallet in the other.

Ellie's eyebrows lifted. "Where'd you get those?"

Olivia grinned. "Brandon's gardening co-workers. They brought them by last night."

Ellie slipped carefully off the stool, protecting her bandaged arm from unnecessary bumps. "I bet those guys wondered what you were up to."

Olivia's teeth sparkled as her smile widened. "You should have seen the size of the other ones they loaned me. There's a mallet the length of my arm lying on my kitchen floor. I can barely lift it."

"Good protection in case of..." Ellie trailed off.

I could have used it last night.

"Nope." Olivia shook her head. "I'm choosing to believe Noa was the only deranged killer on Maui. And now that he's dead, I'm returning all mallets when we're finished."

"So let's get at it." Ellie ambled to the front door. "I'm stoked to see what Brandon left behind."

A gust of fresh ocean breeze carrying a hint of flowers and the sea greeted them when they stepped onto the lanai. The early morning sun bore down with an intensity that foretold afternoon heat.

"I always feel like I'm stepping into a sauna out here." Ellie spread her arms. "Not in a bad, humid way. But in a perfect, warm way. No matter how tense I am, I step outside and some of the stress melts away."

"I know what you mean." Olivia closed her eyes and turned her young face to sky. "It's perfect."

"Guess that's why they call it paradise."

They reached the garden's centerpiece. The hula dancer gazed down at them. Ellie pushed loose stones around the fountain away with her foot, furtively examining the dark red scratches peeking from the bandages on Olivia's knees.

"I'm really sorry about pushing you so hard yesterday." She pointed at the dressings.

Olivia stared at her. "Are you kidding? You probably saved my life."

"I didn't want him to see you."

She let out a slow chuckle. "*That* was clear. Nobody would have looked at me the way you were screaming." She sat cross-legged at the side of the fountain wall. "Seriously, dude, no one's ever done something like that for me before."

Ellie rolled her eyes. "Don't thank me. It wasn't a hard choice."

"That's my point." Olivia shielded her eyes from the bright light and glanced up at Ellie. She positioned the metal chisel carefully against the mortar between two stones.

Ellie looked over her shoulder. "Are you nervous?"

Olivia let the chisel fall gently. Her fingers traced markings in one of the stones.

"Kind of. I wouldn't have seen this if you hadn't pushed me down."

From Ellie's viewpoint, the lines etched in the lava disappeared into the rough surface that was pockmarked with holes left from centuries-old air bubbles. But when she leaned closer, they clearly outlined the shape of a leaf.

Ellie cocked her head. "You've just got good luck."

"I fell and here it was staring right up at me. Brandon's message." Olivia blinked a few times. "Here goes nothing."

She tapped the mallet against the chisel, chipping

away at the mortar that held the leaf-marked rock in place. Tiny specks of brown fluttered down, speckling the grass around them. She worked methodically, digging deeper into the crevice, jiggling the chisel now and then to test for movement in the stone. Ellie watched from above, shading Olivia from the direct sun, cradling her wounded arm with her good one.

After fifteen minutes, the rock began to wiggle. Five minutes later, Olivia pried it free from its resting place. She removed the warm stone, kissed it, and pressed it against her breast.

"It's like his hand touching my heart."

Ellie peered into the dark space. "Is there something behind it?"

Olivia seemed not to have heard, rocking softly back and forth, nestling the lava in her arms.

Ellie squatted and Olivia passed her the stone. Ellie placed it on her knee and traced the leaf with her index finger while Olivia thrust her hand into the dark hole. Olivia's eyes widened.

"There's something in here."

Her arm pulled slowly, fingers clutching a small metal box taped closed with duct tape. The round container was about half the size of Olivia's hand and very flat.

Ellie laughed. "Well, it's not cash."

"Nope." Olivia bounced the box up and down on her palm. A faint clinking issued from inside. "Maybe a bottle opener?"

"Or a binder clip?"

Ellie tried to grab the box but Olivia held it out of reach.

"Come on. I want to see what's inside."

"You and me both." Olivia pulled at the tape, which came away with a reluctant sucking noise. Her fingernails dug into the ridge around the lid and worked it open. A small plastic baggie sparkled as the sun reflected from a tiny yellow flash drive inside it.

In the kitchen, Ellie sat at the counter and pushed the flash drive into a port on her laptop. The rock with the leaf tattoo rested between her and Olivia. Ellie drummed her fingers on the granite, waiting for the drive to register.

"We're in." She glanced at Olivia. "Only one Word doc on here. Okay if I open it?"

Olivia nodded.

Ellie read a few lines and pushed the laptop toward Olivia. "It seems personal."

Olivia slipped onto Ellie's vacated chair and scanned the page, head bent over the screen. Tears left glistening paths, sliding slowly down her cheeks as she scrolled. Ellie busied herself making tea.

"Green tea okay? I'm avoiding coffee after yesterday. I still feel wired."

When Olivia didn't answer, Ellie poured hot water into two cups anyway. She glided one mug across the smooth surface at Olivia. "I'll be in the living room with Viv."

In the living room with the overhead fans whirling silently, Viv jumped on the sofa and stepped carefully around Ellie's bandaged arm, as though he sensed the wound underneath. A few minutes later, Olivia appeared silently in the doorway. She flung herself into the armchair across from Ellie.

"Shit."

"That's not the reaction I was expecting." Ellie wrinkled her brow. "Good news or bad?"

"It sucks and it's awesome, both at the same time."

Viv abandoned Ellie and slunk ingratiatingly to Olivia's chair. She patted her lap and the cat bounded onto it, purring loudly.

"It's like Brandon knew something was going to happen. He writes about why he came here. Why he left Seattle. His plans for a new life." Olivia shuddered. "It's freaky."

Ellie leaned forward. "Maybe it was therapeutic. Maybe he had to get things down so he could put them behind him?"

Viv stretched velvet paws against Olivia's chin, begging for attention. Olivia flipped him onto his back and rubbed his tummy. Viv closed his eyes and kneaded the air.

"Must have been. Everything he ever told me is in there. That he was done with drugs forever. That he came here to make a new life for us, to turn over a new leaf." Her eyes sparkled through the remains of her tears. "I made fun of him when he got that tattoo, you know. I said it looked like ivy crawling up his arm. Not exactly sexy."

"What else did he say?"

"That he left me some money in a bank."

"How much?"

Olivia shrugged. "No idea. But it can't be much. He used most of what he had to come here. He left me the username and password. I'll check later."

Viv clasped his paws around Olivia's arm. Olivia closed one eye, inspecting Ellie with the other.

"What?" Ellie rubbed her mouth with the back of her hand. "Do I have something on my face?"

"There's something else. He said was going to bury the flash drive to wipe the bad things from his mind forever. He said he hoped it would clear his conscience. So he could move forward with a new life for us." She paused and inhaled deeply. "And our baby."

"What?" Ellie sat stunned for a moment and then sprung from the sofa. Viv scuttled with an annoyed meow down the hall. "You're pregnant?"

"Yeah." Olivia stroked her tummy.

Ellie perched near Olivia's chair. "When did you find out?"

"Before Brandon died."

Ellie draped her good arm over her eyes. "It explains so much."

"Like why I wasn't drinking?"

"That. And why you're always throwing up. And eating like a horse. And why I always thought there was something you weren't telling me. Oh, Olivia." Ellie touched her on the shoulder. "Why did you feel like you had to do this alone?"

Olivia gazed at her stomach. "I almost told you a couple of times. But there's really nothing anyone can do. Not like I'm giving up the baby."

"No, but aren't there things you have to take care of?" Ellie studied Olivia. "Like getting some kind of baby check-up? Or think about where you're going to live? Or tell your…" Ellie stopped herself with a quick shake of her head.

277

"My parents." Olivia's cheeks flushed. "No." She looked suddenly exhausted.

"Hey." Ellie pulled her up from the chair. "You look wiped out. Why don't you lie down? I'll bring you some tea."

Olivia trudged to the sofa and flopped on the white material, stretching her legs so that her thin body extended from armrest to armrest. Ellie exited the room only to run back in seconds later. She skidded to a stop next the couch. Olivia stared up at her.

"I *pushed* you." Ellie's gaze flew over Olivia's body as though the incident had only just happened. "I pushed a pregnant woman. Oh my God. Did I hurt you?"

Olivia laughed. "Chill. I'm fine." She flexed her arms and legs. "See?"

Ellie's gaze centered on Olivia's abdomen. "But the baby. I could have hurt the baby."

"Could have." Olivia hugged her stomach protectively. "But my knees hit first. You knocked the wind out of me. That's all. And it was so much less than what Noa could have done." When Ellie didn't leave, Olivia waved her away. "I'm fine. Go get me that tea. Make it herbal."

Ellie trudged into the kitchen. The laptop sat on the counter, still open to Brandon's document. As the water re-boiled, the open page continually drew her attention.

Olivia will look later.

She searched the cabinets for herbal tea.

But she could really use some money now.

She found a tattered bag of mint behind the

278

emergency jar of instant coffee.

She'll need it to help with baby expenses.

The bag expanded in the steaming water, sending up a fragrant cloud.

God, does she even have health insurance?

Ellie dunked the string.

I should see how much he left. It will be a shock if it's not as much as she hopes. She left the computer open. So she obviously doesn't want to keep it secret.

Ellie spun the computer toward her and scanned Brandon's essay quickly. The bank information was bulleted at the bottom. Ellie navigated to the bank's website, entered the information, and clicked on the savings account icon. She took a sip of her now cold green tea.

The liquid caught in her throat when she read the account balance. She barely managed to turn away from the computer before spattering the counter. When she stopped coughing, she looked again. Her eyes widened until they almost merged with her eyebrows.

She's never going to believe this.

Her hand shook so much when she lifted Olivia's mug that she had to ladle half the hot tea into the sink before she could carry it. She carefully transported it to the living room, where she pushed the ottoman close to the sofa and sat on the edge.

Olivia sat up and took the cup, glancing quizzically at the small amount of liquid before taking a sip.

"So…" Ellie brushed her hair back from her face in a gesture she hoped seemed calm and natural.

"Did you and Brandon make any plans for the baby? Did you do anything in advance, like see an obstetrician?"

The color slowly returned to Olivia's cheeks. "No. We were excited, but we hadn't done anything yet. It seemed too early."

"Ah…" Ellie avoided Olivia's eyes. "How about look at baby furniture?"

"Nope."

"Decide on what kind of diaper you wanted to use?"

Olivia put her tea on the floor. "Ellie, I know you want to help, but it's still early days. Believe me."

"How about make your wills?"

Olivia nodded. "Now *that's* something we did do."

Ellie leaned forward. "Seriously? Legally?"

"I told you before, I think. My dad's an attorney. An estate attorney. I wrote my first will when I was five. Left everything to my hamster. That should tell you something about my parents."

Ellie waved her hand dismissively. "But you and Brandon. He had a will too?"

"Sure. It's easy in Hawaii. You just need two witnesses. Don't even need a notary."

Ellie moved her face within a foot of Olivia's. "So you're Brandon's heir?" Her voice cracked.

Olivia shrugged and leaned far back into the cushions. "Sure. But that doesn't mean anything. He didn't have anything to leave. Except that bank account."

Ellie scratched her forehead. "Well, actually, I took a little peek at the bank account."

"Oh, good. I should have looked, but I was a little afraid of being disappointed. How much was in there?"

Only the whoosh of the fan punctuated the next few seconds, as Ellie drew in a breath and exhaled slowly. "A little more than you think."

Olivia blinked. "How much more?"

"I'd tell you to sit down, but you're sitting."

Olivia nudged Ellie with her knee. "Don't keep me in suspense. Is it over five thousand?"

"Um. Kind of."

"So tell me."

"It's one point two million."

Olivia's face didn't register a reaction. She took another sip of tea. "Million what? Pesos?"

"No. One point two million dollars."

The young woman sunk back until the cushions puffed out around her like marshmallows. Ellie grabbed the tea and then snatched a laminated Hawaiian fish identification card from the side table and fanned Olivia's face.

"You had no idea?"

Olivia's voice was barely audible. "Do I look like I had an idea?"

Ellie propped Olivia's feet on the ottoman. "Where did he get that kind of money?"

Olivia's eyelids fluttered. "I think I know." She stared out the window at the lawn and the distant ocean, where white boats sparkled against the azure blue. "There was this guy Brandon knew. They were really tight." She twisted her t-shirt around her fingers. "He got Brandon started in…" She shifted uncomfortably and tucked her leg underneath her.

"The drug business. He always said he'd take care of Brandon. Give him a way out." She closed her eyes, her brow furrowed.

Her fingers wrung the hem of the shirt into knots. Her eyes focused on the loops of material. "But he got arrested. He had lots of enemies. They killed him in prison." She regarded Ellie. "Brandon took it really hard. That's right about when he started talking about coming here."

Viv poked his head around the corner, as though asking whether everything had calmed down. Olivia patted her knee and he sauntered over, still seemingly miffed at the previous disruption.

"We'll be quieter, Viv." Olivia hoisted him onto her lap and concentrated on stroking his spotted fur. "I think the money in the account came from that guy. I think he left it for Brandon to use if he needed it."

Ellie's face wore a skeptical expression. "So do you think it's legal? Or clean? Or whatever it should be?"

Olivia nodded. "Brandon would *never* have left me money he thought could get me in any kind of trouble. He was protective." Her voice dropped. "He would have been an awesome dad. He would have fought to the death to protect our baby."

In the silence that followed, Ellie thought of all the ways her own dad had been awesome and imagined ways Olivia's father might not have been. The question that lingered in her mind burst out of her mouth before she could stop it. "Did your dad protect *you*?"

Olivia shook her head slowly. "No."

Ellie nodded once, decisively. "I won't ask again. If you can't trust him, you don't need him. You've got your friends to see you through."

Olivia smiled wistfully, but Ellie read determination in her eyes. "My friends. And my child. We'll do okay. I guess Brandon's seen to that."

CHAPTER 21

The noon sun glowed high in the sky, roasting cement and asphalt, skin and hair, sand and surf. But the green grass in Ellie's garden remained invitingly cool to the touch of her bare feet as she wandered toward the guesthouse. Small white mock orange and delicate fuchsia bougainvillea flowers peeped from sculpted hedges around the Italian tile roof. Myna bird and spotted dove chirps and coos floated in the still air. Ellie paused and stared at the door, now wound garishly with crime scene tape.

He was living here for weeks. He could have killed me at any time.

She thought back to the conversation with K-Rao in the hospital early that morning. She had stood by his bedside, watching clear fluid drip into his arm as he spoke.

"We know what saved you." He grimaced as he shifted position. "It's that you were unpredictable. You moved Upcountry. And you were never home alone."

An icy sensation had rushed from Ellie's feet to

her heart. Her smile froze. "*You're* the one who told me what I heard was probably people walking on the public beach path." She tried to make it sound more like a joke and less like an accusation.

K-Rao's gaze shifted around the room, never alighting long on any one object.

Ellie inspected the day-old stubble on his chin, the bandages peeping from under the hospital sheets, his generally troubled expression. Beeps from adjoining rooms seeped through the walls.

"I'm kidding, K-Rao. It wasn't your fault. No one saw this coming."

He scrutinized her. "I wanted to make a good impression on Celine that first night I came over. Maybe that stopped me from doing good police work. Did I miss something out in the garden? I go over it in my head, yeah?" He eased himself higher on the sloping bed, his face stretching in pain as he carefully maneuvered his torso against the pillows. "But I think Noa wasn't there yet. You heard him that night scoping the place out. But he hadn't moved in yet."

The white walls of the room reflected the pale pink of the early morning sun. Birdcalls and Wailuku commuter traffic noises penetrated the window. The air smelled of antiseptic and aftershave.

Ellie nodded. "That's probably right. How could anyone have known he was hiding there anyway?"

"I could have been smarter. Noa had a pattern. I just didn't see it. You and Denver were in danger for much longer than last night."

Ellie straightened. "Denver? Why?" She twisted

a few strands of hair around her index finger.

"Think about it. Noa stalked his ex when she hooked up with her new boyfriend. She put a restraining order on him. So then he went after the boyfriend."

Ellie pulled the shock of hair across her lips. "He couldn't get to me. So he…"

"If we'd been on top of it, we would have seen it."

"He thought I hooked up with Brandon. Then he saw me with Denver." She shuddered. Her view of the room narrowed, the edges darkening. She sucked in a deep breath. "I'm not used to people trying to kill me."

"Trust me. That's something you don't want to get used to."

"Don't worry." Ellie laughed. "I won't."

K-Rao slid one hand carefully behind his head. "Talked with Celine earlier. She said you don't have to hide a psycho in your garden just to get her to visit again."

"Sounds like Celine."

His eyes sparkled. "Yeah. That woman likes a bit of drama."

She pursed her lips. "That's not why she's coming. She's worried about you."

"She knows I'm tough," he said, shaking his head.

Ellie examined the foot of his bed. "I don't know if she'll admit it, but she wants to check on you. I think this whole thing reminds her a bit of…another situation that happened a while ago."

K-Rao nodded. "You mean Kenji's accident."

Ellie's eyes jerked back to his face. "She told you?"

"Uh-huh. That night we were up on Haleakala. Said it was important to her that I know. She really loved him."

Shafts of morning sun illuminated the flowers Ellie had brought and placed on the nightstand. The spindly protea glowed magenta, salmon, and caramel, casting otherworldly shadows on the walls.

"You were okay with that?"

"That she's capable of loving deeply?" K-Rao sighed. "How could I be anything other than okay with that?"

Ellie's mouth twitched up at the corners. "Ugh. Romance doesn't sit well with my image of Celine."

"Maybe your image needs adjustment."

"Maybe you two need to save it for the bedroom."

K-Rao smirked. "Would be my pleasure."

Ellie rolled her eyes. "T-M-I."

A nurse pushed open the door.

"Howzit, Gladys?" K-Rao lifted his chin in greeting.

"Howzit, K-Rao."

Ellie glanced at the young woman. "You know each other?"

"Maui's not that big, yeah?" She handed K-Rao a small paper cup with medication. "K-Rao went to high school with my cousin's best friend's nephew."

The nurse's fingers walked her through the connections. Ellie's brow wrinkled. "On the East

Coast, we have a name for that kind of relationship."

K-Rao glanced at her. "What?"

"Strangers."

He laughed so hard his face contorted with pain.

"I'd better get back to the house." Ellie started for the door. "I'll text you later."

He waved goodbye, still unable to speak, holding his stomach to control the guffaws that burst from him.

Back in her garden later that morning, standing in front of the guesthouse, Ellie lifted her gaze from the police tape and turned toward the beach, where the long expanse of cobalt ocean rolled ever darker, ever wider, until it blended imperceptibly with the azure of the sky. Wispy, ephemeral clouds clustered over the remote islands, shifting shapes as she watched. Waves lapped the shore with the intermittent hushed wash of water over sand.

She inhaled deeply and strolled to the lanai.

Time to move on.

She pulled out her cell phone and texted as she walked.

Ellie: Come on over.

In the deck chair, she had a clear view of the shrubbery and trees. The warm air and birdcalls lulled her. An incongruous crunch of footsteps on the driveway drew her attention. She turned to see Denver limping across the crushed stone.

Ellie stood. "You didn't crawl through the hedge."

Denver paused at the foot of the stairs, his gaze circling from her arm to her face.

"My God, Ellie. You can't imagine how good it is to see you."

Ellie advanced. He raised his hand.

"Wait. I don't want to get distracted." He clasped and unclasped his hands. "There's a lot you need to know. Things I never had the chance to tell you before." He shook his head. "Things I never *made* the chance to tell you before."

Ellie read the appeal in his eyes and perched herself on the top step, one arm around her knees, the other lying in her lap. She squinted at him in the strong sun. "I'm listening."

Denver crossed his muscular arms in front of his torso. Bulges of biceps strained the arms of his gray t-shirt. He looked to her like a drill instructor, at ease but ready for action. She quelled a tingling that emanated from a region below her stomach.

Remember, Ellie, he left you.

"That night with Vivyenne. It wasn't what you thought."

She nodded slowly. "Yesterday when you came back and pretended you were the police, I knew it meant you still cared about me." She paused. "But I don't get what I saw with Vivyenne."

"What you saw was a hug of relief. I can't even describe how wonderful it was to see Vivyenne again."

Ellie's face flushed. She turned her gaze from his.

"Let me finish, Ellie. It was wonderful to see her again. Because she was such a contrast to *you*."

Denver enunciated the final words with firm conviction.

Ellie started. "To me?"

"To you. Seeing her made me realize how amazing it was that I'd found you. It made me feel even more how much I wanted to be with you."

Ellie's indefinite tingling pricked back to life. She gazed into Denver's deep brown eyes and read in them everything she'd stopped herself from thinking in the past weeks. She read that she, with all her flaws, her awkwardness, and her lack of trust represented his ideal. That he wanted her and would fight to get her back. That he loved her.

She reached out her hand but he shook his head. She let hers drop, her brows drawn together.

"There's more?"

Denver scuffed the grass. "There's more. Maybe you believe me about Vivyenne?"

"I do."

"Maybe you know Vivyenne's engaged to someone else?"

Ellie nodded.

"It's someone she knew long before me. When she and I left the next day, it was on different flights. I haven't spoken to her since."

"I believe you. You don't have to tell me more." Ellie tried to rise again. But at a gesture from him, she sat back down on the wooden boards.

His eyes locked onto hers. "I tried to call you."

"I blocked your number." Ellie looked away, the hurt in Denver's face stinging her heart.

Creases on his forehead deepened and he dropped his glance to the ground. "I deserved that."

When he didn't continue, Ellie jumped in. "I'm sorry. Maybe I should have trusted you more. But after what I saw…" Her fingers fidgeted with the edge of her bandage. "It broke my heart."

Denver bit his lip. "I know. I've been a total ass. I don't know if there's any going back." He sighed.

"You're not an ass."

"Yes, I am. I have been. Even before you saw me with Vivyenne."

Ellie regarded the line he'd worn into the grass. "What do you mean?"

"I'm an ass because my company's fallen apart, for one. RED's going to declare bankruptcy. My partner left. The business in China didn't pan out. And we've got no money to pay the employees."

Ellie rose and descended the few steps. Denver backed away. She reached for his hands but he hid them behind his back.

She tried to catch his gaze. "Denver. I don't care. You did your best. You'll start something else."

"I'm not the man you think I am. Remember that day by the beach? When you asked me what I'd do over again?"

"Sure. You said you wouldn't have started RED."

Denver frowned. "I have different answer now. My answer is that I wouldn't lie to you."

"You didn't lie." Ellie stretched her fingers toward him. "It's not your fault the company failed." He started at her touch and edged across the grass beyond her reach.

"I did lie. That house over there." He pointed. "It's not mine. It belongs to some family friends."

He sunk his fists into the pockets of his shorts. "I don't have millions." His foot kicked an imaginary rock. "I'm not a success. I'm a failure." He shrugged his shoulders. "So I understand if you don't want anything to do with me." He drew a breath, stood erect, met her eyes, reached out both hands, palms open, and locked his gaze onto hers. "But if there's anything I can do, anything I can say…I'll wait as long as you need. If only you'll let me work on living up to your expectations again."

The noon sun baked her long hair as she stood, unmoving, staring at him. "That's not your house?"

"No."

"And you're not a millionaire?"

"No. There was a point where my company was worth millions. But that was before I even met you. If I come out of these bankruptcy proceedings now with a little more than the average Joe, I'll consider myself lucky."

The shadow of a smile flitted across her face. It gradually settled and grew into a broad grin.

"What a relief." Ellie flung her hands into the air, as though pushing back mountains of incorrect assumptions. "I spent these weeks thinking I shouldn't have trusted you, because someone as amazing as you would never really want someone like me."

"What? Why would you think that?" Denver took a step toward her. "You're incredible. That morning on the beach when I met you…" He advanced again. "You were so beautiful. So engaging. So full of Maui sunshine. My heart never looked back."

Ellie lifted an eyebrow. "Really? I'm Miss Viral YouTube Accident Video, remember? And I had seaweed in my hair."

Denver smiled and narrowed the distance between them to a few feet. "I didn't notice."

Ellie laughed. "Saltwater must have affected your vision."

"Don't sell yourself short." He strode foreword and stroked her cheek with his palm.

She leaned into his caress. "No. I'm not going to do that anymore." She took his hand. "I was pretty kick-ass yesterday. That's the new me. Kick-ass YouTube videos, here I come."

Denver's face sparkled. He tugged her gently against him. "You've always been kick-ass as far as I'm concerned." He hesitated. "But what about me? I'm not who you thought I was."

"Yes, you are." Ellie tugged her hand from his grasp and ran her fingers through his hair. "You're kind. Intelligent. Loyal. You came back for me when you thought I'd given you up."

Denver smiled. "Does that mean you'll give me another chance?"

"I'm not giving you another chance." Ellie maneuvered her wounded arm around his waist and steered him up the stairs. "Your first chance never ended."

***

Denver cradled Ellie's head in the crook of his arm. Afternoon light filtered through the orange curtains of the guest bedroom, casting their naked

293

bodies in shades of copper. Ellie wandered the fingers of her good hand absently around the line of stitches on his smooth chest.

"Does it hurt?"

"Nope. It's only a flesh wound. He hardly even grazed me."

He wound his fingers around hers, tilted her head, and kissed her, a tender, lingering kiss of sated passion and contentment.

Ellie closed her eyes. "I wish we could stay like this forever."

"I eventually have to go to work."

She prodded his ribs. "Why? I thought you said your company was going under."

Denver grinned. "No need to rub it in. But I've already found another job."

"Seriously?"

"You sound disappointed."

Viv jumped onto the bed and poked his head under the covers. Denver shooed the cat away.

"I kind of liked the idea of your being a kept man."

"I'll be working for my parents' company. It's a job I should have taken a long time ago."

Ellie roughed up his hair and then smoothed it again. "What will you be doing?"

"Learning the ropes, mostly. They eventually want to retire. If I'm any good, they might ask me to take over. But that's far down the road, Ellie."

Ellie smiled. "I'm patient."

"In the meantime, it will at least keep a roof over our heads."

Ellie slid her hand into his. "I wasn't worried

about that. I've been pulling in some decent money these past months. And my prospects are good after I finish school. Even at a not-for-profit, I'll pull my weight financially."

Denver coughed. "Yeah, well, speaking of the money you've been pulling in…"

Ellie scooted sideways to look him full in the face. "You're not upset that I'm still taking Vivyenne's money, are you?"

"Um, no. Because you're not."

She leaned on one elbow. "What do you mean?" The sheet fell from her body and Denver's hands reached toward her. "Hold on." She pulled the sheet back up. "Tell me first what you mean."

He reluctantly pulled back. "You've been taking *my* money. Vivyenne wanted me to take Viv back that night you saw us. She wanted to fire you. I didn't want you to lose your job. So I said I'd pay your salary if she'd keep you on."

Ellie fell back onto the pillows and laughed. "No wonder you need another job. I'm costing you a bundle."

"Worth every penny." Denver kissed her again, his lips slowly working their way from the bend in her neck to her mouth.

Ellie snuggled against him. "So I'm a kept woman?"

"You're mine for keeps if you'll have me."

"I'll have you." Her hand encircled his neck.

Viv's paws and ears appeared on Ellie's the side of the bed. He hopped across the pillow and nuzzled her hair. "No, Viv. Not now." Ellie shooed him away.

She nibbled Denver's ear. "Why did you name the cat after Vivyenne?"

"I didn't. Viv's short for *Vivamus*. It's Latin for airplane."

Ellie's eyes opened wide. "That explains a lot."

Denver's hands cupped her backside and pulled her toward him. "Like what?"

She arched into him, rubbing her torso rhythmically against his. "Like why Vivyenne never liked him. And why he never liked Vivyenne."

"The cat's got taste." Denver flipped her onto her back and straddled her hips.

Ellie stretched her good arm overhead. "So I guess you'll have to find an apartment in Seattle that takes pets."

Denver leaned forward and clasped her hand gently. "You mean in San Francisco. My new bosses are good with my telecommuting." He groaned as she wriggled her hips into place.

"A place for the two of us?"

He lowered himself gently onto her. "For the three of us. You, Viv, and me. Any requests?"

Ellie's breath quickened. "Yes. The walls."

Denver groaned. "What about the walls?"

She stared into his eyes. "They can be any color." Her eyelids fluttered. "Except white."

Denver laughed. Ellie relaxed and lost herself in the dazzling sunlight, the warmth of his skin, and the mutual passion of their bodies.

He whispered, his words thick with longing. "Ellie, I'm yours."

He's mine, Ellie thought. *I'm his. And* this, *finally, is paradise.*

ACKNOWLEDGMENTS

Writing, for me, is a group process. My gratitude to everyone who touched this project, both in detailed and fleeting ways, is deep.

The generosity of our cherished friend Sonja Schluter made this book possible. She introduced us to life on Maui in ways we had never dreamed were possible. Once there, countless individuals enthralled me with their enthusiasm, knowledge, and insights about the Valley Isle. I am deeply indebted to Kelly and Rich Brunner, Ivy and Gavin Campbell, Tracy Lamon for their help.

The staff at Limitless Publishing was, as always, outstanding, including my amazing editor, Rosa Sophia. Readers of my Wild at Heart Newsletter, a wonderful group, helped choose this book's title. My husband, Ron Strickland, unfailingly supported me throughout the months of this project. And my best friend, Antje Hofmeister, patiently coached me, once again, through the nuances of writing romance.

Now, on to book three!

ABOUT THE AUTHOR

Christine Hartmann grew up in Ohio and Delaware and loves traveling to exotic, romantic settings. After a college semester in Kathmandu, her first three "real" jobs were all in northern Japan, where she lived for almost 10 years. She currently splits her career between her daytime occupation (improving the quality of veterans' nursing home care) and her nights/weekend avocation (writing both fiction and non-fiction books). Her husband, Ron Strickland, is a well-known long-distance hiker, trail guide writer, and the founder of the 1,200-mile Pacific Northwest National Scenic Trail. Christine loves reading, pilates, bicycling, snorkeling, and health foods that taste like they're bad for you. You will often find her at a keyboard, with Ron whispering sweet edits over her shoulder.

Facebook:
https://www.facebook.com/christine.w.hartmann

Twitter:
https://twitter.com/chartmannbooks

Website:
http://chartmannbooks.com/

Goodreads:
https://www.goodreads.com/chartmannbooks